Martin Middleton was born in London in 1954. When his family emigrated to Australia in 1960, they lived in Inala, Brisbane. After attending Corinda High School, Martin joined the army and spent most of his time at Lavarack Barracks in Townsville. Martin, his wife and children now live in Beaudesert, Queensland, where Martin works for Coles Supermarkets.

Martin has always been an avid reader of science fiction/fantasy novels, though since the success of his Chronicles of the Custodians series he wishes he had much more time to write.

Also by Martin Middleton in Pan

The Chronicles of the Custodians:
Circle of Light
Triad of Darkness
Sphere of Influence

FORTALICE

MARTIN MIDDLETON

PAN
AUSTRALIA

First published 1993 by Pan Macmillan Publishers Australia
a division of Pan Macmillan Australia Pty Limited
63–71 Balfour Street, Chippendale, Sydney
A.C.N. 001 184 014

National Library of Australia
cataloguing-in-publication data:

Middleton, Martin.
Fortalice
ISBN 0 330 27375 2.
I. Title.

A823.3

Typeset in 10/11pt Baskerville by Post Typesetters Pty Ltd
Printed in Australia by McPherson's Printing Group

To Queensland writers

The Fortalice too was shrouded in mist and surrounded by lesser peaks, but it stood out as a symbol of hope in a bleak land.

Contents

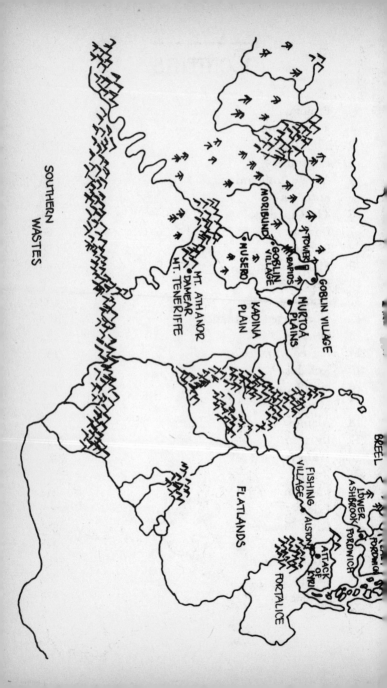

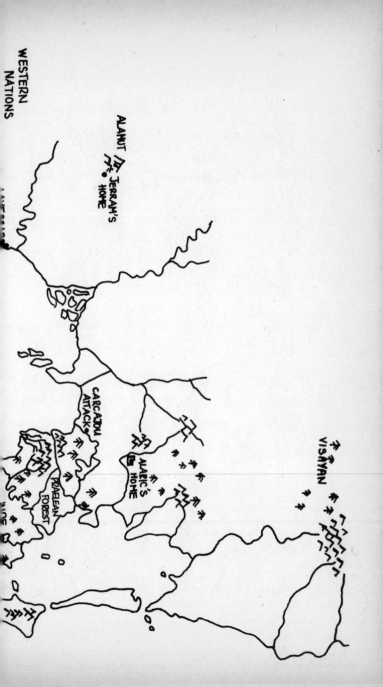

PROLOGUE

In the waste's vastness a shadow appeared. A black shadow which seemed to have a depth beyond all imagining. The shadow was suddenly interrupted as a figure appeared at its centre. Arms flailing, Xularkon stumbled from the darkness and took several paces before waking to his surroundings. Weakened by his journey, the heat of the air around him drove him to his knees. His clothing was torn and stained.

Then he remembered...

Those priests. Those damn priests. If not for them he could have defeated his nemesis.

Clenching his fists he drove them repeatedly into the burning sand. Again those damned priests had aided his nemesis and had stood between him and the power that was rightfully his, but it mattered little. Slowly he raised his head. His jaw stiffened with determination. His face was as grey as the sand around him but his eyes were filled with colour — red, the colour of the blood he would see spilt. In the distance through the heat haze he could just make out the green edge of the southern wastes. Beyond its northern border he would find willing followers to his banner and soon he would be in a position to impose his will over all.

All who survived...

As Xularkon stepped forward, a strange feeling touched his consciousness. The waste was all too familiar, and the thoughts which raced through his fevered brain seemed to echo dreams of a past time. Shaking off those distractions, Xularkon lengthened his stride, his fatigue forgotten. He would take his rightful place in history, but this time he would destroy those accursed priests before they had a chance to interfere with his plans.

1

FOUNDATIONS

Alaric's eyes snapped open. Today was the day. After so long, he was to be free of this prison. In the morning light the four stone walls of his cell seemed to loom over him, making the cell seem even smaller than it was. On the day his father was killed, Alaric had been imprisoned. Since that day he had dreamt only of his coming of age when he would command the respect and loyalty of his father's remaining men.

For so long his whole life had been the four cold stone walls imprisoning him. Every day he would go through his training, keeping his body trim and strong. Once a week he would see one of his silent guards as his rations were slipped through the small bar at the base of the door.

The near naked youth threw the thin covers from him and drew a sharp breath as his body encountered the cold air. Springing from the narrow cot, he tiptoed across the cold stone floor to where his clothing had been readied the night before.

Removing a narrow stone, Alaric paused, staring at the folded clothing. There were still many followers loyal to his late father. For five years he had waited for his fifteenth birthday when he would cease being Alaric the imprisoned son of the dead baron and, if all went to plan, become simply Alaric, a Freesword.

Duncan, his father's brother and murderer, had made one mistake in imprisoning Alaric. His nephew's presence certainly ensured that none of the late baron's liegemen took their vengeance on Duncan — Duncan's men would kill Alaric should his uncle fall to an assassin's blade — but in retaining some of his brother's men, he had left help within reach of the captive.

Alaric began to shiver from the morning chill. Removing his shift, he threw it into the dark hole and began to dress. First his warm undergarments, long-legged and sleeved, woven from the stretchable fibre of a plant grown in the northern regions of Visayan. His mother had sent a gift of clothing for Alaric to a loyal follower as soon as she had reached safety. The undergarments were far too large for Alaric to wear as a ten-year-old but, when word of the gift's arrival had been smuggled down to him, he knew his mother was alive and that she knew he would one day have need of such clothing when he escaped to avenge his father's murder. Loyal liegemen had smuggled the clothing to Alaric over the years, giving the young lad a continuing sense of hope during the five years of his imprisonment.

Next came his hose and tunic. Worn mainly to protect the easily-damaged undergarments, the material was soft yet strong. Alaric lifted out the remaining items and placed them carefully on the floor at his feet. Sitting on a small rough-timbered stool, he slipped on the warm socks his mother had also provided, followed by his high, thick-soled boots, which he laced tightly about his ankles and calves. Then he began to tie on his armour.

First the greaves — shin guards. These were made of thick strong grey leather, laced tightly behind his lower legs. Standing and stretching to almost six feet, Alaric raised the kirtle made of the same material as the greaves, and strapped it about his trim waist. Strips of stiff leather hung from the thick belt, protecting his hips, buttocks and groin from attack. He slipped his black polished lorica over his shoulders, shrugging it into place and lacing it at his sides. The lorica was made of supple

4

leather and covered his upper body and back, leaving his arms free. His kidneys, shoulder blades, collarbones, chest and abdomen were thus covered by the thick leather.

Lowering his arms, Alaric checked each of the kirtle's strips. Each leather strip held a scabbard containing an anhinga, a weighted steel-tipped dart. On the belt about his waist were four pouches, each holding an achico — three strips of weighted leather, joined at one end and used to bring down small game.

Crouching, Alaric lifted the last two objects reverently from the floor. One was a beautifully crafted silver-steel sword. It had been his father's. On that terrible night when the assassins came, Alaric had raced to the main hall to fetch his father's sword, Kilic. By the time he had returned his father was dead. The sword's blade was short but beautifully crafted. His father had come by the sword on his journeys as a youth before he had been forced to return home and take over the barony from his aging father. He had never spoken of how he had obtained the sword. All he had said was that one day it would be Alaric's.

The last item was a helmet made of layer after layer of polished black leather, shaped to fit and protect his head. The tail of the helmet was long enough to protect the back of his neck, while the sides coiled around his head to cover his cheekbones.

Once a week Alaric's rations would arrive: a crock of water and a covered bowl of coarse bread, dried cheese, salted fish and jerked beef. Two years ago Alaric had been surprised when he had unwrapped the bowl and emptied its contents, only to find the helmet he now wore.

Before Alaric had been able to receive anything from his allies, the guard overseeing the kitchen staff as well as the staff themselves had to be liegemen of his dead father. The guard responsible for the delivery of his rations and the sentry on duty outside his cell also needed to be loyal to his late father. In the five years of his imprisonment there had been items smuggled to him on only five occasions. The first was the hastily wrapped

5

packages of undergarments, followed over the years by assorted pieces of armour and finally his sword.

Alaric sat on the stool, Kilic resting across his thighs. Soon the guard would arrive with his weekly rations. If today was to be the day, then when the guard left, the sentry on duty would follow him.

Alaric sat silently staring at the familiar objects in his cell. A tangled web in the furthest corner held a large grey spider that had recently joined him in his imprisonment. For hours at a time Alaric had watched the spider build and rebuild its web. As his eyes moved around his cell they drifted across the uneven stone wall. The rough cut stones had made it easy for him to remove one and use the space behind as a hiding place for his smuggled treasures.

Treasures. Reaching into his lorica Alaric drew out a small rolled piece of parchment. The edges crumbled as he carefully unrolled it. Tall fading letters in a bold familiar script danced across the worn parchment. The writing was his mother's, he was sure of it, but the one word meant nothing to him. Fortalice.

Suddenly Alaric heard the sound of armoured footsteps approaching. As they drew nearer he could hear the sounds of armour and sword clashing. Slowly Alaric stood. The tray holding his rations was placed on the floor outside his cell and a booted foot pushed it through the small opening. His empty tray was taken up and the footsteps started again, this time receding. Alaric waited, holding his breath until finally he heard the sentry move off after his comrade, his steps quickening as he hurried to catch up with the departing guard.

Flexing his shoulders and neck, Alaric moved silently to the door of his cell and, slipping Kilic into his belt, opened the door a fraction and peered out into the deserted corridor. A torch mounted on the wall in a rusted iron bracket burnt low outside his cell.

Leaning down, Alaric removed the cover and saw his crock of water had been replaced by a stoppered bag and his rations were wrapped in waterproof skins. Gathering these, he stepped from the chamber and found himself at the base of a winding staircase. A dark heavy travelling cloak hung from a peg on the wall beside his door. Lifting it down, he was pleased to find a round leather brass-bound shield which he placed on his arm, draping the cloak over it.

Moving silently and with a spring in his step that only freedom could inspire, he quickly glided up the steep stairs past a large timber door. Alaric soon found himself beside a second door, a much narrower one this time. The stairs continued upward, but it was this door that interested Alaric. The leather hinges made no sound as the previously locked door was pulled slowly open. Peering through the small crack he had made, Alaric saw the guards' walkway. A guard stood motionless at the far end of the timber platform, peering out into the morning mist.

With a hasty prayer to the Lady, Alaric stepped silently through the door. Instantly he felt the cold wind slice into his bare hands and face as it tried to drag him from his feet. Leaning into the piercing wind, he began to walk towards the guard. The timber boards beneath his feet groaned slightly with his weight. Halfway along the walkway he stopped and risked a quick look to his right. The mist obscured the forest beyond the open killing ground and it was impossible to see if the horse he had been promised was there. But everything had passed as he had been told it would and so, with a fatalistic shrug, Alaric dropped his cloak-wrapped sword, rations and water over the stone wall.

A look to the left showed the first signs of life in the paved courtyard beneath him as the cook's assistant hurried across the frozen paving stones towards the warmth of the kitchen. The guard had not moved since Alaric had left the tower. He had once served Alaric's father and was part of the escape plan. Silently, Alaric thanked him before lowering himself over the wall. He hung by his hands for several heartbeats before releasing the cold stone and dropping the twelve feet to the rocky ground.

As he struck the ground, he heard the barking of his

uncle's hounds. Alaric froze as he strained to hear any other sounds above the baying. The noise continued for some time until a curse quietened the noisy animals.

Quickly gathering his cloak and sword, Alaric raced for the trees and, hopefully, the promised horse. Moving deeper into the shadowed forest he forced his way past grasping branches and over fallen logs which tried to keep him from the freedom he had craved for so long. A distant whinny caught Alaric's attention, drawing him quickly towards the sound.

Pushing through rather than round a particularly thick patch of brush, Alaric found the source of the noise. A saddled gelding stood in the centre of a small clearing. Bulky saddlebags hung from the rear of the saddle and a large bedroll was strapped atop the saddlebags.

If the escape had simply been a plan to get him away from the watchful eyes in the keep and to murder him in the seclusion of the forest, then the open ground he was about to cross would eventually hold his grave. Stepping away from the protection of the brush, Alaric drew Kilic, took a deep breath, squared his shoulders and walked quickly across the open ground. His steps were sure, yet he felt his heart labouring as he waited for the expected dart to strike him from behind. But none came.

He reached the horse and swung himself up into the saddle. Only now did he pause to throw the dark cloak about his trembling shoulders. His trembling stopped, either from the warmth of the cloak protecting him or from the realisation that he was finally free. He knew that he no longer had to be afraid. With a flick of his booted feet he urged the horse from the clearing, steering it into the obscurity of the forest.

Roland sat upright, instantly alert. Something had disturbed him, a strange sound which was not part of the normal village noises. Even though he had been asleep and was not able to clearly identify the sound, he knew that it meant trouble.

He lifted his blankets and slowly twisted his long legs

over the edge of his cot. Easing his feet to the earthen floor, he climbed from the bed, taking his sword from the floor as he did so. Roland silently crossed to the flap-covered door of his hut and, raising it slowly, peered out into the darkness.

It was still several hours till dawn and in the moonlight he could see no movement between the huts. Dropping the flap, he placed his sword on the floor by the door and began to pull on his boots. He was reaching for his tunic when a piercing scream tore the silence of the village. The flap of his hut was thrown open and a dark shape leapt across the earthen floor, landing on his cot with a growl of fury.

The large black carcajou tore ravenously at the bedding until it realised there was nothing of value to be found. It stood on four short powerful legs which ended in large paws armed with curved claws. Its fur was dark and thick, and long yellow canine teeth protruded from its slobbering muzzle. At a sound from behind, the carcajou raised its broad head and spun around. As the beast saw Roland, the coarse hairs on its back rose; so too did a series of spines from forehead to rump. Its long spike-tipped tail began to thrash madly, slashing bedding and cot with its razor-edged barbs. Roland quickly brought his sword down with all his strength, striking the carcajou between the eyes, splitting its blood-smeared head wide open.

Pulling the flap of his hut open, Roland saw that the village was alive with carcajous of all sizes. They raced frantically between, and occasionally into, the huts. A sound like insane human laughter rose from the pack. The remaining villagers were trying to keep them from the part of the village where a large number of the women and children had taken shelter, but the carcajous were too numerous and soon overran the pitiful defenders.

More screams could now be heard as the frenzied animals forced their way into the last few defended homes. Another carcajou made for Roland's hut. Its insane cackling filled his ears. Stepping to one side, Roland waited. The carcajou could sense a meal within the hut. As the

9

spiked head passed the flap, Roland chopped down hard on the neck, severing the head cleanly.

Letting the flap drop once more into place, Roland moved swiftly to the rear of his hut and began to hack at the woven branches. Soon he had made an opening large enough to crawl through. Taking his waterskin, blanket, and food pouch, Roland slipped from his hut and left the village for the last time. All the carcajous were occupied in the centre of the village, and he reached the tree undetected.

Moving between the large squat trees which made up the majority of the forest, Roland crept further from the sounds of death and destruction that were coming from the village. Slowly circling the settlement, he reached the place where his horse had been tethered. But the animal was down, its stomach torn open by the ravenous carcajous. Running blindly through the dense undergrowth, he headed away from the village, finally reaching the small shallow stream where the villagers drew their water. Roland dropped down on the bank and, leaning forward, began to fill his waterbag with the cool clear water.

Suddenly he heard the sound of horses splashing their way upstream. Melting back into the trees, he waited. Soon four mounted men appeared. The lead rider was dressed in rough furs and Roland could smell him even from where he was hiding well back from the stream. The other three were dressed in leather trousers and sleeveless mail shirts of grey metal over woollen tunics. They rode dark horses and were talking quietly amongst themselves. Roland dropped his hand to the hilt of his sword. Sliding the blade an inch from its scabbard, he waited. He could feel eagerness surging through his arm as if the blade were readying itself for the fight to come.

Without warning, the lead rider stopped. His eyes searched the foliage on either side of the stream. Roland knew that as long as he remained still, his brown leathers would blend well with the shadow-filled foliage. Finding nothing, the lead rider turned to those behind him and pointed towards the village. One of the armoured men nodded and the fur-clad scout turned and kicked his mount forward once more.

Roland pushed the sword home. He felt a tingle of frustration as the blade fought against its sheathing.

Anyon leaned back against the rough bark of the tree. His breathing was laboured. He tried to steady his grip on the axe but found he was shaking too much. He should have built his fire higher when he had stopped for the night but he had been too tired, and that one mistake had cost him dearly.

A sharp noise from the right made him push himself away from the tree and begin a faltering run through the forest once more. His horse was dead, its throat torn open by the first of the carcajous. His pack and bedding were probably still beside the smouldering fire of the camp site. All he had managed to save were his axe and boots as he had rolled from the blankets.

It was the screaming of his horse that had snapped him from his restful sleep. His right hand had dropped automatically to the haft of his axe before he had fully woken, while his left hand had grasped his boots, drawing them protectively to his chest. The remainder of the carcajou pack had sauntered into the camp from the trees. One grey carcajou, slightly smaller than the others, had leapt forward. Anyon had straightened his legs, moving to his left as he did so. The young carcajou then shot past its prey, digging its claws into the soft floor of the forest as it desperately tried to stop and turn. Anyon's axe had descended, stilling the creature.

Anyon had backed from the camp, never taking his eyes from the unwelcome visitors, though they seemed happy enough with the remains of his horse and the dead young carcajou. He could still hear them feeding as he moved further from the dying embers of his fire.

Jerram passed through the well-tended and colourful garden of his parents' home and entered the small shrine which held the statue of the founder of their order. It

11

was not a place of religion, more a place where he or his family would come when they needed solitude.

Jerram gazed at the statue, taking in the ever-familiar armour and clothing, finally coming to rest on the face. His parents claimed direct descendancy from the Founder and, because of this, his family held a place of power in Alamut. Jerram had always felt a close bond with the long-dead Founder after whom he had been named. He continued to stare at the face as he thought over the mission that had just been assigned to him.

How would the Founder have solved the problems which were presenting themselves to Jerram? In the distance he heard the single deep tone of a bell summoning all to the daily training session. Jerram turned and left the shrine, his questions unanswered. Leaving the fragrant garden, he came upon the circular arena where his family would soon be gathering.

As he watched his mother, father and brothers enter the arena he was filled with despair at what would soon be forced upon him — to leave all he held dear and go out into the world in search of four people to undertake a vital mission. But the four knew nothing of his mission. Even Jerram did not know what they would have to do, but he had to be there to guide them. His father had even hinted that his part could possibly be the most important, but Jerram could not bring himself to believe that. His family, and for that matter all those who believed in the ethos of Alamut, had steered lands and rulers from the shadows for many generations, but never had one of them taken an active role in the events which had unfolded in the surrounding lands.

Only the seven Knights had been granted that blessing.

The horse stood by a small pool, its head lowered as it drank its fill. Alaric sat by the fire, the remains of his meal on the ground before him. For more than ten months he had been riding south, crossing many lands, entering villages and towns only when he needed to replenish his dwindling supplies. Twice he had hired on as a freesword, a wandering swordsman of no allegiances or loyalties. Both times the caravan was travelling in a direction which suited him. For the remainder of the time he had travelled by himself.

Three days ago he had entered a dark damp forest. When he had ridden free of his imprisonment, he had intended to turn the horse's head northward. Once reunited with his mother, he would plan his revenge. But at the first crossroad, he had found himself turning south towards a small village. He did not know why he had changed his plans so suddenly. All he knew was that he felt an overpowering urge to enter the village, as if something of great importance would be found there. In the village he heard tales of a place called the Fortalice, a mountain of such enormous size its slopes were continually cloaked in snow, while its uppermost reaches were lost from the sight of man amongst the ever-present clouds. There, men and women were trained in the skills of magic or weapons. This was what the one-word message his mother had sent him meant. Alaric thought on this throughout his first night of freedom. With the dawn's light, he knew that his future lay with the Fortalice. The skills he would be taught would aid him in his quest.

Woken from his reverie, his gaze left the dancing green flames of the fire, distracted by a movement visible out of the corner of his eye. His horse had lifted its head and pricked up its ears. Alaric leapt to his feet, his sword ready.

'What is it boy? More of those thrice-cursed carcajous?' Alaric asked soothingly. He had already been forced to fight off two carcajous who thought him an easy meal. Kilic at the ready, he reached down and took a burning branch from the fire and moved towards his nervous mount. Burning green resin dripped from the branch, hissing as it struck the damp ground. 'By the Lady,' he said, as he stood beside his horse and tried to calm him, 'I've never seen so many carcajous before. You'd think the local baron would put a bounty on the damned beasts.'

The horse stepped back from the pool and whinnied.

'Still out there, are they, boy?' Alaric searched the deep shadows of the forest, but could see nothing. 'Perhaps we should invite them in,' he laughed as he moved back to his bedding and dropped to one knee beside the fire. Reaching forward, he placed the burning branch on the fire. Then, leaning to his left, he took several more branches from his fuel pile and fed them to the dying flames.

He could hear his mount fidgeting nervously behind him. Slowly he dropped his right hand until it rested on his thigh. At a sharp sound, Alaric snapped his head round and peered over his right shoulder. As his head moved, his right hand rose from his hip. With a casual underarm throw, he released the steel-tipped anhinga which sped across the clearing only to be met by a flashing blade.

Alaric leapt to his feet when he realised the intruder was an armed man and not a carcajou.

Anyon took one hand from his axe and reached down to pick up the anhinga. He tested the weight of the small but deadly weapon before flicking it back to its owner.

'Nice toy,' Anyon laughed.

Alaric caught it and rammed it angrily back into its sheath. 'Do you often wander about in the dark like a cowardly thief?' he snapped.

Anyon stepped further into the small camp site. At first he had planned to steal the youth's horse and anything else of value he might have had, but the tone of his voice angered him. Not the insult, but the thought that it might be true. Anyon had survived most of his life by using his wits. To trick or con someone out of their goods was one thing, but to steal something showed no skill whatsoever and could be accomplished by even the dullest thief. Since the night of the carcajou attack, he had been forced to wander the forest taking whatever he needed, but Anyon had never really thought of himself as a thief, he had always seen himself as an opportunist.

'I saw the fire and thought I might share in its warmth,' he lied easily. A half smile touched his lips.

Alaric squatted, scooping his scattered belongings quickly into his saddlebags. Standing, he kicked the last of the fuel into the fire then, with his saddlebags over one shoulder, he moved towards his horse.

'Take the fire,' he threw back over his shoulder. 'I'm leaving.' Alaric saddled his horse and mounted. Without a backward glance, he left the camp site and was swallowed by the darkness of the forest.

Anyon rode slowly through the gates of East Fordwich. Thanks to its planners who had the foresight to construct it so that the city straddled the Lower Ashbrook, controlling all traffic along the great river, the city regulated all trade in the region. It was a melting pot of people: rough skin-clad plainsmen, barefoot canvas-dressed sailors, and merchants of all types. The city, like its population, was an amalgam of land and water. The outer buildings and wall of East Fordwich were constructed of stone, while the buildings closer to the river were timber and much older, with a large number of them seemingly rundown and deserted.

Anyon hated large towns and cities, their crowds and their smells. In such places business for a man such as he was always good, but the streets were always filled with refuse and the sickening smells were trapped within the narrow streets where the sweeping winds of the plains never reached. Beggars lined the narrow avenues, their filthy hands extended in search of the few coppers compassionate travellers might throw them.

Reaching the water's edge, Anyon shielded his eyes against the setting sun and looked out over the still waters. The ferry appeared as a small black dot on the far bank. Turning, Anyon angled his mount to intercept the movements of a nearby worker.

'When will the ferry return?' he asked.

The man looked up from his work and, closing one eye against the glare, examined the speaker. But he made no effort to answer the question.

Anyon pulled the glove from his right hand with his

teeth and reached into the small pouch hanging about his neck. He withdrew a thin triangular coin and held it up for the man's inspection.

'Three hours past the dawn,' answered the man as he reached for the coin.

Anyon returned the coin to the pouch around his neck and, turning his horse's head from the river, ignored the curses and insults from behind him as he searched for a place where he could spend the night.

A weathered wooden sign caught his attention as it swung slowly back and forth in the steadily growing wind. The Boar's Head was a low-class tavern, typical of the places where Anyon had been forced to stay since he had taken to the road.

A thin rag-clad boy appeared at his side as he dismounted. A small dirty hand reached for the reins and began to lead the horse around to the back of the timber building.

The youth reminded Anyon of himself at that age. He had drifted about the back streets and alleys of his hometown trying his hand at one money-making scheme after another. One stormy night he had taken refuge from the drenching rain in a narrow alley behind the popular Black Carcajou bar. He was cold and hungry, but he was used to that, and he lay down to sleep. As sleep finally began to overcome him he heard a crashing of timbers.

A short leather-clad man appeared out of a cloud of splinters which had once been the back door of the premises, and flashed across the alley striking the opposing wall head first. The tankard held in his right hand dropped to the ground and smashed, but an axe stayed gripped firmly in his left hand. Two burly men stepped through the wreckage of the door. They stooped over the unconscious man as a short bent figure pushed between them. A wave of his hand dismissed the two flanking men. They turned without a word and made their way back to the bar. Anyon recognised the bent figure as Orm, the owner of the bar. Anyon had been

16

on the receiving end of Orm's anger several times and still moved with a slight limp from their last encounter.

As Orm reached into the unconscious man's jacket he spoke for the first time since entering the alley. 'If you think that trick of yours is going to work with me, you are sadly mistaken,' Orm laughed as he straightened, a bulging purse gripped triumphantly in his right hand. 'Fortunately, Ducrane my friend, I always win.'

Anyon felt his hand tighten on a piece of broken furniture, a leftover from one of the many bar-room fights that had erupted at the Black Carcajou.

As Orm bent over the unconscious form once more, a knife appeared in his left hand. Anyon slipped from his hiding place and moved quickly behind Orm. With all his strength he brought his improvised club down on the back of Orm's neck. Rolling the small unconscious form to one side, he slapped the axeman about the face until he got a favourable response.

Orm would soon be missed, so Anyon had little time as he helped the cursing Ducrane to his feet. 'We must hurry,' Anyon urged, 'for they will catch us and this time Orm will succeed.'

Ducrane raised his axe. 'Wanna bet?'

Staggering under the weight of the axeman, Anyon made his way down the rain-drenched alley, his mind flashing through a list of safe places where they could hide until the air cleared.

Anyon's thoughts returned to the present as he watched the horse disappear from sight. He hoped the horse would be well cared for. He had trekked seven days through a carcajou-infested forest before he had been able to steal it.

Ivo sipped slowly at the hot spicy drink. It was welcome after her ordeal today. She always hated travelling by water — the continual motion upset her; the odours from the small river villages reached out across the swift-flowing waters and churned her stomach to a point where she thought she would lose her morning meal.

Even as she sat sipping her drink she could not think what had made her take passage on the river packet. In the last town she had stopped at in the vain attempt at finding employment, Ivo had heard stories of a place of great learning — the Fortalice. She had sat and listened to the tales late into the night as the storyteller had woven his magic about the audience. When the tales were finally over, Ivo, like the other listeners, had paid well for her entertainment. When she woke in the morning, the story still fresh in her mind, she had felt a strong urge to seek out this Fortalice and the knowledge it offered.

She had been so happy when the vessel finally reached East Fordwich that she entered the closest tavern and ordered a drink, and a bath: the bath to wash away the clinging stench of the river, while the drink, she hoped, would take away the taste. However, the bath and drink had proved costly.

While she was soaking the aches and odours from her shapely body, a young lad had silently entered her room and stolen her pack. Everything she owned was in that battered pack, everything save the dirty crumpled clothing on the floor by the bath and the unstrung longbow beneath them. Ivo quickly dressed and made after the thief, but in the narrow alleyways, the young thief's headstart proved too much for her and she soon lost sight of him in the crowds.

Left in a strange town, with only the clothes she wore and a longbow, she had wandered the waterfront marketplace. She did not even have any arrows for her longbow as the quiver had been secured to her pack. As Ivo walked between the many gesturing traders, she had happened upon a fletcher's stall. Stopping to admire the workmanship, she recognised her quiver and arrows which were on display.

She had waited all afternoon for her chance to speak with the owner of the stall and when her chance finally arrived, she moved quickly. Following the merchant into an alley, she checked that she had not been seen before quickly catching up with the man. When she reached him, she silently dropped her bowstring around his neck. Once this was done, it had taken little effort to persuade the merchant of the ownership of the goods in question. And with a tightening of the bowstring, Ivo suggested that perhaps she should take a small sum of money to compensate her for her troubles. Naturally the merchant had agreed.

Ivo was now quite content as she sat, a full purse at her hip and a full quiver of arrows with her longbow beneath her left hand. The loss of the pack and its contents was no longer a problem. She now had enough money to replace all the items lost and purchase a horse, and perhaps still have some left.

Ivo looked up from her drink as a short man entered the tavern. She had made it a practice to examine those about her. Perhaps if she had paid more attention earlier in the afternoon she would not have been put through all the trouble. The young man was short but had large shoulders and well-muscled arms. His black hair was long, drawn tightly behind his head and tied with a piece of thin braided leather. He walked with a slight limp, probably due to exhaustion rather than to injury. Judging by the state of his clothes and equipment, he had travelled far and fast. He walked up to the bar and slammed his axe down to get the barman's attention.

Anyon ordered a drink then turned slowly to survey the taproom. It was filled with the type of riffraff he had become used to, save one — a young woman whose raven black hair was cut short except for a plume of hair standing above her forehead. She sat at a table in the far corner of the room, a drink in her slender hand and a longbow on the table beside her. Anyon was surprised to see the longbow — the people of Munde preferred to use the crossbow, and it marked the woman as a traveller, possibly new to these parts. Anyon knew he would have to keep an eye on her, not that it would require any effort. You never knew when your luck would take a change for the better.

*

Jerram strode from the low stone building. His horse was saddled and his saddlebags packed. Without looking back, he placed a foot into a stirrup and stepped up into the saddle. He wanted to look once more at the place that had been his home for so long, but he knew that was not possible. Should he throw even one glance over his shoulder, he would lose his resolve and be unable to go through with what he knew had to be done.

He sat his mount and gathered his strength, his right hand dropping to the hilt of the dirk resting on his right thigh. He ran over in his mind all that was expected of him, his finger gently caressed the decorated hilt. Jerram, as always, wore a long mail shirt of woven metal drawn tight at the waist by a wide leather belt. His coat reached his mid-thigh and a coif hung down between his shoulder blades. Though his arms and legs were bare, his stirruped feet were encased in mid-calf supple leather boots.

With a slight touch of his heels and a gentle pressure on the reins, he left his home. He was across the courtyard and beneath the raised portcullis before another slight pressure sent his mount forward at a brisk gallop.

2
THE GATHERING

Beside a shallow fast-flowing creek several days' travel south of East Fordwich, Alaric sat before a small fire waiting for the two brush wyandots suspended over the glowing coals to cook. He leaned forward and, sliding his knife from its sheath, pressed the tip against the crisp golden skin of the closest bird. Clear juices ran from the small cut and dropped sizzling into the coals. The cooking filled the slight hollow with a delicious aroma.

Alaric's horse was hobbled, feeding on the lush grass on the slope of the hollow, while Alaric sat with Kilic lying unsheathed across his knees. For half an hour he had been aware of the lone horseman moving slowly along the creek's edge towards his camp.

When his horse whinnied, Alaric remained seated by the fire, but now he could hear the sound of a horse entering the hollow behind him. Turning slowly, Alaric watched the man as he reined in his mount.

Roland dismounted and flicked the reins over the branch of a twisted stunted tree. The youth sitting by the fire wore practical well-used armour and there was a naked sword resting across his knees. He also seemed undisturbed by Roland's presence. However, Roland sensed that should he prove unfriendly, the youth would give a good account of himself.

'My horse is all but exhausted,' Roland explained. 'That, and the smell of your meal, drew me here.'

Alaric gestured to the far side of his fire then turned his back on the newcomer and resumed watching the roasting birds.

Roland removed the saddle from his horse and threw it across a dead gnarled log protruding from the creek's clear waters. His horse bent its head and drank deeply. Dropping to the ground, Roland stretched his cramped legs, ran a hand over his light stubble, and threw sideway glances at his silent host. He looked to be about sixteen — the same age as Roland himself — and the silver-steel sword which rested across his host's knees seemed an equal to the blade hanging at his own hip.

'That's a nice sword,' Roland said. 'Fine looking workmanship.'

'It was my father's,' came the sharp answer.

'I'm Roland, a traveller. You?'

Alaric looked up from his cooking meal and answered curtly, 'Alaric, a freesword'.

'Ah! A freesword. Then I am indeed lucky to find you. In the last village I stopped at they said there was a large raiding party of kyri in the area.' Roland looked casually over his shoulder as he spoke.

'Kyri?' questioned Alaric.

'Creatures from the mountains along the coast,' Roland replied. 'They raid for murder and robbery. They are a strange race who believe deeply in their gods. One of their beliefs is that all others are here simply to supply the kyri with what they need.'

This time it was Alaric who threw a look over his shoulder. 'A large party?'

'Yes. Large enough to have every sane traveller holed up in the larger villages and towns hereabouts.'

'You're not sane then?' Alaric asked.

'I'm here, aren't I?'

'So am I.'

'Exactly,' Roland said with a grin. 'Surely those birds

are ready now? If I have to put up with the smell any longer...'

Alaric slipped one of his thick leather gauntlets on and, reaching forward, removed the metal spit from its timber supports. Sliding one bird onto his platter, he threw the spit over the fire to Roland. Roland caught the bird and quickly pulled it from the hot spit. Licking his slightly burnt fingers, he laughed before turning his total attention to the meal.

Anyon kicked his mount to draw on the last of its strength as it began to flounder on the slope. Behind him he could hear the hunting cries of the kyri as they noticed his difficulty and increased their pace. Anyon's horse finally reached the top of the rise. A quick look behind him was enough to reveal two score kyri as they burst from the forest.

The short grey creatures took to the slope with little effort. Even though they had been in pursuit of Anyon all morning, they were showing no sign of tiring. Anyon's mount, however, was tiring fast; the horse had only a few more miles in it before Anyon would have to stand and fight, or abandon it.

Since stealing it, Anyon had grown fond of the black horse. But fighting forty or more kyri was pushing the friendship. On the horizon was a faint smudge of smoke, indicating a campfire of sorts. Forcing the horse into a faltering gallop down the slope, Anyon began to ride towards the fire and the help its builder might provide.

Anyon turned his horse's head at a small creek and followed the stream into the hidden camp. In the centre of a slight depression, a small fire burnt. Two horses stood by the creek, alert. One was tied, the other was hobbled. Both looked to be in much better condition than the horse he rode, so a trade could prove worthwhile. His hopes were dashed when a familiar armoured youth stepped between him and the horses. A long shining sword swung menacingly in one hand, while a leather shield hid most of his chest and face.

Anyon was about to speak when a second youth appeared, also armed, this time with a broadsword. Deciding that a trade was impossible, Anyon forced his mount through the camp and up the opposite side of the hollow. If he couldn't trade his horse with them, perhaps he could trade his problems. Once the kyri saw the two youths, they'd forget him.

Just as he crested the far side of the hollow, his mount collapsed, totally exhausted. As the horse crashed to the thick grass, Anyon kicked his feet from the stirrups and jumped clear. Rolling from the panicking horse, Anyon ended up at the bottom of the hollow. He came to rest against a pair of armoured legs. Looking up, he smiled just as the first of the kyri leapt into the hollow.

Ivo heard the shouting and instantly recognised it for what it was: fighting. After stringing her longbow she slid a long feathered shaft from the quiver on her pack and notched it. Moving cautiously forward, she began to pick her way through the trees towards a small creek. Once through the trees, she could see the reason for the noise. On the other side of the creek, three travellers were battling an overwhelmingly large force of kyri. With their backs to the creek, the three were, for the moment, holding their own. But for how long? The kyri were creatures of the mountains and had a fear of running water. One of their beliefs was that rivers were wounds in the Earth Mother, and that water was her flowing blood. The kyri would not cross these wounds without first offering a prayer for forgiveness for fear of hurting the Earth Mother. Should they offer the prayer, they could cross the creek and encircle the three fighters, finishing them off in a short time.

The kyri were short manlike creatures, not as strong as a full grown person but with unlimited stamina. They had been known to run for days on end without tiring and often raided the eastern lands. They were primitive and used only copper knives. All steel weapons they gained from their raids were sold, or left where they lay if better booty was to be found. The kyri had a strange belief that the skills needed to make their copper weapons were given to them by their gods, and that to use any other weapons would offend them and cause their clans great hardships.

One of the men in the hollow fought behind a large leather shield, while wielding a flashing silver longsword. The second was using a broadsword with great skill, cutting his attackers down with a strong two-handed stroke. The last sheltered behind the two swordsmen, leaping forward occasionally to wreak havoc with a war axe. Should the kyri finish these three off, they might search the immediate area and, though the creek lay between them, offer their prayer and find a place to cross, and then come upon her trail. So decided, she raised her longbow and drew the string to her lips before loosing an arrow into the right eye of a kyri. Slowly and calmly, she notched one arrow after another, sending a steady stream of death at the kyri.

After firing all her shafts, she unstrung her bow and sat, her back against a tree, to watch the three defenders as they finished off the last of the kyri. As the final attacker fell, the youth with the beautiful sword and leather shield sank to the ground. The axe-man staggered to the creek's edge and collapsed into the cool waters. The remaining defender forced himself to cross the hollow and climb the far side, searching the horizon for any sign of more attackers.

By the different actions of the three, Ivo was able to gauge their strengths and weaknesses. The familiar looking short axe-wielder had thought only of himself and had drunk his fill. The youth with the beautiful sword, seeing the last of his enemy fall, had relaxed before being sure there was no further danger. Only the tall one had understood the situation and had searched the area for more of the kyri.

Once satisfied that there was no more immediate threat, Roland returned to the camp and sat beside the trampled fire. As he passed one of the dead kyri, he drew a long feathered shaft from its chest and examined it.

25

Ivo took up her pack and longbow and crossed the creek. As well as the dead kyri, three horses were in the hollow. One was dead on the southern slope, the second was by the creek, also dead, its belly opened by one of the kyri's copper knives. The last mount stood nervously beside one of the fighters.

The four travellers left the clearing and moved further down the creek, leaving the bodies of the kyri and the two horses to the carcajous and other scavengers.

'This should be far enough,' Alaric said. He tied his horse to a low tree branch and removed its saddle.

'Who gave you command, General?' Anyon asked.

'If you wish to continue alone,' Roland said with a smile, 'you are free to do so.'

Anyon moved to Ivo's side. 'We may just do that.'

Ivo looked at the youth beside her and rolled her eyes.

'Come, sit,' Alaric said, smiling. 'There may be other bands of kyri about and it would be safer to travel on in number rather than risk meeting those creatures alone.'

'I can look after myself,' Ivo retorted.

'So we noticed, and we are certainly grateful for your presence,' Roland said. 'But that is no reason to take unnecessary risks, is it?'

Ivo nodded and dropped her pack. She arched her back, stretching herself to her full height, only slightly shorter than Roland.

'Where are you bound?' Alaric asked Roland.

'South,' he answered. 'I'm for the Fortalice. There are many questions I need answered.' He had always felt the urge to do well, to excel. His father had expected too much of him. Perhaps now he was expecting too much of himself. His fingers traced unseen patterns on the pommel of his sword. The Fortalice was still far to the south and even those who dwelt there might not have knowledge of the strange symbols and runes which adorned the sword.

'So am I,' Alaric added. 'I hear it is the best place to be trained in swordsmanship.' Alaric had gained great skill with sword and shield since his escape but he would need more than just skill if his plans for revenge were going to succeed. With the help of the Fortalice, his uncle was going to pay for the murder of Alaric's father, the banishment of his mother and Alaric's own imprisonment.

'Me also,' said Ivo. 'I need a place where I can find answers, perhaps guidance.' Ivo briefly studied the three young men. In them she saw many qualities she remembered from her three brothers. Roland was Ren — always in control. Alaric's uncertainty reminded her of Pel, while the gleam of mischief which had never left Anyon's eye even when he was exhausted from the fight with the kyri reminded her of her youngest brother, Clay. He had always been like that.

'Wanna bet who else?' Anyon mumbled. 'I hear that a dedicated young man can make his fortune there.' Anyon had said make his fortune, but he had meant gain power. Ducrane, who had become his mentor after that fateful night at the Black Carcajou, had always told Anyon that power was the secret to success. No amount of money could help if a man of power decided you stood in his way. Even a poor man wielding power could bring the richest of men to their knees. Ducrane had explained how in some lands a lowly clerk with a stroke of a quill could steal away a man's life faster than any stroke of an axe.

'May the Gods save us — and the Fortalice,' Ivo grinned, shaking her head.

Jerram walked his mount cautiously into the hidden camp site. The bodies of the kyri and the dead horses had drawn others to the site. Carcajous and many other smaller creatures had helped themselves to the banquet which had been left for them. Even though the pickings were bountiful, many of the scavengers fought over the bodies. Portions of the kyri were scattered about the site. In places, some of the small carnivores were still feeding, pausing only to watch the lone rider as he moved slowly past them. His coif was drawn over his head; the single-edged dirk, his only weapon, was grasped firmly in his right hand.

Dismounting, Jerram walked about the edge of the camp, stopping momentarily at the long-dead fire. Stirring the ash with the toe of his boot, he looked about the hollow. There was little remaining of the original scene, and from what there was, Jerram could learn nothing. Climbing into the saddle of his patient mount, he left the hollow and began to make his way southward.

Finally he found the trail. It was old and completely gone in places, but he was still able to follow the four he sought.

Shrouded in mist and surrounded by lesser peaks, the huge mountain, Fortalice, dominated the lands about it. With its peaks lost in the clouds and its slopes cloaked in a white blanket of snow, the Fortalice stood out as a symbol of hope in a bleak land.

The dark, cold, grey rock of the Fortalice looked to have been thrust up from the very heart of the land, a land which had decided that there needed to be a protector for its people, hence the Fortalice was born. Driven upwards through large fissures from the molten mass which made up the centre of this world, the great edifice stood ready to serve any who were chosen to enter it. Nothing grew on its wind-blown slopes. No animal sought shelter against the cold. Step by step the desolate mountain reached up above its brethren.

No enemy had trespassed on the lands overshadowed by the Fortalice in the three millennia of its existence. Within the safety of its towering walls the Ma'goi had brought the teachings of mastery in the Arts and weapons to all who could pass the test of acceptance. A pilgrim's first sight of the Fortalice signalled an end to their journey but only the beginning of their dangers.

Demanding entrance, pilgrims would arrive at the lower portal where a lesser member of the order would determine if they were worthy of acceptance. Once accepted into the

Fortalice, the pilgrims would be taken to a chamber where more questions would be asked before they were taken to the lower levels where they would be trained and tested. They would then wear yellow robes and become Morallie, responsible for all the menial tasks in the Fortalice.

The next rank, Yarracks, the warriors, wore blue robes. They had to protect all levels of the Fortalice, and the two portals which were the only means of entrance into the mountain's interior. The Kungour, wearing red robes, were the true students. At this rank, for the first time, they would be taught the basics of magic.

For years they would study under the greens, Nglelin, the senior students and magical backbone of the Fortalice. Few would ever reach the highest level of the Fortalice — the Wiseones. They were the head of the order, whether skilled in magic or weapons.

Guyon stumbled forward. She knew she was close to the lower portal even though it was lost in the storm which raged about her. Since childhood she had thought of only one thing: to escape her slavery and make her way east to the Fortalice. Only in its heart would she be able to learn the one thing she truly wished to possess — magic.

Suddenly the wind eased and, as its screaming died down, Guyon spied the lower portal. The massive doors towered above her, causing her to shrink back in fear at their size. Shaking uncontrollably, Guyon moved forward and touched the doors. As her hand caressed the timber, she saw an inverted V of silver. Reaching out slowly, she touched the symbol of the Fortalice. A warmth ran up her fingertips filling her inner body with a tingling sensation, and feeling quickly returned to her fingers and toes. She had been told that there would be tests to pass before the Fortalice opened itself to her. Somehow she knew that she had just passed the first: the portal itself had accepted her.

Gurth left the stairwell and turned down the wide well-lit corridor. His six-feet frame was draped in robes of green. A lock of dark hair had escaped from beneath his hood which framed a youthful face. Only the deep etched lines about his eyes revealed the troubles he had overcome to reach his lofty station in the Fortalice. His slippered feet made no noise as he approached the polished timber door.

There was no need for guards to be stationed on these levels of the Fortalice. No outsider had ever walked these corridors. Gurth stopped at the end of the hall and turned to face the only door. There was nothing out of the ordinary about the polished surface, but Gurth knew better than to touch it. Tuning his thoughts beyond the door, Gurth announced his presence.

The room beyond the door was, like the corridor, carved from the heart of the mountain. One wall seemed to be a huge window which looked out over the mountain range to the north. The remaining three walls were covered in shelves holding all manner of books and scrolls. The furniture of the room was, like its only occupant, old but well-preserved. Cymbeline lifted his eyes from the ancient book before him. Turning slightly in his chair, he focused his attention on the door. Flickering between the timber framework was a fine web of green energy. Anyone who was stupid enough to touch the door would find themselves part of the web, trapped until the web's weaver returned.

'*ngiralin*,' Cymbeline said softly, raising his right hand and pointing three fingers at the door. The green web vanished instantly. 'Enter.'

As the door opened, revealing Gurth waiting in the corridor, Cymbeline stood and gestured at the large book with his right hand, saying, '*muriltpun*'. The leather-bound book closed and a thin skin of green appeared over the surface of the cover. Satisfied that none but he could open the book, Cymbeline turned to greet the young student.

'Greetings, Gurth.'

'Greetings, Wiseone,' the green-robed student answered. 'I am sorry I must disturb your time of study but the pilgrim has reached the lower portal and has been accepted.'

'Then allow her to enter and be taken to the room of questions,' Cymbeline ordered.

'At once, Wiseone.' Gurth turned and left the room.

Cymbeline waited until the student had left before crossing the room to where a large silver mirror hung on the stone wall. Cymbeline passed his right hand over the silver and whispered, *'nokuna'*. The shining surface fogged, then quickly cleared, revealing a steep-sided canyon. The grey rock sides were bare, while the floor of the canyon was covered in a thick blanket of snow. As Cymbeline moved his hand to one side of the mirror, the scene changed to show a young girl huddled against the cold. There was frost on her face and her lips were blue. She shivered uncontrollably as she waited for the huge portal to open.

Her features were familiar to him as he had watched her progress for some time now. No one could near the Fortalice without the Wiseones becoming aware of them. As they struggled onwards, they were watched closely for strengths and skills buried deep within them that might one day be released and used in the advancement of the Fortalice.

Reaching the Fortalice alive was the first test. Towns and villages surrounding the Fortalice had their share of people who believed that pilgrims were there to be shorn like sheep. Those pilgrims who avoided civilisation soon learnt first hand of the many wild animals that inhabited the forests and plains bordering the Fortalice. Being recognised by the portal was the second test. Only one more remained before the pilgrim would be allowed to enter the Fortalice proper.

Cymbeline drew his hand from the silver surface. As he did so, the scene faded and was replaced by his own image. Cymbeline stared at himself — long white hair, a short neatly-trimmed beard, and deep-set brown eyes. He knew that anyone meeting him would see a man in his fifties, never imagining his true age.

Gurth returned to the lower level. It took him a considerable time to make his way down from the highest levels to the level which held the lower portal. As he descended, he unconsciously noted the Yarracks who were stationed at every intersection, door and stairwell. The Yarracks wore studded boots and metal greaves, breastplates and helmets. Their kirtles were a deep blue, as were their helmet plumes and the long cloaks they wore. Each held a large round shield, emblazoned with the symbol of the Fortalice, an inverted V representing the mountain which held and protected their order. From each belt hung a long sword, while an eight-feet pike was gripped firmly in their right hands.

On reaching the lower portal, Gurth made a formal gesture commanding the Yarracks to form up before the large doors. A small group of men and women dressed in yellow robes moved silently from a small door hidden in the shadows. Quickly they crossed the open chamber to the portal where half their number operated a winch, which began to draw back the four huge bars securing the doors.

Silently the retaining bars slid from the brackets into recesses in the wall — two to either side of the doors. Once the bars were withdrawn, the remaining Morallie began to work a second winch which opened the heavy metal-inlaid doors.

The bitingly cold wind from the valley beyond whipped into the chamber. Small flurries of snow were blown across the bare stone floor as the doors opened further. The Morallie, with their yellow robes flapping in the wind, huddled about the machinery trying to keep themselves warm. With shields raised and pikes levelled, the Yarracks, their blue cloaks drawn tightly about them, rushed out into the snow and formed a half circle around the opening portal and the lone occupant of the valley.

Guyon felt the hands touch her as she was guided through the open portal into the Fortalice. Quickly the large doors were closed and the blue-cloaked warriors resumed their posts.

Two yellow-robed females led her to a small room and motioned for her to be seated. Guyon sat on a low timber stool, the only piece of furniture the room had to offer.

She watched the two Morallie leave the room, closing the door after them. Guyon studied the stone walls of the room while she calmly awaited a further test.

3

PILGRIMS

Alaric rode slowly towards the gates of Alston. His travelling companions, Roland, Anyon and Ivo, followed. He hoped that the three of them could purchase mounts in the town. While Alaric had little need of their company, he did, however, feel obligated for their help with the kyri. Although it was Anyon who had led the kyri to the secluded camp, it would not have taken the creatures long to smell them out and attack. Anyon had had no choice about whether he wanted to help the pair at the camp or not. With his horse down, it was the only way to save his life. Ivo was different. She could have swung round the camp and left the kyri busy with the hapless trio. But she had decided to stay and lend a hand. Why, he was not sure, but he was glad she had. Ivo brought a feeling of capability to the group, as if she could handle anything; Roland brought dependability; Anyon uncertainty, his very presence seemed to cancel out the other two.

Alaric allowed these thoughts to run their course before finally admitting to himself that for the first time in his life he felt needed. He felt part of something. Watching the other three he thought what it would have been like to have brothers and sisters. There was something about the three of them which drew him to them.

*

Alston was built on the northern edge of a huge plain. Once beyond Alston there was little by way of civilisation. Southward stretched the huge expanse of Flatlands, bordered to the east by the ocean and to the west by a great body of water known as Lake Zeridal. Many religions preached that the southern border of the plain had no end. Some believed that the plain stretched on forever and was a place where the souls of evildoers were sent to pass eternity in unimaginable suffering; but most knew that the southern plain did end. Exactly where was a mystery — no one had ever returned to tell.

But the plain also held a wonderful prize. It rested nine days' journey south of Alston, in a huge range of mountains, any one of which was a match for the impressive mountains of the north. In their midst rested the tallest and most majestic of all: Fortalice.

Alaric rested his mount at the town's gates, and awaited the other three on foot. The guardsmen watched him with suspicion as he sat his horse awaiting the three footsore travellers as they approached the town. He had offered his mount to Ivo, only to have his offer refused and his head almost broken by her longbow.

Alaric had since decided that Ivo was not someone to trifle with. Roland had also noticed this, though Anyon needed reminding regularly. One day Ivo might well break her longbow if she continued to use it to try to press her point home.

'Now where?' Ivo demanded.

'A room,' answered Roland.

'And then we'll have to try to find a livery,' Alaric added, 'which has a high selection of horses...'

'At low prices,' Anyon finished.

'Fat chance,' Ivo scoffed.

'Leave the horses to me,' Anyon said with a smile. 'I'll get us three good mounts.'

Alaric and Roland exchanged looks.

'No, really,' Anyon continued. 'My last horse was a great deal.'

'I'll bet,' Ivo sneered. 'Deal or steal?'

'What's that supposed to mean?' Anyon snapped.

Ivo said nothing. She looked from one of the faces before her to another, and finally to the third. How long ago had she argued with three males, and to what end? She trembled as a slight chill passed through her. Changing the subject she turned to Alaric. 'Where are we going to be staying?'

'I asked one of the guardsmen and he told me of a place on the far side of town which is supposed to be clean and cheap,' he answered.

With Alaric in the lead, the four set off for the inn. Alston was a reasonably modern town. The streets were wide and well paved, and the buildings were all two storeys high made of small blocks of stone scrubbed white by proud owners. The upper levels had large windows used to catch the wind from the open terrain around the town. Alaric could see people standing and laughing just beyond those windows in what they believed to be the safety of their homes. There had been little by way of conflict in the land around Alston for hundreds of years, so little thought had been put into the defences of the town. Even a small well-trained force could easily breach the walls and march through the straight wide streets.

Soon the streets and white walls were behind them and they entered an older section of the town. The walls here had not been scrubbed for a considerable time and the streets were narrow and full of filth.

'Clean and cheap?' Ivo asked as she strode through the front door of the inn, examining her surroundings.

Cheap, Alaric thought, though he had to admit it hardly looked clean. The walls were scarred and covered in stains. The sawdust-strewn floor was littered with rubbish and strange sickly smells drifted up from the refuse every time it was disturbed. Trying not to add anything else to the thick foul air of the inn, the three carefully stepped over to a low filthy wooden counter.

Ivo drew her dagger and brought the pommel down

36

on the top of the counter. She looked around the small room and banged on the counter once more, this time slightly harder. The third blow left a deep round impression on the stained timber counter. As Ivo raised her arm for another blow, a grubby curtain parted, adding stale cooking odours to the fumes already in the room.

A tall thin man passed through the curtain. 'I ain't deaf,' he snarled as he plunged his right hand beneath his shirt to chase some elusive creature. Stepping forward, he placed his left hand on the counter and leaned forward to survey the three before him.

'Four singles,' Alaric stated curtly.

'On'y got doubles,' the thin man answered gruffly.

Alaric reined in his anger. 'Then we'll have three doubles.'

'Just the three a you?' the innkeeper asked. He pulled his right hand out from under his shirt and momentarily examined something trapped between thumb and forefinger.

'There is a fourth, he'll be here shortly,' Roland explained, stepping between Alaric and the innkeeper.

The man smiled as he ground thumb and forefinger together. Then, raising his eyes, he said, 'And who'll be sharing...?' He paused, giving Ivo a long steady look. The corners of his mouth began to curl into a crude smirk, and he was about to say something when Ivo reacted to the stare.

Her hand flashed up then down, driving her dagger deep into the counter top between the innkeeper's spread fingers. The thin man leapt back in surprise and anger, only to have the tip of Ivo's longbow strike him just below his ribs, causing him to fold forward and slump into the counter. The hand that had wielded the dagger grabbed the thin man by the hair on the back of his head and brought his forehead down hard against the timber top. The entire incident had taken only seconds, from the crude smirk to the innkeeper slowly sliding down behind his filthy counter, unconscious.

As Ivo wiped her hands on her leggings a woman came

through the rear curtain. She looked down at the unconscious man and then up at the three. Stepping over the unconscious body, she fronted up to the counter and smiled. 'Yes, how may I help you?'

Later, Anyon joined them in the taproom.

'How did it go?' Alaric asked.

'Marvellous. I acquired three good mounts and a packhorse.'

'Why the packhorse?' asked Ivo.

'I got such a good deal on the three horses, I decided a packhorse would come in handy.' Anyon noticed the knowing looks the three gave each other. 'No, really, it was an incredible deal.' He peered at Ivo, daring her to say something. 'Besides,' he finally added, 'when I found them they looked perfect together and I would have hated to break up the set.'

'Where are they now?' Roland asked, quickly stepping between Ivo and Anyon.

Anyon inclined his head towards the eastern wall. 'In the livery down the road.'

'Why not out back?' Alaric asked.

'Are you kidding?' Anyon grinned. 'I wouldn't leave my horse here.'

'Oh great!' Ivo laughed. 'I need another drink.'

Alaric waved for the barmaid to bring four drinks to their table, then turned to Anyon. 'Did you learn anything of value about the countryside between here and the Fortalice?'

'A little. It seems that it's a little late in the season for pilgrims, though one passed through here several weeks ago, just before the first snowfall of the year.'

'Can we still get through though?' Ivo asked.

'Oh yes,' Anyon answered. 'It may be hard going, but we should still be able to make it.'

'Were you able to find out exactly where the pass we need lies?' Alaric asked.

Anyon looked uncertain. 'Not exactly.'

'Then where can we get exact directions?' Ivo

demanded. 'I'd hate to wander round alone in the snow for the remainder of winter trying to find the damn pass.'

'You wouldn't need to be alone,' Anyon winked.

Ivo turned her back on him.

'All we have to do is ask someone,' Roland said, also ignoring Anyon. 'The owner of the livery should do.'

'That mightn't be a wise thing to do,' Anyon mumbled, turning from Ivo to concentrate once more on his drink. 'It seems that pilgrims are not treated all that well in town. Most think they are going to their death anyway, so they try to get as much as they can from them before they leave town. I even heard a rumour that some of the locals follow the pilgrims from the town and help them on their way by lightening their loads... considerably.'

'Let them try that with me and I'll...,' Ivo said angrily, raising her bow.

Anyon rubbed his bruised ribs, feeling almost sorry for anyone who made the mistake of getting in Ivo's way.

Roland woke with a start. For an instant he thought he was at home, but quickly his eyes adjusted to the darkness and he saw the squalor of the room. His father would never allow such mess within his walls. His walls, always his walls, never had he or his brothers ever felt that the home was theirs.

One day his father failed to return from a skirmish with a rival landowner. Roland and his brothers had ridden out and found the body of their father and the men of his company.

Roland remembered clearly looking down at the still, blood-spattered body and realising that at last his father was at peace. He had turned and mounted, not saying a word to his brothers. Riding from the scene of his father's death, Roland had not looked back. He had needed time to himself and had intended to return, but as he rode further southward, he found himself drawn further from his home. Finally he gave up all thought of returning home for the time being and had simply given his mount a free rein, allowing it to choose its own way southward.

Since the night of the carcajou raid on the village where he had been staying, he had suffered occasionally from bad dreams about his father and brothers, which caused him to wake up sweating profusely; but this was different. He paused, tilting his head to one side. There was someone moving outside his door. Roland's hand dropped to the hilt of his sword which lay on the floor beside his bed. Lifting the sword to his chest, he waited.

As he lay in the darkness, he strained to pick up any sound coming from outside his door. Slowly the door to his room eased open. A faint light from the hall filtered into the chamber. Silhouetted against the dim light in the hall, Roland was able to make out three shapes as they entered his room. One stayed by the door, while the other two moved silently across the floor towards the bed.

As the leading intruder bent over Roland, the second shape drew a knife. Not waiting for the first to follow suit, Roland lunged upwards off the bed. Hurling his blankets at the closest attacker, he leapt for the figure with the knife. Side-stepping a clumsily-thrust dagger, he brought the flat of his blade down against the attacker's wrist. A sharp snap was followed by a shrill scream.

At the same time, confusion erupted from the rooms to either side of his. Roland spun round to avoid another attack. As the man who had been at the door leapt forward, Roland tripped him, sending him crashing into his uninjured companion. In a tangle of arms, legs, and blankets the two fell to the floor.

Roland stepped over the struggling figures and brought the pommel of his sword down on their heads, halting their attempts to free themselves from the blankets and each other. Roland could no longer hear anything from the other rooms. The two on the floor remained motionless as he quickly dressed and began to gather his gear. He was almost finished when the door to his room burst open. A dishevelled Ivo jumped into the room, dagger in hand.

'I shouldn't have been so gentle with that skinny bastard downstairs.'

'Let's see about the others,' Roland said.

'They're fine,' Ivo answered. 'Anyon heard the disturbance and leapt from his room's window.'

'Hopefully he's going to saddle the horses and bring them round back.'

'I wouldn't count on it,' Ivo laughed.

'Alaric?'

'He was in some difficulties,' she answered. 'But I gave him a hand.' She held up a dagger coated in blood.

'Are you all right?' Roland asked.

'Yes. The fools only sent one man to my room. Obviously they thought that as a woman I would be an easy mark.'

Roland smiled but said nothing. He had had enough trouble for one night.

Roland threw his saddlebags over one shoulder and made for the door.

'What about these?' Ivo asked as the forms on the floor began to stir. She squatted down beside the two men and began to wipe the blade of her dagger on the blanket. Both men froze at the sight of the blade slowly and rhythmically being wiped across the blanket's edge. One man managed to drag his eyes from the blade. In the dim light it was still possible to see the sweat beads on his face.

'You won't get out of town,' he croaked. 'We have a way of dealing with thieves around here.'

Ivo leaned forward to speak, but Roland was becoming worried about the time they were wasting. 'Leave them,' he called.

Ivo retrieved her pack from the hall and hurried after Roland. Alaric was just re-entering the taproom through the rear door. He looked nervous. 'Anyon has the horses ready. Let's leave, before more of the innkeeper's friends arrive,' he said.

'You wouldn't think something that smelled that bad could have friends,' Ivo commented.

The horses were saddled and Anyon was mounted as the three left the inn. Quickly securing their gear, they mounted and walked their horses towards the main street of the town. A yell erupted from their left and a dozen or more men ran from the front door of the inn.

'There they are!' one yelled. 'Thieves!'

'Stop the bastards!' another cried.

Several stones fell short of the four as they rode down the main street. The men began to give chase and they were joined by many from the surrounding buildings. After several sharp turns the four lost their pursuers and slowed their mounts.

'That innkeeper sure had a lot of friends,' Roland shouted above the noise of the horses.

'I'm not so sure,' Alaric answered, slowing down to ride beside Anyon. Reaching over, he grabbed the reins, nearly tearing them from Anyon's grip. 'Where did you get the horses?'

'Forget it,' Ivo shouted. 'How are we to get through the gates? They'll be closed and barred this late.'

'I'll see to it,' Anyon said, jerking the reins from Alaric's grasp. He kicked his mount forward and raced off down the street.

'Damn!' Ivo cursed, and spurred her horse after him.

'What are they up to?' Roland asked.

'Who cares?' Alaric answered, glancing over his shoulder. 'They can't get us into any more trouble.'

As Alaric and Roland approached the gate, they saw Ivo lifting the bar, and a saddled horse standing unattended before the guard house. Ivo turned and threw the bar, just as Anyon ran from the guard house and threw himself up into his saddle. With a laugh, Anyon kicked his mount in the ribs, sending it leaping for the open gate. Ivo mounted and followed after the still laughing Anyon.

'I think we missed something,' Roland said, puzzled.

'I think a lot of town's folk are going to find themselves missing something,' Alaric answered dryly.

Roland threw him a puzzled glance.

'When I first met Anyon, before the incident with the kyri,' Alaric explained, 'he had gone to great lengths to approach my camp without being discovered. He was also on foot at the time.'

'You think he was after your horse?'

'And anything else he could get his hands on.'

'You think he stole these horses?' Roland asked, looking down and examining his mount.

'I'd swear it before the Lady herself.'

The pursuit stopped at the town's gates, allowing the four to ride for a few hours before reining in their mounts. Roland leapt from his horse and, throwing the reins to Alaric, strode over and tore Anyon from his saddle.

'What in the five hells do you think you were doing back there?' he shouted. 'We could have been killed.'

Anyon pushed Roland from him, then his hand dropped to the hilt of his axe. Roland stepped back and slid his sword from its scabbard. Quickly Alaric leapt between the two.

'Put down your weapons, you idiots!' he yelled as he slapped Roland's sword away. He then turned and faced Anyon. 'As for you, you idiot, you've caused enough trouble; don't add to it.'

Anyon slowly hung his axe on his belt. 'I'll do as I please, General,' he smirked at Roland, 'and if you don't like it we can always part company.'

'They're the only true words you've spoken since our meeting,' Roland hissed.

'Enough!' Ivo shouted. She was standing a short distance from the three, her longbow strung, an arrow notched and ready. 'Enough of this stupidity. We are all riding for the same destination. Even if we were to separate here, we would virtually have to ride side by side to reach the Fortalice.' She lowered her longbow and stepped forward. 'Already we have been forced to fight together...' Roland gave Anyon a cold look. '... and we may be forced to do so again, so I strongly suggest we stop this bickering and reach our destination as soon

43

as possible as this seems the most logical way to be rid of each other's company.'

'How far to the Fortalice?' Roland asked.

'Two weeks, perhaps sooner,' Alaric answered.

'Then two weeks it is,' Roland declared, glaring at Anyon.

'Or perhaps sooner,' Anyon countered, a cold edge to his voice.

Alaric moved to Ivo's side so only she could hear. 'Do you think it wise to allow Anyon to travel with us?'

'Sooner with us,' she said, 'than following us. I think we should keep an eye on our small light-fingered friend.'

Cymbeline drifted down the vertical shaft. A web of green, invisible to all those not skilled in the Arts, joined him to the shaft's walls, controlling his descent. As his slippered feet touched the stone floor of the lowest level of the Fortalice, the magical web disappeared. Cymbeline stepped from the shaft and began to walk slowly towards the lower portal. It was his task to welcome the new pilgrims and ascertain their worthiness to the Order.

He had thought he had finished for the season with the last arrival. The weather beyond the portal would be quite inhospitable, while the creatures of the snow would make travelling the pass almost impossible.

The creatures were almost man-like and covered in thick white fur which protected them from the cold, biting wind. They lived in caves at the bases of some of the lesser mountains and hunted when the weather was at its worst, while their prey was holed up out of the wind, making them easy pickings for the unseen hunters.

Once, one of the Nglelin had suggested clearing the pass of these creatures, but they played an important role in the defence of the Fortalice. Any large force traversing the pass could be easily detected. A small force, however, trying to approach unnoticed would find the going extremely hazardous. It also meant only those pilgrims who were truly committed to train at the Fortalice would reach the lower portal.

The guards on duty in the corridors remained motionless as Cymbeline passed them, not one movement betrayed the fact that for the entire distance from his personal level he had been watched and warded by them.

Cymbeline had been disturbed by the deep feelings of commitment he had sensed from the new arrival as she had traversed the valley. Many pilgrims were committed to the aims of the Fortalice, but this new one was something different. Because of her, Cymbeline had used his considerable skills and the larger mirror in his chambers to search further afield from the Fortalice.

As he searched to the north, he had found four others who sought the Fortalice. About to pass them up as late pilgrims, Cymbeline suddenly stopped and searched the faces of the four. For some reason he felt a close affinity with the four, an affinity he knew was impossible but important to his plans.

4

A NEW COMPANION

Ivo sat by the fire. Alaric and Roland were lying on their stretched-out blankets. Anyon was standing beside the horses, stroking and talking quietly to them, trying to keep them calm.

With little warning, a tall filthy man dressed almost totally in rags entered the camp. He strode towards the fire as if the camp was his.

'I am Frewen,' the rag-covered man said. He stopped beside the fire and extended his dirt-encrusted hands towards the flames. 'What are you doing here?'

'We are pilgrims,' Ivo answered testily.

'Ah, pilgrims,' he sighed. 'A little late in the year, but always welcome.'

Two more men entered the camp. They were dressed in rags like Frewen, but these two carried ill-tended swords.

'It has become our job,' Frewen continued, 'to help pilgrims on their way by ensuring they are not burdened by too much equipment.'

The two swordsmen laughed, and moved further into the light cast by the fire.

'We have little to burden us,' Roland said calmly.

'I'm sure we'll be able to find something,' Frewen laughed. Four more men left the shadows and entered the camp. They too were armed with rusty swords. 'As you can see, there are enough of us to ensure we miss nothing in our search.' As he spoke, he glanced down at Ivo and smirked. His men burst into laughter and moved towards the seated woman. As they clustered about the fire, a final man entered the light. He carried a crossbow.

As the last man moved towards the fire, Alaric's hand shot up from where it had rested on his thigh. The anhinga struck the man carrying the crossbow with such force that it buried itself deep in his forehead, killing him instantly. As the crossbow fell from his lifeless fingers, the camp erupted in chaos.

Ivo rolled to one side, taking the legs out from beneath three of the intruders. Roland and Anyon drew their weapons and attacked from two different sides, confusing the intruders even further. Alaric threw two more anhingas before drawing his sword and joining the others.

Anyon cut down two of the attackers with short solid blows from his axe. He fought with a careful style, never facing more than one intruder at a time. He fought because he had to... for the moment. Anyon was proud of the fact that he always fought with one eye on an exit, knowing that he'd use that exit if the need arose.

Roland's style of fighting was the complete opposite. Throwing himself at three of the intruders, he parried, blocked, and cut, until he stood over three unmoving bodies. It had been the one thing his father had taught him.

Alaric fought with shield and sword, killing his attacker efficiently and with considerable ease.

Ivo had quickly regained her feet and, taking her longbow from beneath her blankets, she notched and drew an arrow, waiting. It seemed like no time before the intruders were down. They had stood little chance against the fighting skills of the four.

'Eight!' Anyon laughed. 'Exactly as I said.'

'Nine,' Ivo answered, and released a shaft into the shadows beyond the camp. A scream echoed from the darkness, followed by the sound of a heavy body falling.

Roland and Alaric laughed as Anyon strode off into the darkness, cursing. Finding the body, a primed cross-bow beside it, Anyon gave it several swift kicks before searching it for anything of value. Returning to the fire, he passed over the triangular silver piece which Ivo had just won from him.

Early in the afternoon Anyon had returned to camp with word of the bandits. He had claimed there were eight. Ivo had left the camp to spy out the approaching band and returned claiming that there were nine of them. Anyon and Ivo then spent the remainder of the afternoon deep in argument, before they had settled on the idea of a silver piece for whoever proved to be right.

Jerram rode through the town's gates. He was closing in on those he sought. They had stolen three mounts and a pack animal before being forced to fight their way out of town. Jerram drew his heavy cloak about him, hiding his mail coat. How hard it was to gain information now. He was not used to it. All his life he had simply asked, and all around offered whatever they knew. This was indeed a strange and barbaric land where the might of Alamut had not reached. It was lucky for him that the ones he sought were not trying to hide their trail in any way.

Roland guided Ivo into the shelter of the rock face, where they were temporarily shielded from the wind. Looking up through the snow flurry, he could just make out Anyon and Alaric as they struggled against the wind to reach the slight shelter.

Having reached the great mountain range of the south, the four had thought their journey near an end. However, the slow climb up the pass into the heights of the range soon proved otherwise. The weather changed drastically the higher they climbed, until one day the horses were unable to go any further. They stood shivering in the freezing wind, unable to take another pace, even if it would save themselves from a frozen death.

Much to Anyon's chagrin, Alaric had released the horses, chasing them northward back along the pass towards the warmer weather. After several attempts, the horses must have sensed this, because they staggered back along the pass, finally disappearing in another snow flurry. The four pilgrims had continued on foot, carrying what gear they had been reluctant to leave behind.

Jerram reined in his shivering mount and slipped quickly from the saddle. Removing his blanket from his shoulders, he draped it over the suffering horse until he could unroll the large warm horse blanket strapped to his saddle. Once he had secured the blanket, he continued down the snow-filled valley leading his much comforted horse.

There was no chance of finding a trail in the snow flurries which repeatedly whipped along the valley floor, but he knew he was closing in on his quarry. The four horses he had passed earlier showed that they were on foot. Jerram stopped and turned his head slightly, trying to catch the faint sound he thought he had just heard. It sounded like a muffled shout, but in the blustering wind it was hard to be sure.

Unable to quicken his pace, Jerram simply leaned once more into the cold wind and resumed his slow pace. As he moved further into the valley, the sound came to him more often. It was definitely shouting: human voices, and another sound, one he had not heard before.

With no further warning other than a slight increase in the noise, Jerram found himself in the centre of a confused fight. Struggling figures appeared only to vanish almost instantly in the wind-blown snow. A figure stumbled out of nowhere and, seeing Jerram, attacked. Though wrapped in his heavy clothing, Jerram crouched and drew his dirk in one fluid motion. His attacker's true shape was lost in the swirling snow as it raised its arms and towered over the crouched Jerram. At the last possible moment Jerram moved quickly to one side, bringing his dirk up at a steep angle to enter the side

49

of his attacker just above the hip. The figure lurched silently to one side, obviously in great pain, but still it turned to attack. A wide sweep of Jerram's right hand drew the razor-sharp blade across its throat. A quick glance about him showed that there was no sign of more of the figures. Crouching, Jerram rolled the figure over.

The beast was a strange mixture of man and animal. The shape was human but the face revealed a forward pointing jaw and short curved canine teeth. The ears were large, probably for picking up the faint sounds in the frequent storms, and its entire body was covered in a shaggy white pelt.

Suddenly more of the creatures appeared out of the snow, and soon Jerram was fighting for his life against several of the strange beasts. He pulled the blanket from round his shoulders and, wrapping it round his left arm, placed his back against the rock wall of the valley. His mount was rearing and kicking at some of the attackers who thought it might be easier prey than its rider. Jerram had no sooner dispatched his attackers when another of the creatures suddenly appeared, followed closely by a stocky man wielding an axe. A second creature appeared and leapt onto the back of the man, sending him crashing to the ground.

Jerram leapt at the two struggling figures, deftly reaching round and cutting the beast's throat. The first creature had stopped its headlong rush and had turned to attack. Jerram launched himself at the beast, striking it in the chest with both feet. He rolled as he struck the ground, quickly regaining his feet. Before the creature could rise, Jerram reached forward and drove his dirk into its right eye, killing it instantly.

The axe-wielder disappeared and the noise of the fight ceased. Jerram bent over and wiped the blade of his dirk clean on the thick white fur of the closest of the dead creatures. The noise of someone approaching made Jerram leap from the corpse into fighting stance: feet spread, right hand extended, dirk at the ready, left arm raised, giving him the balance he would need should he be forced to attack.

Four figures stepped from the thinning snow. Each was muffled against the biting cold, their features hidden, but Jerram knew they were the ones he sought.

'Welcome, traveller,' Roland said. 'Your arrival was quite timely for our companion here.' Roland nodded towards Anyon as he spoke.

Anyon said nothing. His axe was still gripped in his right hand, but it hung by his side, offering no threat. Ivo held her longbow at the ready, an arrow nocked, her fingers caressed the string as if eager to draw it taut. Roland and Alaric had sheathed their weapons and were stepping closer to Jerram as he surveyed the four. The two drew back their hoods as they stopped before him. Alaric, Ivo and Anyon looked exactly as they had been described to Jerram months earlier by his grandfather, but Roland's appearance caught Jerram by surprise.

There was a sure serenity about the young man, something Jerram had become quite familiar with in his years of training, though he had only noticed it before in the faces of his many teachers. This last one's background had not been known by Jerram's parents, and he wondered if he came from any of the lands bordering on Alamut.

'How is it you travel this valley so late in the season?' Ivo asked.

'I am a pilgrim,' Jerram answered. 'I seek the lower portal of the Fortalice.' As he spoke, he slipped his cloak about his shoulders, drawing it tightly about him.

'As do we all,' said Alaric.

'Perhaps it would be best if we were to remain together for the rest of our journey,' suggested Roland.

'Yes,' Anyon agreed. 'You seem poorly armed to be travelling alone.'

'I do not usually travel alone and I have never been one for unnecessary violence,' Jerram answered, quickly slipping his dirk beneath his cloak and sheathing it.

'You should not leave your weapons on your mount,' Ivo warned. 'In cases such as these, there is little time to arm yourself.'

'I have no other weapons,' Jerram answered. 'I have found a dirk is all I have ever needed.'

'I see,' Roland remarked softly. 'Have you travelled far?'

'Yes.'

'You will scarcely find a knife suitable in this land,' Anyon commented.

'In any land for that matter,' Alaric added.

'Perhaps we should move on,' Ivo said suddenly.

The conversation ceased abruptly. Nothing could be heard, but there seemed to be an unnatural chill in the air.

'Yes,' Anyon said quickly. 'Let's hurry.'

Jerram took up the reins of his horse and followed the others back to their small camp. Quickly Roland, Anyon and Alaric gathered their belongings while Ivo kept watch. Jerram took the opportunity to study them more closely.

Each of the four were about his age, with Roland possibly the oldest and Alaric the youngest. They wore an assortment of clothing and armour depicting the vastly different lands from where each hailed. But regardless of their different backgrounds, Jerram knew that soon they would become the only hope of this land and many others. Because of their efforts many thousands of people would survive the coming time of darkness and he had been chosen to join them and help them in their travels.

Soon the five left what remained of the small camp and began the final stage of their journey. Anyon led the way, continually stopping as he surveyed the valley floor for the easiest and safest route. Ivo followed closely behind the short axe-man, her longbow synchronised with her eyes, ready to quickly rise and fire should danger threaten their pathfinder. Roland walked beside Jerram, saying nothing, but Jerram could feel Roland's eyes flicking over to study him from time to time. Jerram knew that Roland would see an unarmoured, virtually unarmed, stranger.

Alaric brought up the rear. He had changed considerably in the year since he had dropped from the wall of his prison. No longer would he simply be satisfied with the death of his uncle and the reclaiming of his late father's lands and titles. He felt as one with his three travelling companions, as if he was meant to journey with them and fight at their side for the rest of his life. Of the fourth, Jerram, he knew very little, and wasn't sure he could really trust him.

Cymbeline stood silently while the young woman drank the warm beverage. At first her hands had shaken so badly from the cold, she had been unable to lift the high-sided bowl from the tray; but by wrapping her hands tightly about the wooden bowl she had finally warmed them enough to stop the uncontrollable shivers. As she drank the warm liquid, a little colour began to creep back into her ashen cheeks.

'Do you feel better, young one?' Cymbeline asked.

She reluctantly drew the bowl from her lips and nodded. Then she returned to consuming the life-giving beverage. When the last drop had been drained, she placed the bowl on the tray and turned to face the old man who had waited patiently for her to finish.

'Thank you,' she said softly.

'Are you well enough to begin?' Cymbeline asked. A wave of his hand dismissed the Morallie with the tray.

'I believe so, Wiseone.'

'That is good,' Cymbeline answered. He moved closer to the young woman and continued. 'What is it you seek here?'

'Answers,' she replied.

'And you think you will find them here?'

'I do,' she answered.

'Everyone who seeks us out comes searching for answers,' Cymbeline said. 'Unfortunately, there are no answers to be given here.'

'Then what?'

'Only questions,' he explained.

'Then I will hear your questions and find their answers,' she explained.

'And your own answers?'

'I will find them myself if you are unwilling to help me,' she said. Her voice was tinged with anger.

'There is no need for that, young one,' Cymbeline answered.

'Then I will be allowed to stay?' she asked.

'Of course, young one,' Cymbeline answered smiling. 'For as you search for your answers, you may help those here who still search for theirs.'

'Are there many who still search?' she asked.

'All who are here are looking for answers,' Cymbeline replied, placing an arm about her shoulders.

'Even you, Wiseone?'

'Especially me,' he laughed. 'I have a feeling that you may even help me, young one.'

'Guyon, Wiseone. My name is Guyon.'

'I have not heard that name before,' he said with a smile as he did not wish to offend.

'It is an old name, Wiseone. My father once heard it spoken, and it remained with him until I was born,' she answered.

'Then come, Guyon,' he said, offering her his hand, 'I will show you to your room where you will be able to rest and bathe.'

Guyon followed the old man from the small room. In the corridor they were met by a tall young man wearing long green robes. He joined them as they wound their way through the seemingly endless corridors of the lower levels of the Fortalice. At every turn or junction one of the blue-clad warriors stood motionless, eyes staring ahead. Guyon could not see whether their chests rose or fell and, if asked, would not have been able to answer whether they were alive or statues.

'Guyon!'

Guyon raised her head from her work and noticed one of the overseers walking quickly towards her.

'You have lost the distinction of being the last pilgrim of the season,' he said.

Guyon said nothing.

'Five more have just arrived and have been accepted,' he explained. 'That makes eight for this season, the most the Fortalice has accepted in many a year.'

Guyon simply nodded and turned back to her work. She cared little about the others around her. All that mattered was the fact that she was here, and her training was about to begin.

The huge hoof struck the ground tearing free a large sod, as if telling the rider of its impatience. As the leg rose again, the scaled bard which protected the horse jingled. The armoured head rose and fell as the metal scales running along the back of the neck flexed and rippled.

The rider was as protected as his mount. From the armoured sabaton protecting his feet to his massive helmet, every part of the rider's body was encased in steel, a dull black steel with a long white surcoat. A wide leather-studded belt surrounded his waist supporting an enormous broadsword. A huge circular shield hung from his left arm covering half his body, while a long thick lance rested on his right stirrup and was held loosely by his right hand. A black and white diagonally-striped pennant situated just below the steel tip fluttered and snapped in the strong breeze.

As the rider sat motionless, and his mount vented its anger by pawing the ground once more, six more mounted men appeared, three moving to either side of him. The six reined in their mounts and sat as motionless as their companion.

In the valley below them, two large armies were readying themselves for an onslaught which would leave thousands dead or maimed. As the two armies positioned themselves, large tents were being set up well to the rear to accommodate the two generals.

One rider leaned forward in his saddle. 'Do we intercede?'

The Knight in the centre answered without moving. 'Not as yet, Seth. We must bide our time and wait for the right moment.'

Another Knight spoke. 'But, Daniel, if we wait too long, the battle may commence while we sit here.'

'They will camp, William, and ready themselves for battle,' Daniel explained.

'And us?' Thane asked, his head turning to left and right as he sought an answer from all present.

Daniel turned and faced the speaker. 'During the night we will make our move and by the dawn all will be ready.'

'For the beginning,' Sibbald said softly.

'And only Azyr knows the outcome,' Geruaise said. He shifted his shield slightly to a more comfortable position as he spoke.

'As is predicted,' Zenias intoned.

'As is predicted,' the other six Knights repeated.

5

FORTALICE

Jerram, Alaric, Anyon, Roland and Ivo, after their meeting with Cymbeline, were taken to a huge gallery which held their rooms. As they entered the gallery they were met by five yellow-robed figures, who each took one of the travellers by an arm and began to steer them away. As Jerram turned to follow his guide, he saw the backs of the four he had sought for so long as they disappeared into the dim light. His first thought was that he would lose them, but then he remembered his grandfather's words. 'There may come a time when you are separated from those you must guide. Fear not, for the time will be short and you will soon be reunited.'

Roland surveyed his room carefully before entering. It was small, with a plain low ceiling and bare walls. A low, narrow cot in one corner was the only furniture. In the ceiling in the far corner of the room was a small opening covered by a fine metal grid. A gentle but cool breeze drifted through the small opening filling the room with cool air.

Anyon was shown through a narrow door into his room. He paid scant attention to his surroundings, but simply sauntered across the room to throw himself heavily onto the low cot.

Ivo seated herself carefully on her bunk, blending into

the surroundings. Absent-mindedly she placed her long-bow across her knees and began to gently rub a soft rag along its polished length. As she examined her room a nameless tune passed her lips.

Jerram's first thought on entering his room was to see to his privacy, but there was no door, only a thin, slightly-tattered curtain. Drawing the curtain, Jerram began to remove his heavier clothes, quickly dropping them on the floor at his feet. Finally he was left standing in his long black mail shirt, the small dirk on his right hip. He removed his belt then slowly slipped the coat over his head, and crossed to the narrow bunk. Lifting one end of the thin mattress he laid the mail coat out on the bunk, then lowered the mattress to cover it. He placed his belt and sheathed dirk at the head of the cot, carefully arranging the pillows to ensure that nothing of its hidden treasure could be seen.

Alaric slowly walked across his room to the bunk and sat down. He didn't move for some time, then his eyes seemed drawn to the walls and ceiling of his room. How much they reminded him of the stone walls which had made up his cell, the cell which had been his prison for so long.

Cymbeline stood on a slightly raised platform at the end of his long low-ceilinged chamber. Winter was over, though the valley beyond the lower portal was still blan-keted in snow. It was time for those of the Fortalice to renew their contact with the outside world. Even as winter had raged beyond the thick protective walls of the For-talice, Cymbeline and the other Wiseones had maintained communications with their ambassadors via their ornately-bordered mirrors.

But now was the time when the forces of the Fortalice should be seen abroad in the land. Those the Fortalice favoured would be comforted, knowing that their pow-erful ally was once more free of its snow shroud. It had been many centuries since the Fortalice had been forced to send an army of any size from its mountain stronghold and decades since it had had to interfere in the affairs of the surrounding lands. In all that time, the forces of the Fortalice had waited in the mountain, occasionally sending ambassadors and advisers to troublespots in the ever-warring west. But alarming news had reached Cymbeline from one of the western advisers. Another pinnacle of power had asserted itself in the affairs of the west, and threatened to spread its power beyond the western borders.

Cymbeline crossed his chamber and sat at his desk. Open before him lay a thick book he needed to study further, but his mind refused to take in the neatly scripted words. First unsubstantiated rumour, then eye witnesses' reports had begun to filter into the western cities and towns, creating a buzz amongst the population wherever they met. The little visited walled cities from the lands across Lake Zeridal had united. One of the rulers, Edelmar Rhys, had made himself regent over their combined forces.

The feat of bringing the many warring independent city states together was thought to be impossible, yet Edelmar Rhys had accomplished it, though not without aid. Behind the new regent of the western army was a small force. Little could be found out about them, only that those who opposed the will of Edelmar Rhys tended to disappear mysteriously.

Also, at the head of the marching army, rode seven armoured Knights of remarkable prowess. They spoke only to each other and Edelmar Rhys. These Knights wore black plate armour overworked with strange silver patterns. Likewise their warhorses were armoured. Each courser was protected by a full bard of plate armour. This armour was also black, patterned with silver, though the designs were different.

They were always seen on the battlefield or sitting patiently beneath the walls of besieged cities. Only on one occasion had they been called into battle by Edelmar Rhys. Survivors of the fighting had taken their stories to Landscarp, a walled city on the shores of Lake Zeridal.

The ambassador had gathered the survivors and heard their tales; now Cymbeline was waiting to be informed of what she had learnt.

At the sound of his name, Cymbeline looked up from his study. The voice was soft as if calling from a great distance. Cymbeline rose and crossed to a small oval mirror. 'I am here,' he said softly.

The face of the ambassador filled the mirror. Her youthful face seemed aged. The smile which had started to appear on Cymbeline's face quickly dropped.

'Wiseone,' she began, 'as you know, one of the walled cities refused to join the new western alliance. Rather than be besieged and die in their own city, the ruler, Abdi, decided to take the field against the forces of Edelmar Rhys, hoping that he might cripple the advancing army sufficiently to allow his neighbours to defeat what remained of the enemy. Abdi gathered what forces he could, including several companies of freeswords from the far north. At either end of a shallow valley the forces met. Both armies prepared themselves for battle, but neither moved as they each waited for the other to strike the first blow.

'The seven armoured Knights rode through an almost solid wall of arrows as they crossed the open ground between the two opposing armies. Arrows struck the armour worn by the Knights and their mounts, rebounding with no effect. With a crash like the thunder of a mighty storm, the seven struck the front rank of pikemen, hurling bodies from their paths as their momentum carried them deep into the enemy's lines.

'Even surrounded as they were, Wiseone, no blade touched them as they opened a space about them. Slowly they moved deeper into the enemy army, their intention to reach Abdi and his generals. Seeing that the day was lost and that to continue would cost more lives of his countrymen and do little damage to the enemy, Abdi ordered his generals to lower their pennants, signalling an end to the fighting. Almost immediately, the seven Knights stopped and withdrew. This is what I have learnt from those who survived.' Her message completed, the ambassador bid Cymbeline farewell and disappeared from sight.

Cymbeline thought long on what he had been told. He doubted that a force of that size with such strange allies would be content to remain in the western lands once they had been conquered. He must meet with the other Wiseones and suggest a small force be sent to learn what they could about Edelmar Rhys, his seven Knights, and his unseen allies.

As Cymbeline returned to his chambers he wondered why Edelmar Rhys had chosen this precise moment in time to unite the west. Had he and his cursed assassins learnt something or was Cymbeline's long-awaited scheme still safe?

It had been decided that one of the Nglelin, a wearer of the green robes, should take ship to Lakescarp and learn more of the new enemy. Gurth had been chosen. With him would travel three of the Kungour, representing three of the many orders of the reds.

To protect the party, a half company of thirty Yarracks had been assigned to Gurth. The remainder of the party would be made up of Morallie. There were to be two groups of Morallie: one to see to the comforts of the numerous camp sites, the other to act as waggoners, loading, unloading, and caring for the horses. It was for the last group that Guyon and the others were to be tested.

'I can still see no reason for this test!' Anyon snapped angrily.

'We must prove ourselves worthy,' Guyon answered. When at first she had been allocated her role, she had been extremely happy, but soon her enthusiasm waned. She had been assigned the five latecomers and it seemed that they did not share her happiness. 'It is a great honour,' Guyon explained further.

'To be tested to see if we are fit to care for horses is hardly what I call an honour,' Ivo retorted.

'I've cared for horses most of my life,' Anyon said.

'Other people's,' Ivo added, and continued quickly. 'I'll be glad for the opportunity to be out of this place, even if only for a few months.'

'Well, what exactly do we have to do?' asked Roland.

'We are to be taken to the lowest of the galleries, where we will be left,' Guyon explained. 'After a short time has elapsed we are to make our way back here.'

'That's all?' Ivo asked incredulously.

'That's all,' Guyon replied, though she too thought there might prove to be more to it than that.

'Is there a certain time to complete this impossible task?' Jerram asked with a laugh.

'No,' Guyon answered. 'We are simply to make our way back here.'

'Then let us start,' Alaric said. 'I agree with Ivo; once this test is over it will be pleasant to be out of this mountain, even for a short time. These stone walls remind me too much of home and I miss the openness of the free road.'

Once their guides had left, and the designated time had passed, Guyon began to lead her party back the way they had come. However, the task was not to prove as easy as she had first thought. Following one of the passageways, she came upon a solid wall of stone.

'We must have taken a wrong turn,' she said, confusion sounding in her voice. 'I could have sworn...'

'This is the right way,' Ivo said quickly. 'Look!' Lowering the torch till the passage floor could be seen easily, Ivo pointed down to where, in the thick dust of the ages, scuff marks could be clearly seen. 'We passed this way on the way down.'

'How do you know those marks were made by us?' Anyon asked. 'Anyone could have passed this way before us.'

'No,' Ivo answered. 'Look!' She pointed to one almost complete footprint. 'See the small pockmarks? Those were made by the metal studs on the sole of Alaric's right boot.'

Alaric slowly lifted his boot and in the torchlight they all examined the pattern of the studs.

'So if this is the way we entered,' Anyon asked, 'what now?'

'We find a different route,' Guyon answered.

'We'll try one of the side passages we passed,' Roland said and turned back down the passageway.

Five days later, footsore and hungry, Guyon and her party reached a familiar gallery. Waiting for them was a small table set with several meals and three flasks. Standing beyond the table was a Nglelin, a glowing green ball of light rested above the open palm of his right hand and filled the small chamber with a dim light.

Cymbeline and Gurth stood before a face-sized mirror in Cymbeline's quarters. A miniature scene from the lower gallery filled the surface of the mirror.

'You saw?' Cymbeline asked.

Gurth nodded.

'Well?' the Wiseone asked.

'It is possible,' Gurth answered, moving closer to the mirror. The mirror showed the six travellers as they stood before the table filling their empty stomachs.

'Did you notice the expression on the woman Guyon's face when the Nglelin informed them that the wall which had stopped them from leaving the lower galleries had been merely an illusion?' asked Cymbeline.

'Yes, she was angry,' Gurth replied. 'But only with herself, no one else.'

'And the others?'

'Each has a unique quality which will one day, with training, serve them well,' Gurth answered.

'Then they are acceptable to you?' Cymbeline asked, an unusual zeal in his voice.

'They are, Wiseone.'

'And when will you leave?'

'Three days' time,' Gurth answered.

6

THE CITY STATES

'**A**re you sure word reached them?' Edelmar Rhys
asked.

'Yes, Great Lord.'

'Good, then it has begun. Are my staff waiting?'

'Yes, Great Lord. They are in the outer chamber.'

'Have them enter.'

The colonel bowed. As he crossed the ornately patterned stone floor, he readied himself to greet those who
waited beyond the heavy doors. At a nod from the colonel,
the sentries slid the bars from the twin doors and drew
them open.

Waiting patiently in the outer chamber were Edelmar
Rhys's generals, each of them a ruler in his own right.
To one side stood the seven Knights. The silver designs
on their black armour seemed to dance in the torchlight.
Behind them, in the corner of the chamber, stood a
solitary figure. His face was hidden in the shadows.
Unlike the others, the only armour he wore was a black
sleeveless mail shirt with a thin belt around his waist,
which supported a small scabbard.

The Knights entered Edelmar Rhys's chamber first,
followed by the generals. The black-mailed figure was
the last to enter, staying at the rear of the chamber while
the rest crossed to stand before Edelmar Rhys.

'The first phase of my plan has ended,' Edelmar Rhys began. 'The west is united under my banner.'

The generals nodded in agreement. Each of them had been the ruler of one of the many city states. As each city had fallen, the rulers had been taken before Edelmar Rhys expecting only death, but to their surprise they had found a different offer.

At first it seemed like madness, but as Edelmar Rhys explained what he had learnt, and when others came forward to substantiate his story, the rulers understood what had to be done. Strange happenings were reported from the southern forests. Creatures long since believed extinct were to be found in alarming numbers. Raiding parties of goblins had ventured far from the security of their forest homes and were plundering the countryside.

But worse was still to come. Other creatures had been sighted: large reptilian beasts and tall armoured figures, and it was this last sighting which worried Edelmar Rhys the most. He had taken the description to his counsellors, and his worst fears had been confirmed. Kobalos.

Edelmar Rhys then continued explaining what was to be done next. Even he doubted he could have got as far as he had if not for the arrival one morning of the seven strange Knights at the ridge beyond the camp. When Edelmar Rhys investigated, he had found the seven armoured Knights waiting, sitting motionless on their huge armoured mounts.

The seven Knights had not answered his questions about their homeland, but had simply stated that they had been sent to aid him in his task. It was not until several weeks later that Edelmar Rhys met the rest of his new allies — the black-mailed assassins.

7

DAMEAR

Far to the southwest, in a land never travelled by the men of the city states or coastal lands, a low range of mountains lay. On the eastern spur of that range, tucked protectively in a wide valley between the mountains Athanor and Teneriffe, squatted the city of Damear. Huge stone walls forty feet in height surrounded the city. Walls of even greater height sealed off the entrances to the valley, turning it into a well-protected haven.

The city of Damear lay in the centre of the valley. Fed by four springs, and with nearly a quarter of the city being storehouses, the inhabitants, who simply called themselves Damear, felt safe and secure in their mighty home. In the centre of the city there was a long building. Only in rare times of war was this building visited, but recently it had had many visitors.

The building consisted of one long hall, large enough to hold the commanders of all the legions of this warrior-dominated land. In decades past, their attention had been turned southward, but now a new war arena had presented itself.

The hall was long, a tall curved ceiling stretched high above those who waited. Armoured men filled the hall, leaving only a narrow aisle running its length. Down this clear passageway a tall man strode. He was dressed completely in grey plate mail. The visor of his helmet was lowered, revealing only piercing blue eyes which surveyed those assembled. A sheathed broadsword hung from a thick metal-studded belt about his armoured waist.

At the top of a short flight of stairs, Phelan turned and stood silently, allowing his gaze to sweep the great hall. There had been silence before, but now an even deeper silence gripped those in the large hall. Robed Ma'goi, long trained in the arts of magic, lined the stairs.

'Those of the city states have learnt of our preparations,' Phelan said quietly, yet his voice reached even the furthest corner of the long hall. 'To this end we are forced to make slight adjustments to our plans.'

Not a sound came from those assembled.

'The Lord Beleth,' Phelan gestured to an enormous armoured figure wearing a helmet in the shape of a horse's head, 'has agreed to undertake this new, and unexpected aspect of our plan.'

Beleth gave a slight inclination of his head in agreement.

'Duke Zepar, Duke Tesmond, and the Marquis Leraie will aid the Lord in this work.'

Leraie wore a plain helmet, while Tesmond's was shaped like the head of a lion. Zepar also wore a plain helmet, but the visor was raised showing the handsome features of a young man.

'Should the Lord Beleth require any other assistance, he is to be given it without question,' Phelan ordered and stepped from the dais.

Phelan strode from the building, leaving the buzz of conversation behind him. It had been many years since the Damear had had an enemy worthy of them. For far too long they had been forced to act as gatekeepers, holding back the twisted hordes of the southern wastelands; but in the fast-approaching war, the Damear would find themselves facing a truly formidable foe.

Phelan stopped in mid-stride and turned his troubled gaze to the north. The western lands were ready, his spies had informed him of that, but was the Fortalice aware of what was really happening?

8

INITIATION

The party left through the upper portal shortly after first light. The blue-cloaked and armoured Yarracks rode ahead of the small convoy as they wound their way down the mountain to the open plain to the west. Gurth rode surrounded by the red-robed Kungour, answering their questions about the surroundings.

Guyon flicked the reins, urging the horses to maintain their fast pace. She resented being given the role of teamster but she would take each task allotted her and perform it well. She would show everyone she was equal to any task, and from these menial tasks she would build a future of power and position.

Anyon, seated beside her, cursed his luck at having been paired off with this morose female. No matter what he did, she would find fault with it and ridicule him in front of the others. She even found fault in the way he wore his short yellow robe. But he had made a promise to himself that he would not allow her to annoy him on this journey. He had learnt more in the short time he had been at the Fortalice than he had thought possible, and even though most of his time had been spent on menial tasks, it would not be long before he could turn what he had learnt into profit.

Roland and Alaric rode in the second wagon. Alaric

had been so glad to leave the confines of the Fortalice that he had kept up a continuous chatter since passing through the upper portal. Roland understood how his companion felt. He had heard Alaric's story and realised that after such a short amount of freedom the stone walls of the Fortalice must have seemed like another prison.

That left Ivo and Jerram, the third and last wagon in the small convoy. Ivo was enjoying the scenery. It was vastly different from her barren rocky homeland. She had travelled extensively over the years but this was the first time she had had a chance to relax, and actually examine her surroundings. She remembered well the first time she left the village in the attempt to escape the stares and whispers. The further she travelled from her home the more she came to realise that the entire world was made up of nothing but barren rocky slopes. How very different to the land through which they now travelled.

The countryside below the upper portal was different to that which the four had travelled through to reach the lower portal. The trees to either side of the road were short but straight limbed, which gave the impression the Fortalice was even taller than it really was. Low shrubs covered the ground beneath the trees, harbouring an enormous variety of fauna, and a peacefulness hung in the air about the convoy as they travelled, leaving only the sounds of the wagons and their teams.

Jerram gave the horses their head as they plodded on behind the other wagons. Of all the luck. Why had they been chosen for this journey? At least he had not been separated from the other five. It would have been ironic to have travelled so far to find them, only to be separated from them a short time later, though it did surprise him that ones so new to the ways of the Fortalice should be chosen for such a mission.

The terrain was flat and heavily cultivated. The party was forced to cross many irrigation ditches as they made their way westward. The fields were full of farmers and their families and each small group stopped and waved as the party rode by. Their prosperity and safety was solely due to the work of the Fortalice. No war had touched this land for almost a century, and any law-breaker who dared operate so close to the Fortalice was soon hunted down and dealt with.

With an hour till sunset, Gurth called a halt. The teams were unhitched and the horses unsaddled. Anyon, Jerram, and Roland began unloading the items which would be needed from the wagon. Guyon, Ivo, and Alaric saw to the horses. The other party of Morallie set about preparing the camp site. A spot was cleared and enough dead wood to see them through the night was gathered. A small tent was erected for the Nglelin, and the Yarracks set up a watch for the night. Light rain had fallen shortly before the party had stopped and one of the Morallie was finding it difficult to light the fire with the damp fuel available. Gurth, seeing the young man's difficulties, crossed to the smoking fire.

'*ngarrin kudla wiena*,' he muttered. The pile of damp timber began to smoke. The Morallie stepped back from it as the smoke increased even more. Suddenly the timber burst into flames, giving off a strong bright light which lit up the centre of the camp site. The three Kungour gathered before their teacher and immediately began asking questions. Gurth studied the eager students before nodding in agreement. He then broke into a short explanation, his hands moving in small, sharp movements.

Once the impromptu lesson was over, the Kungour separated and moved from the light of the fire. Soon small fires could be seen beyond the boundary of the camp.

With the Yarracks wrapped in their heavy blue cloaks patrolling the perimeter of the camp, the remainder of the party settled down for the night. The Morallie had again been paired off. It would be their responsibility to maintain the fire throughout the night.

'Did you see how Gurth lit the fire?' Guyon asked.

Anyon was caught off guard by the question, not so much that the always silent Guyon had spoken or even that she had spoken to him, but the fact that she was so enthusiastic about what she had seen. He had to admit that the small display of power had fuelled his drive to return to the Fortalice and continue the steady climb until, one day, he too would be able to wield the same power, but on a much larger scale and for a greatly different reason, a reason which would fill his life with gold and all the pleasures it would buy. No longer would he have to fight to survive. No longer would he be forced to live by his wits, constantly on his guard. He would be able to hire others to do all the menial tasks he had always found unpleasant.

'Impressive,' he answered. 'But...' Anyon glanced at the dancing fires beyond the camp site, 'perhaps a trifle dangerous.'

'Don't be ridiculous,' Guyon snapped. 'They are serious students. They know what they are doing.'

'Oh really?' Anyon said, leaning forward slightly. 'Wanna bet?'

Guyon was about to reply when there was a startled cry from behind her. One of the Kungour leapt into the camp site with his two companions beating wildly at the lengthening flames which were eating their way up his robe. Finally the flames were extinguished and the Kungour, including the slightly singed youth, returned to their studies.

'Serious students?'

Guyon ignored Anyon's comment. Instead she fed more fuel into the fire before turning to watch the Kungour as they returned to practise their new skill.

The wagons, like the days, rolled on. The land changed little as the convoy approached the inland sea. Six-wheeled, the cumbersome boxlike wagons rolled onwards, their unsprung bodies riding rough over every bump.

Alaric leaned to one side and massaged his rump. 'Thank the Lady we leave these cursed wagons today,' he mumbled.

'I doubt you'll find passage on one of the coastal fishing boats much better,' Roland said.

71

'Why didn't we make straight for Breel?' Alaric continued to try to work the aches from his pained rump.

'The forests of Munde are alive with carcajous,' Roland explained. 'Many large packs of carcajous have, over the last year, gradually worked their way south, terrifying the populace as they moved.'

'I know all about the carcajous,' Alaric snorted. 'They dogged my steps through Munde's many forests. I was glad to be rid of them.'

'Well, it seems they have travelled even further south than when you had your run-in with them,' Roland explained. 'They have reached the Ashbrook and are in great numbers from the coast to Lake Zeridal. Fortunately they are unable to cross the Ashbrook, though little is being done to reduce their number.'

'When did you learn all this?'

'Shortly before we left.'

'Then there has been little time for the situation to change.'

Roland nodded. 'Once we reach Breel, we'll probably book passage on a larger more comfortable vessel and continue our journey.'

'More comfortable?'

'Have you ever travelled on a fishing boat?' Roland asked.

'No. Never,' Alaric replied. 'Why?'

'You'll find out soon enough.'

Slowly the wagon crested the long rise. For almost the entire day they had been forced to crawl their way up an ever increasing slope. The horses were completely spent as they neared the top. Jerram leapt down from the wagon and, walking beside the exhausted animals, tried to urge the last effort from them.

From her high position on the wagon's seat, Ivo saw the waters of the great lake stretching out before her. Pleased to reach the end of the first leg of their journey, she was very apprehensive about the voyage that was still to come; but she had to push those thoughts from her mind as the wagon started down the lake side of the ridge.

Jerram jumped to the side of the wagon and climbed up to the seat beside Ivo as she struggled with the team.

'Need a hand?' he asked.

'I can handle it,' she answered curtly.

'If you say so,' Jerram said with a smile. He leaned back and watched his companion as she fought against the horses. Her right leg was braced against the brake, muscles straining as she locked it down, slowing the wagon's descent.

By the time the road levelled out, Ivo was soaked with sweat and her body quivered with the effort of holding the vehicle in check. Without asking, Jerram leaned across and took the reins from her trembling hands. She didn't resist. Once Jerram had the team under control, Ivo leaned against the hard back of the seat and closed her eyes.

She remained that way until the wagons rolled into the small fishing village which was to be the end of the first leg of their journey. Ivo had paid little attention to where she was, until the first whiff of the village reached her. Wrinkling her nose, she slowly opened her eyes and began to examine her surroundings.

The small village could have been any one of the many she had seen over her years of travel. The buildings were small and constructed of a rough weather-worn timber. The street was wider than most, but that was the only difference. The thick mud slowed the wagons' progress even more, and covered the wheels with a coating of black fish-smelling mud.

There had been a village like this at the end of the long valley which held her home. When her father had taken her there for the first time she thought they were standing at the edge of the world. Her brothers had stood to one side trying not to be overawed by the situation, but Ivo could see that they were as overcome as she was. In the light rain that was falling she could see the barren landscape slowly dropping away in all directions save homeward. Little had she realised the true extent of the world and the wonders it held.

Gurth stopped before the largest building and dismounted. Even though the mud was thick and covered the entire street, he made no effort to avoid it. Stepping down into the mud, he walked the short distance to the decking of the nearest building. As Gurth crossed the decking, several of the Kungour began to murmur and point. Gurth's boots were clean, not one spot of mud was to be seen.

'Nice trick,' Ivo exclaimed.

'That could be useful,' Alaric said with a wink.

'Have you seen the scow we're to travel on?' Ivo asked as she entered the small room and seated herself before the well-tended fire.

'The fishing boats here are all the same,' Guyon answered. 'It will make little difference which one we travel on.'

'Really,' Anyon laughed. 'Wanna bet?'

Ivo stared at Anyon, trying to work out if he was laughing at her. Anyon continued, unaware of the stare. 'I've spent a bit of time travelling these shores not so long ago,' he explained. 'Some of these villages have certain vessels put aside that they deem... unseaworthy. It's generally these that they hire out to strangers.'

'Why?' Alaric asked.

'They have found in the past that they very rarely get the vessels back once they have been hired. This way they get the money for the hire but lose nothing in the process.'

'But who'd hire the vessels if they are so bad?' Roland answered.

'People who need transportation in a hurry,' Anyon answered.

'Like us?' asked Ivo.

'Like us,' Anyon nodded.

'Damn,' Ivo cursed. 'I'd hoped that when the state and condition of the vessel was seen, Gurth would hire another.'

'No chance,' Anyon grinned. 'We're stuck with it.'

*

Gurth had decided that, due to the condition of the village, they would board the vessel and leave immediately. That news was greeted with mixed feelings from the group. Some, like Alaric and Roland, were glad to be free of the mud-splattered village, while Ivo seemed reluctant to cross even the short distance from the tumbledown timber jetty to the waiting vessel.

It had been planned at first to transport the horses below decks, but the size of the vessel available made that impossible. Anyon was just pleased to see the end of the wagons and horses. From the start he had been unhappy with his position in this group, and now for the first time he felt as if he was taking an important part in things. With the timbered hull creaking alarmingly, the vessel slowly inched its way from the sheltered bay and out into the offshore wind.

Alaric positioned himself at the bow, enjoying the strong salt tang in the freshening wind. So far their journey had been fascinating, and he intended to milk the remainder of the trip for every new experience he could.

Roland and Guyon sought out Gurth to see if there had been any further change in their plans. Although the green-robed leader of their party did not generally confide in them, it was not difficult to learn what was happening by simply keeping their eyes open.

Ivo had disappeared below deck as soon as she had come on board. She knew there was no way out of this voyage and had resigned herself to a terrifying trip.

Anyon had taken himself below deck as well, though he was there for different reasons. Though the crew was small and not well paid, they carried enough coinage to make the odd game of chance worthwhile. And Anyon was there to see that there were games, but without as much chance involved as some would like.

For the first time in many months, Jerram allowed himself to relax. There was no way he could be separated from his companions for the next leg of their journey. Though the voyage looked to be uncomfortable, and slightly cramped, it would be his first chance to simply rest, free of the continual danger which had threatened his mission since its beginning. So many accidents could have befallen the four before Jerram had found them. A slip in training could have rendered one of them unfit to travel, separating that person from the group. And one slip was all that would have been needed for those about him to find his true origins. If it was even hinted at that he was from Alamut, his mission to watch over the four could end.

The wind gradually strengthened through the night so that as the sun rose above the eastern horizon, the small vessel and its occupants were speeding towards their destination. Ivo had not left her cabin since the voyage began. All through the night she had remained seated on her bunk, her legs drawn up tightly to her chest. In the darkness of the cabin, the creaking of the timber and the sound of the water rushing past the hull were magnified until no other sound could be heard. Slowly Ivo drifted back to her childhood, the rocking of the vessel and the sound of the water gradually putting her to sleep.

It had been midsummer when a young Ivo and her three brothers found the small cave opening. They had searched out the many passageways and caverns over the next few weeks until they had at last found an underground lake with a small narrow beach.

At some time deep in the land's past, the water must have been forced below ground where it was finally trapped. The four adventurers had not taken long to explore the water. They found it icy cold yet somehow totally invigorating. During one of their many swims, Ren, Ivo's older brother, discovered that the lake was inhabited by a multitude of strange fish. Clay, always the fisherman of the young group, caught several of the almost transparent fish, only to find that they had no eyes. But, regardless of what they looked like, once roasted slowly over a very small fire they tasted superb.

On their many visits, Ivo and her brothers brought many items to their dark realm: firewood and dried food, spare clothing, and larger lengths of timber which were to be used for building a small shelter. It had been Ivo who first suggested that they use the timber to construct a raft so they could investigate more of their new world or, as she so often quoted, her new realm.

Pel was immediately against the idea. He was worried that they did not know how deep the water might be once away from the safety of the small beach. But Ivo was quick in shouting him down. She liked it when her brothers did as she wanted and relished her power of manipulating them.

Soon the raft was constructed and loaded with everything the group thought they might need for exploring. Without another thought, it was launched and the children set out on their big adventure.

The raft was large enough to be comfortable for the four occupants as well as their gear. In each of the corners a torch was tied to a tall pole. Many spare torches had been prepared and they rested safely in the centre. The four laughed and splashed the water as they slowly paddled their way along the wall of the cavern.

For hours they worked their way along the cavern's curving wall, expecting to find themselves at their small beach any minute. But as time wore on they realised that the lake was much larger than they had first realised. Though the water remained calm and flat, there seemed to be more disturbances caused by unseen creatures than there were in the shallower water where they had often swum.

First one set of torches burnt down, followed by the second set then the third. With only eight torches remaining, Pel began to panic. He wanted to turn back immediately. But Ren explained that their remaining torches would be gone long before they reached their starting point. The thought of making the rest of the journey in darkness terrified Pel.

Clay, always ready with an answer, suggested that they

extinguish two of the torches and that in the half light they could reach the beach in safety. Ren and Pel agreed but Ivo suggested that they leave the wall of the cavern and make their way back straight across the dark water. Ivo had always got her way with her brothers by suggesting that what she wanted to do was what a man would do, and that any who opposed her were merely children playing at being men.

Pushing off from the wall of the cavern, the raft was soon surrounded by darkness. In their small flickering circle of light, the raft and its small crew moved further out into the centre of the lake. Suddenly the raft was buffeted from below, throwing Pel and Ren to the timber floor and lifting Clay from his feet and hurling him into the water. Quickly Clay was dragged from the dark waters. As he was drawn onto the raft, he cried that something had brushed past his legs. In the light of the two torches, Ivo and the others could see that the skin had been scraped off his right leg from knee to ankle.

The four took up their paddles and bent their backs in an effort to reach the wall of the cavern. A second shock from beneath the water struck the raft, tilting it to one side. All the gear and the remaining torches were lost as the four held on for their lives. When finally the raft settled, only one torch remained alight; everything else had been lost, including their paddles.

Suddenly the raft tipped as a large dark shape tried to draw itself up onto it. Clay drew his knife and slashed at the dark shape. His attack was answered by a strangled cry from the creature before it slipped back into the still water. In the flickering light of the remaining torch, Ivo had caught a fleeting glimpse of the attacker. It had been reptilian, long necked and short limbed. Its hide was grey and looked coarse.

Just before the last torch died, Ivo sat in the centre of the raft surrounded by her brothers. Each had drawn a knife and was waiting, grim-faced, for another attack.

How long she sat there unmoving Ivo could never remember. Even when the raft touched the small beach, she remained seated. It wasn't until large warm hands had lifted her from her cramped seat and had drawn her to a warm leather-clad chest that, at last, the tears she had held back for so long poured from her red eyes. Through the tears she could see her father looking anxiously about the beach for any sign of his other children. Slowly he looked down at the small shivering child in his arms and realised the awful truth. Then, drawing Ivo even closer, he turned and began to make his way up to the light above, while his companions continued their fruitless search.

9

FIRST MISSION

Hugging the ever-visible coast, the small fishing vessel made its way northward. Soon the Flatlands gave way to a heavily forested coastline outlined by a thin strip of white sand. Guyon spent as much time as she could watching the changing coast through a set of lenses encased in a tube, which Gurth had produced from his luggage. Fascinated by the beautiful scenes she observed through the strange device, she was horrified one morning to find the beach full of carcajous. During the night the party had passed the mouth of the Ashbrook River, and the land north of the river was known to be alive with a plague of carcajous. The creatures were prowling through the remains of a small fishing village. Thin plumes of smoke rose above several of the huts which, until recently, had been in use. Several of the carcajous broke into a fight over something that Guyon could not quite make out.

'They're a curse,' Roland said quietly.

Guyon lowered the tubular lenses as if to answer; then, changing her mind, she raised the brass instrument and continued her search of the coast, ignoring Roland.

'Did they cause you any difficulty?' he asked, trying to draw Guyon into a conversation.

'I did not pass through this land,' she said.

Roland nodded and thought about what he had just learnt about his latest travelling companion. If what she said was true, then she had not travelled from the north. Then where had she come from? In truth she did not have the look of a northron about her, and her weapon skill was somewhat lacking, which was a thing unheard of in the far north. She had taken a great interest in the voyage so probably she was seeing things along the lake's shoreline for the first time. That left east or south as her probable homeland.

To the east lay a powerful island empire. Its ever-present navy patrolled the narrow strips of water which separated the many islands. None had ever entered the empire's lands without permission, and very few who had permission ever returned.

To the south lay a vast desert and wasteland. Only a few scavengers and trappers eked out a meagre existence along its border, and there was no chance that she was one of those as they were noted for their ferocity in combat and their ability to live off the land in all conditions.

Roland risked another quick glance at the woman leaning on the rail beside him. She disturbed him. Something about her drew him closer; he felt that he could trust her, depend on her for strength. Travelling as much as he had, he knew the mannerisms of the many lands and peoples, but Guyon's origins were a mystery. There was nothing extraordinary about her appearance. Her brown hair was loose and hung to her shoulders. She was slightly shorter than Ivo, and her grey eyes were never still in her search for knowledge.

Alaric, on the other hand, was a typical northron, in dress and action. Ivo was from one of the mountainous regions to the far north and Anyon was typical of the type to emerge from the troubled areas around the Prae-lean Forest, north of Fordwich — a thief and an opportunist.

Jerram also troubled Roland. His actions and mannerisms spoke of a good upbringing, yet his lack of weapons and fighting skill seemed strangely out of place in these troubled lands.

Alaric shifted his position on the hard bench before the raging fire. Shortly after their arrival, a severe storm had rolled in from across the vast lake bringing with it high winds and heavy rain. With the arrival of the winds the town of Breel had simply closed up. Crews were called back on board the many vessels in the harbour, while businesses closed their doors and lowered the storm shutters to wait out the torrential rain.

The steeply-sloped roofs of the small town soon seemed alive as the heavy rain danced about on the red clay tiles. The timber-decked walkways on either side of the quickly disappearing streets were empty, save the occasional town dog as it sought cover from the worsening weather.

Ivo was resting for the first time in days. She had hardly had the strength to make her way from the fishing vessel to her room at the waterfront tavern, and once she reached her room, she collapsed on the bed, exhausted.

Alaric had taken a seat by the fire and was listening to the sounds of the storm as it threw itself at the small town. Alaric turned at a noise from behind him; it was Anyon. He was making his way somewhat unsteadily across the taproom towards the fire. He carried a massive pewter mug in each hand and was expending a great deal of energy to ensure that none of the mugs' contents spilt.

'Here,' Anyon said. He thrust a mug into Alaric's hand and dropped to the seat beside him.

Alaric took the offered mug and sipped the warm beverage. As he did so, the storm suddenly increased in fury. 'Doesn't sound like it's going to stop today,' he commented.

'Who cares,' Anyon answered. He extended one hand towards the fire. 'I'm warm, fed, and entertained.' He raised the mug to his lips and took a long pull at his drink.

'Aren't you interested in continuing?' Alaric asked.

Anyon shrugged and took another drink. 'I'm in no hurry,' he explained. 'The sooner this mission is over, the sooner we return to the Fortalice and all the menial tasks that are expected of us.'

'But that is part of our training,' Alaric said.

'Your training perhaps,' Anyon mumbled. 'I've got other things to do and there are several lands I want to see before I am too old to enjoy them. Besides, all this work and stuff is bad for your health.' With each gulp his speech was becoming more slurred and his eyes were gradually losing their focus.

Anyon tilted back his head and finished his drink. 'Yeh, I've definitely got more important things to do with my life than waste it as somebody's menial.'

'Then why did you bother to make the pilgrimage in the first place?' Alaric asked.

Anyon looked into his empty mug and then slowly raised his eyes to stare into the dancing flames. 'A slight misunderstanding,' he answered. 'A small thing that grew out of proportion.'

'But why the pilgrimage?'

'I needed to disappear for a time. A place where I was free to move about, yet was safe from prying eyes,' he answered. 'Besides, there's money to be made with what could be learnt at the Fortalice. Unfortunately there's too much work involved.'

Alaric said nothing as he refilled Anyon's mug.

'I grew up in the back streets and alleys of a place you probably haven't even heard of. I spent half my time persuading the rich that I was totally trustworthy and the rest of the time hiding from those who found out I wasn't.' Anyon laughed and gestured for Alaric to move closer. 'Sometimes I acquire things, not steal, mind you, but acquire. Ducrane always said that it was easier to convince a person to give you something than it was to actually steal it from them.' Anyon finally noticed his mug was full and took a long drink.

'Was Ducrane your father ... brother?' Alaric asked.

'Just a friend,' Anyon answered and turned his full attention to his drink.

Alaric laughed to himself. He could very well imagine why his companion had had to disappear for a while — probably something to do with the ownership of a horse, or the mislaying of an expensive piece of jewellery.

Alaric glanced at his suddenly silent companion. Anyon's head had dropped, his chin rested on his slowly heaving chest. Smiling, Alaric prised the mug from Anyon's unfeeling fingers and placed it on the floor beside his seat. As Alaric straightened, a woman's scream tore the night above the howling of the storm.

Kicking the door open, Alaric burst into the kitchen as a second scream tore from the lips of the terrified serving girl. The back door was open, slamming back and forth against the wall in the storm's fury. Heavy rain was being driven through the open door, covering the floor of the kitchen in a steadily growing pool of water. The cook's assistant was struggling on the floor with a large grey carcajou. The cook was leaning against a large table in the centre of the room trying to stem the flow of blood from his badly mauled arm. Bleeding heavily from several bad cuts to his face, the cook's assistant was rapidly losing his struggle with the carcajou. Both his hands were locked about the straining creature's throat, but he was quickly weakening. The carcajou's spiked tail thrashed wildly from side to side as its jaws drew closer to the throat of the cook's assistant.

Alaric drew his knife and drove it deep into the carcajou's ribs. The beast screamed and tried to tear itself from the young lad's grip. But Alaric struck twice more before the carcajou was able to free itself. Twisting, the creature turned towards the door but collapsed before it had taken two paces. Grasping the door, Alaric tried to force it closed. A second carcajou struck the door frame, trying to paw its way into the tavern's kitchen. Kicking the struggling beast in the head, Alaric slammed the door closed and dropped the bar into place. The insane laughter of the carcajous sounded even more eerie through the closed door.

He was soaked to his skin by the driving rain before he turned from the barred door. Flying pieces of timber heralded the arrival of another carcajou as a small black shape crashed through the lightly shuttered window of the kitchen.

The carcajou slid on the wet floor and crashed into the far wall. Before it could gain its feet, the cook pushed himself away from the table and brought a large meat cleaver down on the beast's rain-soaked head, splitting its skull.

'This way!' Alaric called, dragging the terrified serving girl towards the taproom's door. The assistant got to his feet just in time to receive a push from behind by the cook. Both literally fell through the open door.

Alaric drew the door closed, throwing the two large bolts. 'Upstairs,' he said quickly. The walls of the taproom held many windows, all of them shuttered, but they were no stronger than the one which had shattered in the kitchen.

Anyon was still asleep before the fire, oblivious to the danger which threatened. Charging across the room knocking furniture from his path, Alaric reached his companion's side as one of the shuttered windows exploded in a shower of splinters.

The noise of the storm increased, almost drowning out the shrieking laughter of the carcajou. The large beast was wedged tight in the shattered shutter, unable to enter the taproom or fall free. Dragging Anyon to his feet, Alaric steered his unsteady companion around the upturned furniture and up the stairs. Halfway up the first flight, the carcajou freed itself and gave chase.

Bounding up the stairs, it was stopped in mid-stride by a long feathered shaft. Alaric threw a glance at the second landing in time to see Ivo notch another arrow.

'Quickly!' she shouted. 'Get that drunken idiot up here before we have more company.'

Ivo maintained her watch on the taproom until Alaric and Anyon were safe on the topmost landing. 'Get him into the room at the end of the hall,' she said with disgust as Alaric staggered past under the weight of the protesting Anyon. 'Drunken fool,' she added.

'Plague on you,' Anyon mumbled by way of an answer.

Ivo backed along the landing following her two companions into the end room. The rest of the party were already crowded into the small room. Gurth stood by the shuttered window listening to the sounds of the storm. Occasionally other sounds could be heard above the screaming wind.

'We have to help them,' Alaric said.

'How?' Roland asked. 'We are too few to help the entire town.'

'But we can at least try,' Ivo said hotly. 'We can't ignore them.'

'Wanna bet?' Anyon said suddenly, still leaning against Alaric.

'Useless . . . ,' Ivo started.

'Fool,' Anyon interrupted.

Ivo leapt forward but Alaric released Anyon and moved to intercept her. As soon as Anyon was released he fell against the wall. 'Plague on them all,' he mumbled as he slowly slumped to the floor.

'Alaric is correct,' Gurth said softly. 'We must help these people. The question is how?'

'There must be a break in the town's wall,' Alaric explained. 'If we could find the opening, we could seal it.'

'What good would that do?' Jerram asked. 'By now the town is already infested with carcajous.'

'True,' Roland conceded. 'But this will stop more of them from entering.'

'And a concentrated effort will rid us of those which remain,' Ivo added.

'Then it is settled,' Gurth said calmly. 'This is how it will be done . . .'

Gurth stepped from the protection of the tavern into the full strength of the storm. Rain lashed Ivo and Jerram as they followed the green-robed Nglelin out into the blinding storm. The wind struck Ivo and Jerram like a hammer, throwing them off balance. Jerram grabbed Ivo's arm and, bracing his feet, leaned into the wind. Shielding their eyes against the stinging rain, they peered through the heavy downpour.

Gurth stood in the centre of the small street. The wind howled around his body and the rain hammered down, but he was undisturbed by this. His green robes hung limply, unaffected by the wind. His unruffled hair was dry, as was his robe. He surveyed the street and buildings about him for any sign of the invading carcajous.

Jerram and Ivo stood supported in each other's arms, eyes wide as they stared at Gurth in disbelief. The Nglelin finished his search and turned to face the pair. A faint smile came to his lips as he saw their surprised stares.

'Come,' he said quietly. 'Let us continue our search.'

Gurth turned and strode off effortlessly towards the waterfront. Unfortunately for Ivo and Jerram, Gurth was moving directly into the tearing storm. With arms locked, the two made slow progress as they followed Gurth.

Ivo tilted her head and said, 'We'll never keep up with him.'

Jerram looked confused. 'What?' he shouted.

'We'll never keep up with him,' she shouted.

Jerram shrugged, but continued to struggle forward against the wind.

Ivo tightened her grip on Jerram's arm and moved forward with him. Only slowly did she realise that she had heard Gurth's voice above the howl of the storm when he had stood several paces away. Yet her voice, so close to Jerram, had been torn away by the wind.

Without warning, the two found themselves beside Gurth.

'There is something out of place,' Gurth said quietly.

Ivo noticed that she had no trouble hearing him, even though the wind still howled about her.

'Something is different,' Gurth added. He drew a small mirrored amulet from beneath his robes.

The section of the town seemed no different from

anything they had seen on their arrival, and the storm had not lessened in its intensity.

'What...?' Ivo began. She stopped speaking as she realised she would not be heard above the storm.

'There is something wrong here,' Gurth explained. 'Something that should not be.' The amulet was clutched tightly to his chest as Gurth began to turn slowly. Eyes unfocused, his head was cocked to one side as if trying to pluck a scent or sound from the air.

Ivo and Jerram began to search the street and buildings around them, looking for danger, yet not knowing exactly what it would look like.

Gurth reached for his companions and drew them towards him. 'Back to the tavern,' he said softly.

Ivo and Jerram found they were able to keep up with the tall Nglelin now that the wind was at their backs. Almost running, the trio reached the tavern's door simultaneously. Gurth raised his hand and spoke a word. This time Ivo was unable to hear the word, but she saw its result because the door swung open before them.

The taproom was a mess. Broken furniture was strewn about the room. Intermingled amongst the wreckage were many yellow-robed bodies. Ivo rushed into the centre of the room and began to search the figures for any sign of life. Jerram had stepped clear of the door and was searching the destroyed room carefully. On the stairs were five of the Yarracks. They lay side by side on the first landing where they had obviously made a stand to delay the attackers, while those of the party who remained made good their escape.

Dotted between the furniture and bodies were what seemed to be several scorched patches. With his hand resting on the pommel of his dirk, Jerram crossed to the closest scorch mark and knelt. He touched the black mark lightly with his fingertips and raised them to his nose. A strange sickly-sweet smell filled his nostrils.

'It's all that remains of their slayers,' Gurth said, nodding towards the unmoving yellow-robed bodies on the taproom floor and the blue armoured bodies of the Yarracks on the stairs.

'Slayers?' Ivo asked, raising her eyes from one of the bodies. 'But the carcajous . . . ?'

' . . . did not do this,' Jerram finished.

'No,' Gurth explained as he crossed the taproom towards the stairs. 'The carcajous were merely a diversion, something to keep us occupied while they located us and readied themselves for their work.'

'Who?' Ivo asked.

'We may yet learn,' Gurth answered softly as he silently began to climb the stairs.

Ivo drew an arrow from her quiver and notched it. With her longbow at the ready, she started up the stairs after Gurth. Jerram began to follow but was stopped by a sharp word from his female companion.

'No!' she snapped. 'If they are still here you would be next to useless with that toy. Wait here and see if there are any left alive.'

Jerram was about to argue but instead he clenched his teeth and removed his hand from his dirk. With fists locked in anger, he began to examine the bodies. He found no sign of Alaric, Guyon or Roland, but Anyon's body was in an untidy heap beside the dying fire. Faint wisps of smoke were rising from the leather jerkin Anyon wore. He must have made his way back to his seat beside the fire after Gurth and the others had left.

Jerram sat down heavily amongst the broken furniture. He had known Anyon for a short time only but the loss of a comrade-in-arms was always a sad moment.

But as he rolled the body over, Jerram could not stifle the laugh which escaped his closed lips. Anyon's chest rose and fell steadily and on his face was a ridiculous grin. An empty crushed ale mug was held tight against his chest.

'You drunken idiot,' Jerram laughed, drawing Anyon's head to his lap.

Ivo reached the top of the stairs. Her bow was drawn, and followed the movement of her eyes as they flickered from door to door, the arrow ready for immediate release should she see or sense any danger.

All the doors were open; many were broken, with only lengths of timber hanging from brass hinges to show where they had once been. One door was still closed, untouched, though the wall to either side and above the door was scorched black. The young serving girl from the kitchen lay dead beside the door.

'Those we seek have fled,' Gurth said quickly.

'And the others?'

'They are in there,' Gurth answered, gesturing at the closed door.

Ivo lowered her bow and reached for the door.

'No!' Gurth's hands flashed out and grasped Ivo's wrist. 'Their locking web still stands.'

Raising one hand, Gurth held it palm open towards the door. 'They are weak,' he whispered, barely loud enough for Ivo to hear. 'There!' he said suddenly, and leapt for the door.

His booted foot struck the door, throwing it back into the room. Guyon knelt on the floor beside one of the Kungour; his head was on her lap and she was stroking his forehead with a soft piece of cloth. Another of the red robes was lying beside the door. One look was all that was needed to see that he was dead. The other Kungour leaned against the wall by the door. Alaric and Roland were standing at the rear of the room, their bloodied swords drawn and ready. Both men were covered in blood. The remaining twenty-five Yarracks were seated on the floor to either side of the room. Their armour showed signs of heavy fighting and they were bloodied and tired.

Gurth looked at the Kungour beside the door. But there was no response to his questioning gaze. Gurth then knelt beside his injured companion and placed his hand on his wet forehead.

'How goes it?' he asked gently.

The injured Kungour smiled slightly and shook his head. His lips moved and Gurth was forced to lean closer to hear what was spoken. Gurth's face lengthened as the dying man spoke. When the lips stopped moving Gurth placed a hand on the dying man's forehead. Seen only by Gurth, wide bands of green light spread from his fingers and began to wrap around his injured companion. At last Gurth rose, and Guyon lifted the still head from her lap and lowered it gently to the floor beside her.

'What did he say?' Ivo asked. 'Who did this?'

'He did not know,' Gurth answered slowly. 'Someone of great skill in the Arts attacked them here, and won. Someone so strong that he was able to do all this, and still escape. And we have no idea of who he is, where he came from, or why he attacked us in the first place.'

'Could he be sent by those from across Lake Zeridal?' Ivo asked.

'I have no idea,' Gurth answered. 'No idea at all.'

10

BELETH

The scout wound his way between the large rocks which in times past had fallen from the cliff above. He was dressed in leathers rather than the grey mail of his comrades, but that did not bother him as he was good at his job, the best scout the great Lord had. Approaching the waiting men, Manaz steered his mount towards the tall armoured figure wearing the horse-head helmet. As he neared him, he lowered his eyes in respect.

'My Lord?'

'Yes?'

'There is a large village ahead which should be suitable for our needs.'

Beleth raised his eyes and examined the scout. He had seen the young man before, many times in fact. It was rumoured that there was a touch of the Arts in his family. If so, it would explain why he could continually gather information and move where others could not.

'How does the village lie?'

'It sits at the bottom of a deep depression, Lord,' Manaz answered. 'There is little cover on the slopes and even less as you near the village.'

Beleth knew the answer to his question before it was asked, but he had to be sure. 'Were you seen?'

'No, Lord,' Manaz answered with a smile.

'Good.' Beleth then turned his attention to one of the other mounted men. 'Tesmond!'

'Yes, Lord?' the armoured man answered. The visor of his lion-shaped helmet was down, giving his voice a deep ringing tone.

'Secure the village!'

'Yes, Lord,' Tesmond answered. Drawing on his horse's reins, he turned its head towards the waiting camp hidden behind them in the shadow of the cliff.

Within minutes Duke Tesmond rode from the camp, his armoured war company riding behind him. Each man wore grey chain mail and a small round helmet, while a short sword hung from his belt. Long spears, each flying a dark pennant just below the head, were held in the right hand, reaching skyward.

Across the plain the company rode. Manaz was at the head of the column with Tesmond, aware that many eyes watched him. For one so young to ride beside a Lord was a rare honour indeed. Leaning slightly forward, Manaz pointed to the easiest approach to the village. Tesmond nodded and angled his mount towards the large clump of trees.

'The trees will hide our approach to the village, Lord,' Manaz explained.

'And beyond the trees?'

'Once clear of the trees we will be in full view of any of the villagers who happen to be looking in this direction, Lord.'

'By the time they see us it will be too late,' Tesmond said absent-mindedly.

The head of the long column reached the trees. Tesmond moved his mount from the well-travelled trail and waved for the column to continue past him. As the men rode silently by, Tesmond's officers moved to their duke's side.

'Gentlemen,' Tesmond began, 'it is my intention to clear the village of its occupants and contain them on the slopes on the far side of the village. When we reach the edge of these trees we will open up into extended file and sweep down the slope in three waves.'

Tesmond stopped and examined the faces of his officers. Each man was known to Tesmond and had been chosen carefully for his position.

'The first wave will ride through the village creating havoc. The second wave will dismount and clear the huts. The third will herd the confused villagers from the confines of the village where they will be stopped and contained by the first wave which will have reached the far side of the depression.'

The officers nodded and, at a hand gesture from Tesmond, rejoined the column, passing on the information to their sergeants.

With no need for further orders, the column reached the grove's edge and shook itself out into three ranks. Tesmond positioned himself to one side of his men and surveyed the village below him. As he studied the peaceful scene he raised his right hand, readying his men. With a chopping motion of his hand, the first wave spurred their mounts forward.

Panic broke out in the village below as the armoured men were seen for the first time. Squat women grabbed their misshapen children and ran for the shelter of the huts while the men grabbed what they could in the way of weapons and raced forward to meet the fast approaching danger.

Some of the hastily armed villagers managed to bring down two or three of the riders, but for the most part the poorly armed men were ridden down by the speeding rank of horsemen. The first wave continued through the village, reaching the furthest side as the second wave entered the settlement.

Hardly slowing their mounts, the second wave leapt from the saddles and rushed into the closest huts. Screams erupted from many of the huts as the families were driven from the flimsy protection of the thatched walls. The dismounted troops moved quickly from one hut to the other while the third wave slowly made its way through the village herding all before it.

The first wave, having reached the edge of the depression,

had turned and were moving steadily back towards the village, gathering the first of the panicking villagers.

Suddenly, from one of the huts, ten figures burst into view. They made no effort to help the panicking villagers, but simply turned and ran for the edge of the village. An arm rose and a section of the first rank broke off and rode towards the ten fugitives. Seeing that escape was impossible, the ten stopped their headlong flight and formed a hasty circle. Swords glinted in the sunlight as the mounted men rode their horses through the circle without pause. One of the men dismounted and heaved one of the bodies from the ground, throwing it over the saddle of his horse. Quickly remounting behind the corpse, he turned his horse's head and rode to where the officers waited. Reining his mount to a sliding halt, the Damear warrior threw the corpse to the ground. The Lord leaned forward and examined the body. The creature had grey skin and wore well kept armour. Its almond eyes were open and stared blankly upwards.

'Forest goblins!' Tesmond exclaimed.

'Then it seems I was correct,' Beleth remarked.

'Yes, Lord. I would not have thought them this far east,' Tesmond answered.

'Send word to Damear,' Beleth ordered. 'We have less time than we thought.'

As Tesmond watched, one of the officers of the second wave mounted, and rode from the village. The officer soon reached Tesmond's side.

'The village is clear and secure, Lord,' the officer reported.

'The villagers?'

'Being taken care of now, my Lord,' the officer answered.

Tesmond nodded and began to ride down the slope towards the empty village. Beleth and his officers sat their mounts and watched the small party ride down towards the settlement.

Above the noise of the horse's hooves, the screams rose

as the grey-mailed soldiers mercilessly cut down the tightly-packed villagers.

The curved horizon, generally uninterrupted for miles, was broken in two places. The first was a small sail far to the south as the fishing vessel which had brought them to the village made its return voyage. On board were the injured Kungour and half the remaining blue-armoured Yarracks.

The second break was a similar sail, only much larger. That vessel had been hired to take the remainder of the party westward across Lake Zeridal.

As the two vessels had sailed from the small dock of the village, many of the villagers had left their homes to watch the tall figure in the green wind-flapped robes as he stood on the deck surrounded by small blue figures.

The two vessels had seemed to pace each other as they left the harbour, but suddenly the smaller of the two had leaned into the wind turning her bow southward.

On the hilltop high above the village, a leather-clad scout watched the two vessels claw their way over the horizon. His almond-shaped eyes squinted as he strained to make out every detail of the scene below him. The tips of his grey teardrop-shaped ears touched the leather cap he wore. With a snarl, he climbed quickly to his feet and sprinted down the reverse side of the hill and vaulted into the saddle of his feeding mount. Leaning forward and taking up the reins, he kicked the frightened horse into a gallop.

As the mounted scout rode southward, urging his horse to even greater speed, another figure rose slowly from the foliage on the hill. With an axe gripped firmly in his right hand, the short figure jogged down the gentle slope of the hill. At the base of the hill he turned north and, following the low ground, circled the hill to a large stand of trees which had been just out of sight of the leather-clad scout.

If the scout had noticed the stand, and had bothered to investigate it, he would have discovered a shadow-hidden camp deep within the protective branches. The camp held six people: two females and four males. As the axe-carrying scout entered the camp he was greeted quickly.

'Well?'

'He waited till both vessels were out of sight before he was satisfied,' the scout answered. He dropped his axe beside a small fire and sat beside it, taking up a wooden bowl and sniffing its contents.

'We will leave at once,' the tallest of the group said. He was dressed in a coarse woven cloth shirt and baggy trousers, both of which seemed ill-fitting and ill-suited to the tall straight-backed man.

The scout still sat by the fire sipping slowly at the liquid in the wooden bowl.

'Haven't you had enough?' one of the women asked.

'What's it to you?' Anyon answered, draining the last of the liquid from the bowl before flicking it into the fire. 'There was something strange about the fellow,' he mumbled to himself. 'Something damn strange. His skin was almost grey in colour, and looked to be scaled.'

The others seemed not to have heard as they continued to gather their packs, settling the unaccustomed weight on their shoulders.

'It will be some time before those who seek to hinder us realise that we were on neither of the vessels,' Gurth explained. 'So we must put what time we have to good use.'

'Then why didn't we steal some horses?' Anyon asked as he slowly got to his feet. 'If time is so crucial, why must we walk?'

'We managed to leave the town unnoticed because of the panic the carcajous caused,' Gurth explained patiently. 'But to try to bring seven mounts with us would have been impossible.'

'But why all the secrecy?' Anyon asked, slightly angered. 'Surely we could have taken the mounts we needed and waited till the vessels were out of sight before starting out?'

'How can you remain unseen if you steal seven out

of the nine horses a town has?' Guyon asked. 'Someone would have noticed and then there would have been no secrecy.'

Anyon dismissed the argument with a wave of his hand as he bent to retrieve his axe. 'I hate walking,' he muttered.

With Anyon as reluctant scout, the small party set out to the southeast. It had been Gurth's idea that the information about the strange attackers was more important than learning what was behind the western war. Sending the remaining red-robe and Yarracks westward would convince those following them that they were continuing with their mission. This would give Gurth and the others time to lose themselves in the forests to the south.

Gurth had been reluctant to use his skills to send a message to one of the Wiseones as the message might well have been intercepted by the unknown enemy. Though walking to the Fortalice would take the longest time to pass on the information, it would be by far the safest way.

Ivo stood huddled in her cloak against the chilly night air. When they had first set up camp, they lit a small fire to cook their meal, but that had long since turned to cold ash. In the darkness her longbow would have been useless, so as she walked her sentry, she held a naked shortsword beneath her cloak. She felt uncomfortable with the strange weapon, but she knew that thanks to the training at the Fortalice, she would be able to use it if the need arose.

Jerram watched the far side of the camp. He had refused to take the offered sword, saying that he would rely on his dirk should danger threaten. Guyon had started to protest but Alaric had quietened her, saying that it would be useless to force Jerram to carry a sword if he did not feel comfortable with the weapon.

Ivo drew the cloak tighter about her shoulders as a gentle but cold breeze blew through the camp. A shiver ran down her spine leaving her trembling. How she longed for a warm fire to chase the chill from her bones and the shadows from the camp.

Even though the sun had begun to warm the upper reaches of the trees some hours ago, its warmth had not yet reached into the heart of the timbered land. The seven travellers were still wrapped in their cloaks as they followed one of the many paths.

'You realise what side of the river we're on?' Anyon asked.

Roland nodded without taking his attention from the surrounding trees.

'You know what that means?'

'Why don't you keep your mouth shut and your eyes open,' Roland answered.

Anyon took the first piece of advice and closed his mouth. But the second part had not been necessary — he had not stopped searching his surroundings since leaving their cold night camp. He disliked walking, and he also detested being cold. But worst of all he hated the carcajous that were prowling the lands through which they were now passing.

Jerram moved silently from tree to tree. His feet seemed to caress the floor of the forest, scarcely disturbing the leaves in his passage. He had been scouting ahead of the party when the remains of a small fire had first alerted him to the fact that they were not alone in their travels. It was then that he became aware of the waiting outlaws. Moving silently from the path, Jerram disappeared into the surrounding foliage. A quick search of the area revealed nine outlaws waiting in concealment, with a tenth high in the branches of a tree.

Rather than return and inform the others, Jerram decided to resolve the problem himself. Firstly he removed his stained and torn yellow robe; then, kneeling beside the dead fire, he began to rub the dark ashes across his face, arms, legs, and chest. As he did this, Jerram began to whisper to himself; the words were old and familiar.

How often he had recited those words during his training. One after another the words tumbled from his lips. At first it had simply been his training, but now as he spoke the words, he realised their true meaning.

Slipping round behind the waiting outlaws, Jerram drew his dirk and moved slowly towards his first victim.

Osveld and his men always found it hard going surviving on the edge of the forest. There was always an element of danger. Stay close to the open plains where the pickings were best, and risk being surprised by a patrol of the local soldiers; stray too far into the dark interior of the forest and risk the danger of the shadows. He had heard from the locals he had captured — shortly before they were killed — that the forest held strange creatures that hunted any who entered their domain.

Osveld put the stories down to carcajous. Packs of the damned beasts roamed the edge of the forest seeking out travellers and villagers, keeping the much-needed caravans out of his reach. But at last a party of travellers was nearing his camp. One of his scouts returned, the first in several days to do so, and reported that a small party of seven travellers was fast approaching.

Osveld was perched in a tree above the trail the travellers were using. His men were positioned in the thick foliage beside the track. A fallen tree and several large moss-covered boulders caused the trail to bend from its generally straight course. It was at this bend that Osveld's men would attack.

Without warning, a man appeared around the bend. He was young and wore a soiled yellow robe. The youth stopped and searched either side of the trail before continuing towards the unseen outlaw chief.

Osveld waited for the youth to reach the spot where a small tree had fallen across the path. Once half the party was across the obstacle his men would attack, splitting the party in two. The youth stepped over the fallen tree. He was followed closely by another young man, and then a lithe young woman carrying a strung longbow.

As Osveld watched, the woman whipped an arrow from the quiver on her hip and nocked it. Drawing the string back to its full extent, she raised the bow and let the arrow fly. Osveld looked down in surprise as the shaft struck him squarely in the chest. First there was no pain, simply the shock that his men had not attacked. Then the agony of the shaft penetrating deep into his chest reached his brain and with a whispered scream he clutched the shaft and fell from his precarious perch.

Ivo stepped forward and nudged the dead outlaw with the toe of her boot. 'I wonder what he hoped to achieve by himself?'

'Perhaps there are others?' Anyon said.

'There are no others,' Jerram answered as he stepped into the trail.

'What have you been up to?' Ivo asked. Jerram was still covered in the dark ash.

'Scouting,' he answered.

'Not too well,' Ivo said, looking down at the dead outlaw.

'Perhaps,' Jerram answered.

Gurth watched Jerram closely as the young scout joined the others as they searched the dead outlaw.

11

TRAINING

The small weary party reached the safety of the Fortalice after many hard weeks of travel.

A squad of blue-cloaked Yarracks quickly ushered the group through the upper portal, while several more squads stood watch. When the party had first been approaching the closed and barred portal, the waiting squads had poured forth.

Guyon and the others were immediately taken to the lower levels where they were fed and given a place to wash and rest. For Gurth there was no such luxury. Once the upper portal had been secured, three green-robed figures had emerged from the shadow-filled corridors and whisked him away to a vertical shaft. Surrounded by a web of flickering green light, each of the Nglelin rode effortlessly up the smooth shaft until they reached one of the upper levels. With not even a sound of rustling robes, the four made their way down a corridor, stopping finally before a large timber door.

Guyon and the others were left to their own devices for several days before they were summoned to one of the upper levels. With the summons was an order for them to bring all of their personal gear with them as they were not going to return to their small chambers. After climbing four steep ramps, which were heavily guarded by armed Yarracks, the six were shown into a long barracks-like room.

As with all the rooms and chambers of the lower levels of the Fortalice there were no windows. The longer walls of the barracks held nothing but beds. Each one was attached to the wall along one length, while the other side was suspended by two chains from the ceiling. It was possible for the beds to be raised and locked against the wall, leaving a majority of the room's floor space free for other activities.

Guyon estimated that the room would hold at least sixty people: thirty bunks per side in two rows. Most of the bunks were locked tight against their respective walls, but six were open, as if inviting each of the newcomers to choose. The six open bunks were positioned about the room in such a way as to ensure that no two of them were too near each other.

Anyon glanced at Ivo. 'It seems we are to be separated,' he said with a wink. He crossed the room trying to work out which of the unoccupied bunks would prove the most beneficial.

'Perhaps not,' Ivo explained. 'At least we are in the same chamber.'

'But for how long?' Alaric asked.

'True,' Roland added. 'Just because we have managed to stay together so far does not mean it will always be so. There are hundreds of trainees on nearly every level of the Fortalice. To believe that we could remain together throughout our training is ridiculous.'

'But why separate us?' Guyon asked. 'We have performed well to date.'

'And what of plans for our future?' Anyon asked. 'Surely they will not be the same for each of us?'

'I plan to study the Arts,' Guyon volunteered.

'Weapons,' Alaric offered.

'And I,' added Roland.

'Power is all I'm interested in,' Anyon said calmly. He had found a bunk to his liking and had thrown his gear on the floor beside it.

'Ivo?' Alaric asked.

'I have not decided yet,' she answered. She inclined her head towards Jerram. 'And you?'

Jerram simply shook his head.

'But the next level is that of the Yarracks. In the blue order we will still receive the same training. It is not until the level of the reds that the training takes its first branch into specialisation,' reasoned Ivo.

'Then we will probably remain together for a while longer,' Jerram concluded.

'You think we should remain together?' Ivo asked Jerram, curious at his interest.

'It matters little,' he answered, turning his back on them and dropping his gear onto an empty bunk.

For the next eight weeks the six were tested to their utmost limits. Each awakening was the beginning of a new day of pain; a day where the companions were pushed until they collapsed with exhaustion and then were expected to rise and continue with their training.

They were put through drills and exercises designed to strengthen and test them. The exercises reminded Alaric of the time when he was imprisoned in his own home, forced to maintain his fitness and skills by training in his small cell. Of the group, Anyon found the going hardest. Never before had he been forced to endure such hardships. In the past he had been his own master and when something became too hard or tiring he had simply stopped.

If Anyon's lack of commitment surprised the group, then the ease with which Guyon passed the tests surprised all. Like Jerram, she had still not revealed her past as the others had, and no one had managed to discover where her homeland was. Perhaps those who ruled the Fortalice knew the answers. If that was true then they shared her secrets with no one.

'Now what?' Alaric asked as he threw himself down on his bunk. His body was soaked with sweat and his every joint ached, but he had to admit that it was the best he had felt for a long time.

'Weapons!' Roland laughed. 'The next step of our training will be skill-at-arms.'

'At last, something worthwhile,' Anyon mumbled.

Their conversation was interrupted by the arrival of a red-robed Kungour. He raised his right hand and pointed a red-gloved finger at Guyon. 'You are to accompany me,' he ordered. 'Fetch all as you will not return.' Lowering his arm, he turned and left the chamber.

'It seems that we have at last reached the point in our training where we are to receive separate instruction,' Ivo announced.

'What of the rest of us?' Anyon called after the Kungour. When there was no answer he too threw himself down on his bunk. 'Damn!' he cursed.

Guyon still stood in the centre of the chamber.

Anyon lifted his head. 'Well, you had better hurry and do your master's bidding,' he shouted.

With a scream of rage Guyon snatched up the first object that came to hand and hurled it at the reclining Anyon, who barely managed to cover his head with his arms before the chair struck the wall over his head, showering him with broken pieces of timber. Before Anyon could untangle himself and rise from his bunk, Guyon had gathered what few possessions she had and was stalking from the room.

'What's her problem?' Anyon asked.

'The same as ours,' Ivo answered, glaring at the short axe-man.

The remaining five companions were shown to new quarters. The chamber was similar to the last, only this time there were ten bunks in a row down the centre of the room. They were set up parallel and about three feet apart. At the base of each bed was an open-topped chest. But unlike their last rooms, the walls were covered with an incredible assortment of weapons: daggers to swords, light javelins to heavy cavalry lances, as well as a good number of projectile weapons.

'This is more like it,' Anyon laughed. He threw his equipment onto one of the unmade beds and began to walk around the chamber examining the selection of strange and exotic weaponry.

Alaric had a broad smile and stood in the centre of the chamber trying to take in everything at once. Roland approached him from behind and placed a hand on his shoulder. Alaric turned his head slightly and caught his companion's questioning look.

'At last,' he said by way of reply. 'At last.'

Ivo joined Anyon on his tour of the chamber, while Jerram sat himself down on one of the beds. The displayed weapons meant little to him, but he still examined the chamber carefully. In one corner he noticed a fine collection of knives; there were daggers, stilettos, combat knives, and what looked like a dirk. Lifting himself from his bed he crossed the room and took the dirk down from the wall. It was almost identical to the one which lay hidden amongst his spare clothing — short bladed and single-edged, with little by way of a guard. Jerram flipped the dirk end to end several times to test the weight and balance of the weapon.

'Company!'

The five companions turned in the direction of the voice and were facing the chamber's entrance as a group of youths entered.

There were five of them, two females and three males, and they were dressed in leather training armour, functional, but well worn.

'More meat for the grinder,' one of them said as he collapsed on a bed.

'Colbrand will have your guts, Mycroft, if he catches you on your cot wearing soiled armour,' another newcomer warned. This time it was a woman.

'Who cares?' Mycroft answered with a sneer. As he spoke, he stood and straightened the top cover of his cot.

'Greetings,' another said. 'I am Einor Val. My tired companion is Mycroft, and these are Chrestella,' he waved firstly to the young woman who had warned Mycroft, then to the second female, 'Walen,' and finally to the young male who stood at the rear, 'and Jason.'

Roland took a step closer to the newcomers. 'I am Roland, and my companions are Alaric, Ivo, Anyon and Jerram.'

A tall man wearing leather armour entered the chamber and stood surveying those before him.

'Colbrand,' Einor Val whispered.

'There will be no training for the second half of the day. Get to know each other.' With that he turned and left.

'Our trainer,' Einor Val explained.

'For weapons?' Roland asked.

'In all things,' Einor Val answered.

'Not all things,' Mycroft added. He raised his right hand and extended his index finger. A small flame appeared at the tip of his finger and danced about as if in a strong breeze.

'Our own human fire-lighter,' Walen laughed.

'Pay no attention to him,' Jason added. 'He started his training in the Arts, but due to several minor problems which arose, it was thought it would be in his best interest to continue his training in weaponry.'

The newcomers drifted into the chamber and began to strip off their armour and weapons. Every Yarrack they had seen on duty had worn a sword, yet it seemed that during training they would be expected to master one other weapon as well.

'I think the idea is to give everyone an individual identity,' Einor Val explained.

'And Mycroft?'

'He's all right,' Einor Val answered. 'Having someone with us who understands the Arts may be of value later.'

'Another of our companions was taken away for training by a Kungour,' Roland explained.

'And the rest of you?' Einor Val asked.

'I don't understand. The rest of us what?'

'Your skills,' Einor Val explained. 'Each of us has skills that the training will expand. For instance, Jason's father was a healer and he has a great knowledge of herbs and other medicines, though he has little skill in combat. Mycroft, as you know, has an understanding of the Arts and a good sword arm. Chrestella was raised in a forest and has had to survive by her knowledge of woodcraft and her skills as a hunter. She is a superb shot with a shortbow, and can handle a sword well enough. Walen was an urchin in one of the larger cities and has a knack for acquiring things, many different things. Unfortunately, that is her only skill.'

'And yourself?'

'I was training to be a Priest,' he answered. 'But when I saw for the first time what was happening in the world and how little I could do to solve the problems I decided that this was the only true path I could take.'

Roland thought for a short time before answering. 'I am a wanderer who has spent most of my life making a living from my sword. Anyon is like Walen, a thief, though he is also good with an axe. Ivo is at home in the mountains and is an excellent shot with her longbow. Alaric, the son of a northern Baron, was imprisoned for most of his childhood. He has taught himself swordsmanship. Guyon, as I said, is away being taught the Arts.'

'And the last member of your party?' Einor Val asked.

'He is a strange one, a good scout, but he only carries a small knife and would be of little use if trouble were to arise,' Roland answered.

'Perhaps,' Einor Val said. 'But it seems we have an excellent variety of skills.'

'How does that help us in our training?'

'During the training, each group is separated from all others save their trainers. They are responsible for the cooking of their own meals and the treatment of all injuries sustained during training.'

'Then it seems we are fortunate. Are all groups set up this way?' Roland asked.

'Yes,' Einor Val answered.

The training commenced early the next day. One of the lesser trainers woke the group and took them through a series of exercises similar to the ones they had learnt in their previous training. This was followed by a two mile run through many of the semi-dark tunnels on their level of the Fortalice. Other groups could be heard in the darkness, but none were seen. After the run, food was provided. Jason and Ivo prepared the first breakfast the group was to have together.

The morning session of training started with sword handling; those familiar with this weapon were paired off with those who were less skilled. They began with the basics. After a rather rushed midday meal, the afternoon session consisted of training with the weapons of their choice. Alaric fought with Kilic, his father's weapon, and Roland retained his sword, Jerram his dirk, Anyon his axe and Ivo her longbow.

Of their new companions only Mycroft used a sword. Jason, claiming he had only a need to defend himself, used a knife. Chrestella wielded a shortbow with great skill and accuracy. Walen preferred two thin-bladed stilettos, while Einor Val used a war hammer. Each used their preferred weapons with considerable skill, but none of them were able to beat any of their trainers, who were armed with a strange assortment of sticks, clubs and staves.

The first day was a blueprint for all others and the following days differed little. Week after week the group trained, first in individual weapon handling, then later in fighting as a team. After several months, many of the lesser trainers were occasionally beaten by one member or another of the group. But no one had ever come close to matching Colbrand's skill.

Many holidays and festivals were observed in the Fortalice and these breaks were the only rest the group were allowed from their training. By the time five months had passed, the group was allowed to train against other groups using blunted swords. Einor Val slowly rose in stature until all looked to him for answers and leadership. Under his instructions the group fought their way to the top of the trainees.

A further month and they were finally issued with the blue armour and cloak of a Yarrak and were moved once more, this time to one of the regular barracks which would be their home for some time. Their chamber was larger than any they had had to date and much more comfortably furnished. They shared a training arena with three other squads, forming a company. When on duty, the company was stationed as a unit to guard one of the many secured areas of the Fortalice.

It was on one of many such duties that Alaric saw Guyon for the first time since her separation from them all those months earlier. Alaric was on duty at the top of a steep ramp when a party of Kungour passed. As the last one passed his position, the red-robed Kungour stopped and offered him a smile. Before Alaric could say anything, which would have landed him in serious trouble, the party moved on and Guyon was gone.

12

UNEXPECTED RESISTANCE

'Are you sure it was her?' Ivo asked.

'It hasn't been that long since she journeyed with us,' Alaric answered sharply.

'True,' she conceded. 'I wonder how she is progressing?'

'Better than we will be if we are late for muster,' he answered.

Ivo and Alaric were the last to arrive at the barracks and had only just taken up positions at the foot of their beds when Colbrand arrived. He scowled at the latecomers but said nothing as he stepped to one side to allow those who accompanied him to enter.

A Nglelin entered the chamber; three Kungour followed close on her heels. 'The first level of your training has finished,' the Nglelin explained. 'Tomorrow, after morning prayers, you are to present yourself at the upper portal with full field equipment. Your squad will join two others in a routine mission to one of the outlying kingdoms.'

The Nglelin and her three followers turned and left.

Colbrand remained at the chamber's entrance allowing his steely gaze to travel from one frozen figure to another. 'Remember all you have been taught,' he said before turning and striding from the chamber.

It was some time before the first of the trainees moved.

'Well I'll be damned,' Anyon cursed.

Einor Val looked on the point of protesting when Chrestella interrupted him. 'At last we are to be free of this grey-walled prison.'

'By the Lady, I hope the journey is a long one,' Alaric added.

Einor Val raised his index finger to his lips and kissed it then quickly touched it to his forehead. It was a gesture he had thought he'd never use again after he abandoned the Priesthood.

Cymbeline was seated behind his small oak desk, an open book rested on the polished surface before him. For long hours he had searched the dry pages of the ancient tome. He had read and reread every piece of relevant information in the hope of finding something he had missed in his earlier studies. But there was nothing new.

Closing the tome Cymbeline slowly leaned back in his chair and closed his eyes. He placed his right palm on the leather covered book. How many times had he been forced to make a decision like this? How many times had people died because of the plans which had been made in this very room? And now more were to die. No matter how close his plans came to fulfilment, Cymbeline was still angered at the senseless waste of life.

In the far reaching tome on his desk were many lesser works: *Words of Sacred Magic*, the *Volumes of Nel*, and all the gathered letters of Abra-melin, but perhaps the last was by far the most powerful. Simply known as the *Book of Secrets*, its age-worn pages held many a word the world had not heard for many thousands of years.

This smaller work told of a city far to the south surrounded by a gigantic plain. The city was called Musero, and it had once given shelter to a race known as the Kobalos, who were reputed to have ruled all the lands in the distant past.

Many thought the city only a legend, but Cymbeline knew otherwise. The Kobalos had been a cruel race of Ma'goi who had mastered both the Arts of magic and

112

the skill of weapons. Very few had been able to stand against their armies which had swept the land clean of all enemies.

But their reign had come to an end when Xularkon, their leader, vanished mysteriously from his very throne room, never to be seen again. His Kobalos fought for control of the massive empire. When they threw their vast armies at each other, the lands united and drove the remnants southward into the Southern Wastes.

The plain the book had spoken of which surrounded Musero was now a gigantic forest. Its pathways and clearings unwalked for many a century.

Opening his eyes, he raised his right hand until it hovered over the golden inlaid script.

'*koolkuna*,' he whispered. A shining green web opened up between his hand and the tome. '*wakkalde*.' The web settled over the tome, wrapping itself about the leather.

Another whispered word caused the web securing the door to Cymbeline's chamber to disappear.

'Enter,' Cymbeline spoke aloud.

The timber door swung inward. Two Nglelin dressed in traditional green robes entered the chamber and approached the seated Wiseone.

'How may we be of service, Wiseone?' one asked.

'I have consulted the *fer tem hru*,' he answered.

The Nglelin who had not spoken cast a nervous glance at the protected tome resting on the Wiseone's desk. 'To what end, Wiseone?'

'I believe that a means of heading off this possible war with the west lies lost in the centre of the southern forest in a city called Musero, and it is my hope that those sent on this important mission will be able to locate and return with this power so that we may put an end to the useless waste of life.' Cymbeline paused. 'I have conferred with the other Wiseones and they agree with my plan.'

'I will see to the selection at once, Wiseone.'

'There is one limitation I will place on you,' Cymbeline added.

'Wiseone?'

'A youthfulness, a new approach, may be needed. To that end the mission must be undertaken by recently trained Yarracks who have just joined us, and they must leave the Fortalice and travel disguised so as not to alert our enemies to what we may have discovered.'

'It shall be done.'

'Also,' Cymbeline added, 'ask any of the new pilgrims from the south if they have heard of this forest and what it might hold.'

The two Nglelin left the chamber. At a whispered word from Cymbeline the door swung closed and a green web appeared over it. Placing his hands upon his desk, Cymbeline levered himself from his chair and slowly crossed the room. He felt tired, drained of energy. He repeatedly told himself that it was the long hours that were the cause, but really he knew different. This was driven home as he turned and noticed his reflection in the silver etched mirror beside his door. This mirror was smaller than the one he generally used, and the golden scroll work about its border bespoke its true age.

'*iuyulawarrin musero.*'

The mirror misted over before a view of an immense forest appeared. In the centre of the mirror's image a large grey area could be seen.

'*kringgun.*'

The grey area seemed to draw closer until it could be recognised as the remains of an enormous city. The thick forest which surrounded the stone buildings had overrun it in many places, adding to the look of long abandonment.

'*maremuntunt.*' Cymbeline spoke this word sharply. The scene in the mirror faded and then returned clear once more. This time the mirror held a view of what seemed to be a large circular chamber beneath the city. Three-quarters of the walls were hewn from natural grey stone, while the final quarter seemed to be a wall of darkness alone. No matter how he tried Cymbeline could not pierce the darkness. Suddenly the dark section began to waver. With a speed that caught Cymbeline by surprise, a figure leapt from the darkness, hands extended. Even though Cymbeline was by now several paces from the mirror, the hands still encircled his throat.

Grasping the tightening hands, he was unable to draw them from his throat. Releasing the hands, Cymbeline lowered his arms and concentrated.

'*wakkalde koradji*,' he gasped.

Slowly at first, then gradually growing in size, a small green light appeared between the attacker's hands and Cymbeline's constricted throat. As the green light expanded, it opened out to a wall which protected the Wiseone from the mirror. Once the wall had reached sufficient size, it folded itself about Cymbeline sealing him in a green transparent shield. Where the hands touched the green wall briefly a red glow appeared, but the light quickly faded.

'Well done,' whispered a croaking voice from beyond the mirror. 'This time you were able to protect yourself, but next time?' There came a soft terrifying laugh which made Cymbeline stagger back from the glowing mirror in horror. 'Next time I doubt you will be as lucky, old companion. You have interfered with my plans for the last time.'

Colbrand strode into the barracks and noted the activity as his charges packed the few belongings that would be needed on their journey. As Einor Val and the others noticed Colbrand at the door, they stopped their work and turned questioning faces towards their trainer.

'There has been a change of plans,' he informed them. A look of disappointment showed on many of their faces.

'Your uniforms are not to be worn,' he explained. 'You are to wear the clothes you arrived in, plus any clothing or equipment from the quartermaster you feel you may need. All such extras are to be vetted by me before departure. Understood?'

The ten companions nodded and began to remove their armour.

*

115

'All this training and the first time we leave here we are forced to wear the same clothes we came in,' Walen complained. She wore soft supple leathers, and low-cut shoes made for silent climbing rather than walking. A small pouch and two stilettos hung from a thin woven leather belt. Her long brown hair was tucked away under a leather cap. Her small eyes and tapering nose gave her a rodent-like appearance.

Chrestella wore a jacket and hose of some type of cotton material, stained green, with high thick-soled boots. A quiver of arrows for her short bow hung from her right hip, a hunting knife on her left.

Jason wore soft city clothing, with the exception of a fine pair of riding boots. About his shoulders was a small dark cloak with a hood which hung between his shoulder blades. A short-bladed knife was his only weapon.

Einor Val wore a light chain-mail knee-length hauberk, as well as a coif, high metal-plated re-enforced boots, and a wide leather baldric. The baldric supported a war hammer with a three-pronged head and curved blade as a counter balance. A short thick blade extended from between the head and curved blade.

Mycroft wore leather armour consisting of a small helmet with an adjustable half visor, a decorated lorica, and greaves. A long slim sword hung at his waist in a well-adorned scabbard. All the decoration was worked in fine silver thread, forming strange intricate symbols.

'It's time,' Einor Val explained.

With bedrolls and travelling cloaks thrown over shoulders, the party left their barracks and made their way towards the upper portal. Mounts with bulging saddlebags had been readied for them and the rest of their party waited patiently.

Gurth was dressed in soft brown leathers with light riding boots, a long cloak draped about his shoulders. With him were four others. One was another Nglelin, Hasin Jurisa, who had been seen in the presence of Gurth on many occasions. His hair was cut very short, and his face seemed to wear a perpetual sneer. The remaining three were Kungour. Two looked uncomfortable, as if the loss of their red robes was too much for them. Both were strangers; but the third was Guyon, a Guyon who had changed considerably in the short time they had been parted. The loss of her recently acquired robes meant little to her. Even without them she was more confident of her newly learnt skills than of anything else in her life, skills that each day grew in power until Guyon began to believe that nothing was impossible.

The party left the Fortalice and rode northward along a much-used trade route. With their five packhorses in tow the party didn't seem out of place amongst the many merchants who used the well-travelled road. The further north they rode the sparser the traffic became. It seemed that during the many months of training the problem of the carcajou plague had not decreased. Soon, signs of abandoned farms were to be seen beside the road. Waystations and inns were surrounded by hastily constructed timber palisades. At the waystations where the party rested, they heard more stories of carcajou attacks; some travellers even claimed that a large pack of carcajous had attacked a small town well north of Fordwich. Livestock was seen roaming freely in many of the untended fields, which simply added to the carcajou problem — a problem that had grown out of all proportions since some of the party had last travelled through these parts.

After crossing the Upper Ashbrook River, the party turned towards the coast where they intended to pick up transport at Breel. But after only two days of travelling, they found the road clogged by refugees fleeing inland.

Questioning any of the refugees who were willing to stop, Gurth learnt that Breel had been attacked by a large pack of carcajous, even larger than the one which had attacked the coastal town all those months earlier. Steering his party from the trade road, Gurth ordered a night camp be prepared. Large fires were readied around the outer edge of the camp in case the carcajous had followed the refugees. Many of those fleeing called out warnings as they passed, telling them of the dangers which followed close on their heels.

As the sun set, Gurth ordered the sentry fires lit. Large supplies of deadfall had been gathered to ensure enough fuel to see the camp through the night. Jason, Anyon, Ivo, and Dylan, a red robe, took the first watch. When patrolling the outer edge of the camp site, well inside the sentry fires, nothing beyond the leaping flames could be seen but inky darkness. It was hoped that, though there might be unseen dangers lurking beyond the fires, the flames would hold the carcajous at bay.

Jason and the others were relieved by Mycroft, Roland, Walen and the remaining Kungour, Sacha. During the early hours of the morning when Alaric, Chrestella, Einor Val and Guyon were on watch, the forest-wise Chrestella sensed something beyond the dying fires.

'Einor Val!' she whispered.

Einor Val quickly moved to her side, followed by Alaric and Guyon.

'There's something out there,' she explained. 'Something just beyond the fires.'

'Can you tell what it is?' Einor Val asked as he studied the darkness.

'No.'

Einor Val placed a hand on Alaric's shoulder. 'Wake Gurth.'

Alaric quickly made his way across the camp, quietly slipping between the sleeping figures. As he reached Gurth's side the Nglelin woke and sat up, his blankets falling from him.

'Trouble?' he asked.

'Chrestella says there is something just outside the camp in the darkness,' Alaric explained.

Gurth stood and followed Alaric to where Einor Val and the others waited.

'*coleenie*,' Gurth whispered. He stood as if listening to something, but no matter how hard the others strained they could hear nothing above the crackling of the fires.

Hasin Jurisa, the second Nglelin, joined the small

group. Gurth turned and faced his companion. 'There is something hiding in the darkness.'

'Carcajous?' asked Hasin Jurisa.

'Yes,' Gurth answered. 'And something else, something I just can't make out.'

'Perhaps...' Hasin Jurisa stepped forward. *'orucknurra,'* he called. The fires before the group flared up, revealing a large number of carcajous slinking along the tree line.

'Damn carcajous!' Anyon cursed. He moved beside Alaric, axe in one hand, rubbing sleep from his eyes with the other.

Hasin Jurisa raised one hand, pointing it in the general direction of the carcajous. *'reyin.'*

A green glow appeared in the trees behind the slowly advancing carcajous. In the growing light, manlike shapes could just be seen. Suddenly the green light took on a red tinge around its outer edge. Before either of the Nglelin could do anything, the red border flashed once, engulfing the green light.

'Get behind us,' Gurth called as he stepped forward to stand beside Hasin Jurisa. By now all of the party was awake and moved quickly to obey him. A red haze appeared over the fires directly before them, opening out until it covered the two fires completely. As they watched, the red light settled to the ground, smothering the flames.

'nagarin baringa gravwe,' Hasin Jurisa called. As he held up his right hand a large sphere of light appeared. The sphere seemed to have sprung from the tips of his fingers throwing light out past the dead fires. The sudden appearance of the light brought the carcajous to a sudden stop. Whining and growling, they stalked back and forth.

A small red point of light appeared from amongst the trees.

'wakkalde,' Gurth shouted. He raised his left arm and stepped in front of Hasin Jurisa. A disc of green light appeared on his forearm just as the red light shot from the trees towards them. The red ball struck the glowing green shield and exploded in a shower of red and green

sparks. The green shield disappeared just as another red point of light appeared in the trees.

Gurth raised both hands. '*wakkalde alie.*'

A green wall of light appeared between the party and the trees. The red ball raced from the trees and struck the shield. This time it exploded in a shower of red sparks only, as the green shield remained intact.

One of the carcajous, either braver or hungrier than its brethren, leapt forward with a snarl. Chrestella drew and released in one fluid motion. A shaft took the beast in the right eye, killing it instantly. The dead carcajou struck the ground and rolled to a halt just beyond the dead fires.

'Light the fires again,' Hasin Jurisa called. Anyon and Roland leapt for the closest of the piles of fuel and began throwing logs on the heaps of ash. Another ball flashed from the trees and exploded against Gurth's green shield.

Then another of the carcajous made a start forward. This time two arrows struck the beast before it had taken a second step. Simultaneously Ivo and Chrestella reached for arrows and nocked them.

'*baringa nemmin,*' Hasin Jurisa called. The sphere of light disappeared. '*orucknurra,*' and both fires sprang to life. The attacking carcajous were brought to a sliding halt as the flames spread hungrily across the timber.

'*reyin,*' Hasin Jurisa closed his eyes and concentrated. 'They're gone,' he said.

Cymbeline rose and stretched his arms, arching his back to remove the kinks that had developed during his long hours of study. He had read the book so many times that he was sure he knew the relevant passage of the book by heart. Each time he had sought an answer to the questions which had bothered him since the conception of his plan. Who could have bested Xularkon? For what reason had the Kobalos leader disappeared?

Cymbeline left his desk and moved slowly across his study. Xularkon had reached the pinnacle of the Arts. No one before or after had attained the power that

Xularkon had controlled, yet his power had not aided him in his final battle. Somehow he had been bested in his own city and had disappeared, leaving a massive army poised for victory but without a leader. Those who had witnessed the final battle had vanished without a trace. Also, many of Xularkon's closest followers and lieutenants had disappeared over the same period of time. Within a few years the threat had been put down and the surrounding lands had returned to their peaceful way of life.

He stopped his pacing and turned to find himself standing before a tall mirror. The face staring back at him was that of a tired old man. Tired beyond his years.

Cymbeline shook his head at the decision he had made. There was no going back now, no matter what occurred.

13

DECOY

'The carcajous are still out there,' Chrestella warned. 'They're keeping well beyond the fires, but they're still there.'

'What of the others?' Anyon asked. His axe was gripped in both hands and he had moved closer to the sentry fires in an attempt to pierce the darkness beyond.

'Hasin Jurisa says they're gone,' Guyon said.

Chrestella and Anyon were surprised to find Guyon had left the small fire where she and the other Kungour had remained since the attack.

'Gone,' Anyon laughed, 'but gone where?'

'Gurth and Hasin Jurisa have no idea. They disappeared as fast as they appeared,' she answered. 'But it's possible that they may still follow us and try again.'

'The question is were they working with the carcajous or were they just taking advantage of their presence?' Roland wondered as he joined them.

'Working with them?' Guyon asked.

'When I was journeying south to the Fortalice, I spent the night at a small village; I don't even remember its name. During the night, carcajous attacked the village, not a hit-and-run raid, but a concentrated attack. After the attack, a short distance from the village, I saw several strange mounted men. One wore rough furs while the others wore armour. To me they seemed to be part of the attack. I never actually saw them with the carcajous, it was just a feeling I had.'

'Could you describe these men?' Guyon asked.

'Only roughly,' he answered. 'Why?'

'Gurth should know about this.'

The two made their way towards Gurth's tent, while Anyon remained at the camp's edge, tired yet unable to sleep. After all these months he was no closer to the power he craved. He was deep in a forest, surrounded by danger. The one redeeming factor was the chance of learning — or finding — something of value on this journey.

'What have you learnt, Manaz?' Lord Beleth of the Damear asked.

'My Lord,' Manaz bowed deeply, hands on his chest, wrists crossed. 'The Fortalice has sent out a small group. They left several weeks ago and are travelling northward, I believe, towards Breel.'

'And their final destination?'

'At every village or town they passed they asked the same questions. The questions were confusing, having little to do with us or the coming war in the west. They deal with a myth that I heard as a child before I began my training. They ask people about a lost city in the Moribund.'

'I have heard these tales of the lost city of Musero.' Beleth stood and began to pace about his spacious tent. He spoke as if he were alone. 'The Great Lord Phelan, in his wisdom, has sent many expeditions into the Moribund, as did his father and grandfather. Each expedition was made up of great warriors and Ma'goi well versed in the Arts. But it mattered little as none ever returned. If those of the Fortalice are interested in Moribund and the city it hides, then perhaps we should take another look into that evil place.'

'It is possible that those we watch could take ship to the coast which borders the northern edge of the Moribund,' Manaz explained.

'True,' Beleth looked up at the waiting scout. 'You have served me well since your promotion to commander of my scouts.'

'Thank you, Lord.'

'Keep close watch on these people and there will be other promotions,' Beleth promised.

'Thank you, Lord,' Manaz answered, and paused.

'Is there more?'

'One other thing, my Lord.'

'Yes.'

'My men have reported that the ones we follow were attacked west of Breel by carcajous...'

'I should hope that all who travel the northern forests are attacked. The confusion is helpful to my plan,' Beleth stated.

'... the attack, my Lord, was backed by warriors skilled in the Arts.'

Beleth sat down, his chin rested in his armoured right hand. Manaz stood nervously waiting for his Lord's answer.

'It seems someone has exceeded his orders,' Beleth said softly. 'Find out who was in charge of the squad and see that my orders are not exceeded again.'

'And the squad itself?' Manaz asked.

'Perhaps they will volunteer their skills for a mission which may soon arise.'

'Into the Moribund?' Manaz asked cautiously.

'Exactly,' Beleth laughed.

By the time Gurth and the others reached Breel, many of the town's population, those who had fled along the coast, had returned. Gurth wasted no time in hiring a suitable vessel, and soon they were leaving the small harbour. As Roland studied the gradually shrinking village and coast, he was not surprised to see a troop of horsemen gallop into the village gesturing wildly towards the fleeing vessel.

Before the town of Breel and its small harbour disappeared from sight, another sail was seen on the horizon.

Gurth was confident that the vessel he had chosen was the best available in the harbour and that though the vessel might trail them for a few days, he was sure they would slowly outdistance their pursuers.

Seven days after leaving Breel, Gurth removed a small medallion from his saddlebag. It was oval shaped and bordered with a rich golden laurel leaf pattern. Opening the medallion, he stared deeply into a small reflective surface. He whispered one word. *'tuyulawarrin.'*

The mirror's surface fogged and then rapidly cleared showing Gurth an expanse of clear calm water marred only by a small blemish. The blemish grew into a small vessel similar to the one which bore Gurth and the others. A closer view showed its crew working the vessel while several passengers paced the deck.

'gravweru,' he whispered.

The scene wavered, and when it steadied a small schooner could be seen clearly. Passing his hand slowly over the medallion the scene vanished, returning the mirror's reflective surface.

'cymbeline coleenie ngan,' Gurth said slowly.

The mirror's surface wavered once more, this time revealing Cymbeline. The Wiseone sat in his study behind his desk, an open book on the surface before him.

'We are still being pursued, Wiseone. What am I to do?' Gurth asked.

'Are they sufficiently close to cause you difficulties?' Cymbeline enquired.

'No, Wiseone.'

'Then continue on as planned. You must reach your objective as soon as possible.'

'Yes, Wiseone.' Gurth slipped the medallion inside his shirt, and removed a small cloth-wrapped package from his open pack. Carefully unfolding the cloth, Gurth held up a broken section of mirror.

'cymbeline coleenie ngan.'

Again Cymbeline's features appeared, this time in the small section of mirror.

'All goes well, Wiseone.'

'Good,' Cymbeline answered. 'Do not lose your pursuers before reaching the forest.'

'I understand, Wiseone.'

Gurth rewrapped the mirror and replaced it carefully in his saddlebags. When two, or more, open mirrors were used to communicate, any Ma'goi with sufficient training could overhear what was said. The only way to be sure of total privacy was to use two or more fragments of the one mirror, a mirror which had been constructed with the exact purpose of being broken into several small sections. A special chant was whispered as the mirror was broken, ensuring that the fragments of the mirror remained as one, no matter how far apart they were. The mirror had been specially constructed for this journey as none other had been available. The spells used to construct the mirror were long and involved and had a short life span, making it impossible to construct a mirror and then store it.

'I think the best thing we could do is to stop at three or four places along the coast before we disembark,' Roland explained. 'And once we are safely on shore, the vessel should continue along the coast stopping several more times. That way our pursuers will not know exactly where we were put ashore.'

'The idea has merit,' Alaric said,

'I agree,' Ivo added hastily. Her brow was covered in perspiration. 'It may be the only way to lose those who have so doggedly followed us and to allow us to land.' She glanced about nervously as she spoke.

'It would make no difference,' Guyon explained. 'One of our pursuers must be trained in the Arts or we would have lost them long ago.'

'Then perhaps we should let them follow us ashore,' Anyon said suddenly. 'And once ashore, see to it that they no longer have the means to follow us.' He reached into a small pouch on his belt and drew out a whetstone. Spitting on the grey stone he began to work it along one blade of his axe, stopping now and again to admire his handiwork.

'Can we hide ourselves from those who follow?' Einor Val asked.

'Not without certain rites and chants which we would not be able to carry out here,' Guyon explained.

'Then we stay with Anyon's idea,' Mycroft said. 'We cannot afford to have a hostile force behind us as we enter an unknown forest. There is too much at risk.'

'You forget,' Guyon interjected. 'Gurth leads this mission, and he will make all the necessary decisions.'

'We hardly have the chance to forget,' Anyon snapped. 'You throw it at us every time one of us has a thought.'

Before Guyon could reply, Sacha entered the cabin. 'We are to be put ashore here,' she told them. 'Gather what you will need and move up on deck.'

Nothing more was said as they separated to gather whatever gear they had brought with them. Soon they were on deck waiting as the crew lowered the two long-boats into the slight swell. To starboard the lake was clear to the horizon, to port a tall wall of green stood waiting for them. The cries of strange birds filled the air as the group followed Gurth and Hasin Jurisa into the waiting boats.

Ivo was one of the first over the side and she almost fell into one of the longboats in her eagerness to get ashore. The others were more cautious in their climb and soon the longboats were making their way towards the beach.

With a thump, the first of the boats struck the sloping sandy beach. Some of the crew leapt into the water and began dragging the boat further up onto the sand. As soon as the boat was safe, the remaining crew began to heave the stores they had brought over the side. Those already on land carried them almost to the tree line.

'I think they are in a hurry to be off,' Walen laughed as she watched the last crewman tumble over the side into the arms of his waiting companions.

With a sharp order, the oars were readied and soon the first longboat was cutting its way back to the waiting vessel. The second longboat was not far behind in the dash back to safety, and soon the companions were watching as the boats were raised onboard and the vessel made sail.

'What now?' Anyon asked as he eyed the inhospitable-looking tree line.

'First we get the remainder of our stores and water off this beach and ourselves out of sight,' Gurth explained. 'Then I have something to explain to you all.'

In no time the stores were moved a short distance into the trees and a small area was cleared for a fire. No one knew if Gurth intended for them to stay the night, and no one asked. Gurth had sounded strained when he had spoken, and this had worried them all.

'You were told our mission was to reach this forest and the city of Musero,' he said, 'but that is not totally true.'

Anyon threw his axe to the ground at his feet. 'I knew it!'

Gurth ignored him. 'Our mission was in fact to reach this forest, but we are to go no further inland than we have to. Our mission was to decoy the scouts of our enemies away from the true mission, which was to reach the western kingdoms and gain their aid in the forthcoming war.'

'But what about those who follow us?' Anyon asked, picking up his axe.

'They no longer matter,' Gurth replied. 'It is too late for them to do anything about the other party, and once they learn they have been tricked, I'm sure they will not even bother landing.'

'You forget one thing,' Ivo interrupted.

'Yes?'

'Revenge.'

'Damn right,' Anyon shouted. 'We've probably cost those poor bastards their lives, and you think they'll just turn tail and run home hoping to be forgiven.'

'It was not their fault,' Hasin Jurisa argued. 'What else could they do?'

'Come ashore and make us pay for what we have done to them,' Walen suggested. 'If you weren't locked up for so long in that anthill of yours, you'd know that that was exactly what they are going to do.'

For the first time Gurth looked worried. But the look lasted only a second before his usual calm expression returned once more. 'If you are correct,' he said, 'we had better prepare ourselves for their arrival.'

'Dead right,' Anyon muttered.

'What's wrong with him?' Einor Val asked.

'Probably the fact that there are no horses about for him to steal,' Ivo answered quickly. 'No horses, no escape.'

Walen laughed loudly as she moved towards the beach to help the others wipe clean any sign of their arrival.

The moon was bright and some of the reflected light worked its way between the canopy of branches to throw a weak light into the small camp. The companions lay silently as they watched the approach of the longboat. The creaking of the oars and the curses of the sailors could be heard clearly over the small breakers which had risen since the setting of the sun.

The nose of the longboat grated against the beach, and the crew busied themselves with steadying their small craft as its occupants jumped into the water and waded ashore. As the first of them left the water, a shout echoed out from the trees and the companions launched themselves from the shadows.

The enemy wore grey mail shirts and helmets. They fought with sword and shield and though caught off guard soon reformed themselves with their backs to the longboat. Ivo and Ghrestella dispatched the crew of the longboat with calm efficiency. When any of the enemy tried to climb into the longboat, the companions gained the numerical advantage they needed to finish them.

A shout from behind brought Alaric flashing about. One of their party, Alaric couldn't see who it was in the half light, was pointing down the beach at a large number of armed men racing towards them. A quick look up the beach showed an equal number of armed men approaching from the opposite direction.

'It's a trap!' Alaric yelled. 'Fall back to the trees.'

But the defending enemy heard the shout and began to force their way up the beach, not giving the companions the time they needed to break and run for cover. Just as the two parties reached the fight, the moon went behind a cloud and the beach was thrown into total darkness. Soon the beach was in chaos. Men swore and swords clashed as the four groups fought blindly.

For a brief moment a red glare appeared above the beach, but in a flash of green the light disappeared, destroying what little night vision the combatants had acquired. Alaric had somehow found Roland, and the two were fighting back to back, cutting down anyone who came near them and hoping that it was not one of their own companions.

A terrifying scream tore out over the fighting, bringing all but a few to a stop. The scream was repeated, much closer. A bright green light appeared over the beach throwing strange dancing shadows among the now stationary combatants. Shapes should be seen leaving the tree line and slowly walking down the beach towards the silent fighters.

On the edge of the beach could be seen the remains of the one who had warned them and one of the attacking warriors. Both had been literally pulled apart by the hideous beasts and, even as they watched, several of the creatures stopped to feed on the dismembered bodies.

'The longboat!' one of the defenders shouted.

As if the shout acted as a trigger, the creatures sprang forward. Unarmed, they attacked the armed men, their hands reaching forward ready to grasp an opponent. The two parties were hit with the full force of the attack. The attackers were manlike in shape, yet fought with hands, fists and teeth. No orders were heard and none were needed as the strangers cut a wide swathe into the defenders. The creatures clawed at eyes and throats, their filthy nails raking armour in their attempt to maim or kill the defenders. As the creatures were cut down they tried to drag their slayers with them to the sand, and even those already down reached out, grasping ankles in their last attempt to pull down their prey.

Einor Val led his companions towards the now undefended longboat. The first to reach the vessel threw themselves at the oars in an attempt to drag the boat from its sandy resting place. Some who followed saw that this was futile and, sheathing their weapons, threw their weight against the prow of the longboat, pushing it from the beach.

Once the longboat was afloat, eager hands reached down and plucked men from the water. When no more could be found the oars were manned and the longboat rowed steadily from the beach.

'The salt-backed bastards are leaving us!' shouted a voice from the darkness of the longboat.

In the dim light, they watched as the vessel which had brought the pursuing force moved quickly from the beach and out into the waiting lake.

A curse was called after the fleeing vessel, but for the main part, those on board the longboat were quiet as they realised their fate. With the schooner gone, so too was their only real chance of getting off this beach. They were safe for now, but soon thirst would force them ashore and when it did, they were sure the strange creatures would be waiting.

A red light appeared in the stern of the vessel. In this quivering light the occupants of the longboat could see each other for the first time. Alaric, Roland and Anyon were seated at the prow of the longboat. Einor Val, Jason, Mycroft and Ivo were at the oars. So too were six grey-armoured strangers. Chrestella lay amongst the rowers, her head supported by Sacha, a large bruise on the forester's forehead. Guyon and Jerram sat in the stern with the creator of the light. The red light radiated from the Ma'goi's fingertips, and reflected from his grey armour. A look of surprise was on the Ma'goi's face as he too surveyed the crew of the longboat.

There was no sign of Gurth, Hasin Jurisa, Dylan or Walen.

14

FORCED ALLIANCE

When the sun rose it made little difference to the survivors. They had rowed and rested through the night, travelling many miles down the coast, but their troubles had changed little.

In the darkness they had worked together with little regard for their differences. But with the morning's light came the realisation that they were enemies, searching for the same thing. Armoured bodies shuffled in the confined space, and hands hovered near weapons.

'It would be stupid to come to blows,' the strange Ma'goi said suddenly. 'At least for the moment,' he added quickly, gesturing to their surroundings. 'For the moment we must work together. I am Queron, of the Damear.'

Einor Val looked at their surroundings and then at his companions. 'We seem to have little choice in the matter. If we don't work together, neither party will be strong enough to survive.'

'Work together, be damned!' Anyon exclaimed. 'The boat's a bit crowded for my liking.'

'Then perhaps we should ease the cramped conditions,' one of the grey-armoured men said with a slight laugh. Again hands dropped towards weapons.

'Enough!' Queron ordered. The tone of his voice made

132

both parties snatch their hands way from the hilts of their weapons. The last hand to back off was the warrior who had answered Anyon. His armour was identical to the other grey-clad warriors except for the lion-head insignia embossed on the right shoulder.

'Whether you like it or not,' Queron continued, 'we must work together to survive. Those creatures who attacked us were forest goblins. They generally prefer to live their miserable lives in forests, deep in forests. In my land they are seen only rarely and it was thought they were dying out, but it seems we were wrong.'

'Will they follow us?' Einor Val asked.

'Most definitely.'

'Food?' Roland asked.

'Amongst other things,' Queron explained. 'They will take weapons, clothing, armour and, finally, what's left will be used for food.'

'They weren't armed last night,' Ivo said.

'Luckily for us,' Alaric replied. 'But now they are armed.'

'Yes, many good warriors fell last night,' Queron acknowledged solemnly. 'If the opportunity arises, and time permits, I intend to take suitable repayment for the inconvenience they have put me through.'

Roland felt a shiver run down his spine as he listened to the Ma'goi speak. There was an edge to his voice that made Roland glad he was not to be on the receiving end of that revenge — at least not yet.

'Then I suggest we put into the shore,' Roland said. 'Our supply of water will not last much longer and it would be best if we landed during the hours of daylight. This may at least give us a chance if attacked.'

'I concur,' Queron answered. 'Man the oars and make for the shore,' he ordered. The grey-armoured men took up their oars immediately, while Einor Val and the others followed the orders slowly but without question.

With the longboat beached and sentries in place, the search for water began. Several small parties made their way into the interior while others searched further up the coast.

Ivo and Anyon found themselves paired off and detailed to search up the beach. 'Who made him general?' Anyon said once out of earshot of the makeshift camp.

'Would you like to go back and argue with him about his right to give the orders?' Ivo asked.

'No.'

Ivo shaded her eyes and searched out over the small swell of the lake. 'I wonder what happened to Gurth, Hasin Jurisa and Walen?'

'Breakfast,' Anyon answered coldly.

Ivo spun round and faced the short axe-man. Anyon took a hasty step back when he saw the anger on her face. He could see she was shaken by the loss of Gurth.

'We had only known them for a short time, but they were still our companions,' she snarled. 'And even if they were my enemies, I would not wish that kind of death on them.'

'Who cares? They're gone, and we're still here. Here on some godforsaken coast, in the company of enemy warriors, and under the command of a strange Ma'goi. Who knows, perhaps soon we may wish it was us who had fallen on the beach that night.' Anyon strode off along the beach and soon disappeared from sight around a tree-covered point.

Ivo stood and thought about what her companion had said before she began to follow him. As she neared the point, Anyon suddenly appeared. Head down and arms pumping, he sprinted around the point and began to head straight for her. Ivo opened her mouth to call out a question when a band of goblins appeared.

Taken by surprise Ivo watched as Anyon and the goblins neared her. In the darkness the night before, it had been hard to make out any details about their attackers, but on the sunlit beach she could see the goblins quite clearly. They looked roughly like men, only their skin was grey and looked dry or slightly scaled. Their ears were long and pointed, while their eyes were small and oval and drawn upward towards the temple. They wore a strange mixture of clothing and armour and carried an assortment of weapons, from sticks to old rusty swords.

'Don't just stand there!' Anyon shouted.

The shout snapped Ivo from her thoughts. Quickly she whipped the longbow from her back and, bracing it against her left instep, strung it. Drawing a long feathered shaft, she nocked it and took careful aim. Anyon was between her and the goblins so she waited for the right moment, then let fly. The shaft flashed past Anyon's ear drawing a strangled gasp from the near exhausted axe-man.

The arrow fled straight and true and took a goblin through the right cheek. Quickly she drew and fired again, dropping another. As Anyon staggered past her she sent a third shaft into the closest goblin and turned to run.

One of the creatures let fly with his wooden club. The rough wooden weapon spun through the air and struck Ivo squarely in the back. She crashed to the ground. Quickly she rolled over and was in time to raise her booted feet, catching one of the goblins as he threw himself at her. Flipping her attacker over her head she leapt to her feet and, wielding her longbow like a staff, brought it down on the head of the rising goblin.

A loud howl broke from the lips of the beasts. This was the first noise they had made since coming into sight. Spinning round, Ivo crouched and waited for their attack. They were too close, and there would be no time for her to draw an arrow from her quiver. With her bow gripped firmly in her left hand, she drew a knife from her right boot.

She struck the first goblin across the throat with her bow, knocking him to one side. The second attacker struck her head on. Both Ivo and her attacker fell to the ground, the attacker with Ivo's knife buried deep in his chest. Getting to her feet, she reached for her trapped knife, but before she had time to withdraw it, she was knocked from her feet by two other goblins, while a third reached for the body of his dead companion.

After drawing the knife from the bloodied chest, the goblin turned and grinned down at the pinned Ivo. The grin revealed yellow canine-like teeth. Straightening his right arm, he slowly ran the knife's blade down Ivo's cheek, releasing a flow of blood which ran down her cheek and dripped from her chin. The two goblins who held the straining woman laughed and urged the knife-wielder on in a harsh guttural tongue.

The goblin raised the knife and licked the blood from the blade. Reaching forward once more he placed the blade beside Ivo's left breast. Blood splashed in Ivo's face, blinding her as her torturer's head split open.

Her arms were released and by the time she was able to wipe the blood from her eyes, she saw Anyon finish off the last of the goblins. Getting slowly to her feet, she took her knife from the still fingers of her attacker. Anyon bent and took up her bow, throwing it to her.

'Quickly, before more of these things get here!' he called.

Ivo nodded a silent thanks; then, following Anyon, she staggered down the beach past the bodies of more dead goblins. Anyon must have stopped as soon as he realised she had fallen, but he had been unable to come to her aid until he had finished off the remainder of the pursuers.

Ivo's cheek had begun to throb and her breath was coming in short gasps. Anyon slowed down and put an arm under her shoulder, taking some of her weight.

Anyon and Ivo turned briefly when howls and screams erupted from the beach behind them. A large number of goblins had just rounded the point. At the sight of the two fleeing humans more screams were vented. Almost dragging Ivo, Anyon started down the beach once more.

'We're not going to make it,' Ivo gasped.

'What would you suggest?' Anyon asked.

'Let's take some of the bastards with us,' she growled, and shook herself free of Anyon's arms.

Turning to face the attackers she took a wide stance to steady herself, before drawing a shaft from her quiver. Releasing the shaft, she took the closest goblin in the

136

chest. At such close range the force of the blow knocked the attacker from his feet. As quickly as she could, she nocked and let fly one shaft after another.

The remainder of the goblins reached her as she fired her last arrow point-blank into the face of the best-armed goblin. Anyon leapt between her and the attackers giving her time to draw her knife. Cutting to left and right he chopped the attack apart. Ivo did what she could to protect Anyon's back but she knew it was only a matter of time before a sufficient number of the goblins would close in on them and pull them down.

The goblins began to call out in their guttural tongue, and with the calls came a renewed effort to reach the pair. Anyon was bleeding from several minor wounds on his arms and legs, but he still kept his axe swinging in a deadly pattern.

Suddenly the beach around Anyon and Ivo was filled with shouting and cries of pain. Unseen by the two beleaguered warriors, the rest of their companions, hearing the cries, had come to their aid.

In a matter of heartbeats all the goblins were down, save two who had fled when the rescuers first arrived. Chrestella dropped one with a well-placed shot. Queron raised his right hand, palm uppermost.

'doom-gara pulyugge,' he whispered. A ball of light appeared on his right hand dancing on his open palm. Queron closed his right hand and extended his index finger. The ball of lightning shot from his hand and struck the goblin in the back, throwing him from his feet.

'Get them back to the camp!' Queron ordered.

Eager hands dragged Ivo and Anyon to their feet and half carried them to their temporary camp.

'Here, drink this,' Alaric said handing a mug to each of them. 'Did you find anything else apart from your friends?'

Anyon took a deep drink and looked at Alaric in dismay. 'Water?'

Alaric ignored him.

Anyon looked down at the mug, then shrugged and drained it. 'There's a large river just beyond the second point,' he explained.

'It may be our way out of this place,' Alaric said.

'It's just more water,' Anyon mumbled, looking once more into the empty mug.

Alaric placed a hand on Anyon's shoulder, then rose and walked off to search out Queron with the news. Jason had cleaned Ivo's wound and had started on Anyon when Queron and Einor Val arrived.

'How large is this river?' Queron asked.

'I could barely make out the far bank,' Anyon answered.

'And the current?' Einor Val asked.

'I didn't notice. I wasn't really there long enough. If you get what I mean.'

Einor Val laughed aloud.

'The longboat has a mast and a sail,' Queron explained. 'With a favourable wind we may be able to make our way inland.'

'Inland!' Anyon exclaimed leaping to his feet. 'Haven't we got enough problems here on the coast without venturing inland?'

'Possibly,' Queron conceded. 'But there is a chance that once inland we may be rid of the goblins. And who knows, perhaps there may be a settlement just upriver.'

'It's worth a chance I suppose,' Einor Val answered. 'We could hardly be worse off.'

Ivo and Anyon were left to themselves as the preparations to leave were made.

Ivo sat struggling with her thoughts. Finally she spoke. 'Thanks for the help.'

Anyon just shrugged and began to examine one of the stitched wounds on his upper arm. 'I didn't really do it for you,' he answered.

'Then why?' she asked, feeling her anger rise.

'It would have been a shame to separate such a fine pair,' he laughed and he dropped his eyes to her leather-covered breasts.

*

First thing the following morning, and with the incoming tide, the longboat, under sail, moved into the mouth of the river. There had been no sign of goblins since the run-in on the beach the previous day, but all eyes watched the tree line for any sign of movement.

The wind blew steadily all morning and soon the river's tree-lined banks closed in about them. Keeping to the centre of the river, the party felt fairly safe as they were well out of bow range from either bank, but still they did not stop searching for any sign of goblins. Queron's main worry was that the goblins had noticed the party moving upriver and that they would follow them, waiting for another chance to attack.

'The wind's dropping. Lower the sail!' Queron ordered.

'Yes, General,' Anyon whispered as he moved to obey.

Roland and Einor Val sat in the bow, watching for snags, but the river seemed deep, and at this stage, safe.

'Man the oars!' Queron ordered.

Anyon moved to obey, mumbling to himself once more.

'It might be wise to warn Anyon not to antagonise the Ma'goi. We may have need of him later,' Roland warned.

'But will he have need of us?' Einor Val asked. 'Once we find some type of help, or safety, will we still need each other?'

In the stern similar questions were being asked. 'I don't trust these men of the Fortalice,' one of the warriors said. 'I think they will backstab us the first chance they get.'

'Why have we not cut their throats and fed them to the fish?' another asked.

'Because, Kendrick, they may be needed,' Gideon answered.

'You were ready enough to spill their blood just a short time ago,' Kendrick laughed.

'That was personal,' Gideon answered. 'I didn't like some of the things the short axe-wielder was saying.'

'Ignore him,' Kendrick replied.

*

Working in shifts at the oars, the conscripts moved steadily upriver. At the end of each day, as the sun dropped below the trees of the thickening forest, Queron ordered the longboat into the overhanging foliage along the bank. If the forest goblins they encountered on the beach were still following them, then they were slowly being outdistanced.

Roland was sure their luck would not hold for much longer. The river had narrowed considerably since leaving its mouth, and the current had increased, slowing their progress. Einor Val had thought it best that the fact that Sacha and Guyon were Kungour be kept secret from the Ma'goi. Roland agreed that it might prove useful to have someone other than Queron skilled in the Arts.

The deeper the longboat penetrated the forest, the easier it became for the mismatched crew to work together. Only Ivo seemed ill at ease. She spent much of her time in the bow, her knees drawn tightly to her chest, haunted by the terrible memory from her childhood.

As the long shadows of evening stretched across the river, the longboat touched its nose gently against the western bank. Anyon was the first ashore and quickly disappeared. Alaric secured the boat and the rest of the crew climbed wearily to the solid ground. Quickly a watch was set and a small fire readied. During these preparations, Chrestella made an important discovery. Close to the river's edge, beneath a thin cover of leaves and dark soil, she found a layer of rock. Not natural rock, but a stone which had been worked by the hands of man.

She called the others and, clearing away more of the cover, found that it was more than just one rock. It was a paved area, so large that they were not able to find the edge of it in the small light from their fire.

'It looks to be a pier, and some type of storage or loading area,' Chrestella explained. 'Whatever it is, or was, it's old... very old.'

Building up the fire, the party began prodding the soil in an effort to find an edge to the paved area. Soon several more fires were lit and finally all reported an end to the stonework. The area was quite large — several hundred paces across at its narrowest point — and flat, except for a few places where trees had forced their way between the stones.

'Could this be what we were sent to search for?' Anyon asked, having reappeared once the work was done.

'Hardly likely,' Queron answered. 'We are not deep enough into the Moribund yet.'

'Then what's this place — some type of outpost?' Mycroft asked.

'Outpost, trading post, garrison, it matters little,' Queron explained. 'What matters is that for the first time something has been found to show that the city of Musero may actually exist.'

'Not necessarily,' Einor Val stated. 'There may have been many others who have found this site, and because of it continued on deeper into the Moribund when they might have turned back. And even though we have found this place, it doesn't mean we will leave this place to tell of it, or that the city of Musero exists.'

'Lord Queron!' The Ma'goi turned to answer the call and saw one of his warriors running towards him.

'There is no end to the paving stones in one section,' he explained. 'They narrow into a path and wind off into the trees.'

'Have you followed this path?'

'Yes, Lord. It travels a short distance into the trees where it circles a large stone building.'

'Gideon!' Queron snapped.

'Yes, Lord?'

'Remain here with three others of your choosing and watch the longboat. I will take the remainder and see what this structure has to offer.'

Gideon stepped back and pointed at Ivo, Chrestella and Kendrick to do the same. The rest drew their weapons and followed the scout off into the forest. Even amongst the trees enough moonlight filtered through to enable them to see where they were going. The paved path wound its way through the vegetation in what seemed a random pattern. In places it was interrupted by large trees which had pushed their way up from beneath the stones. It followed some long-lost route between trees which had long since died.

The stone building was in fact a squat tower. It was constructed of large well-fitted stones and was circular in shape. Queron sent several warriors around the base of the tower and learned that there were no windows and only one opening. A large portcullis blocked the entrance. The portcullis was locked and no amount of effort could raise it.

'If this tower is as old as it looks to be, then this should not be here,' Anyon said. 'It should have rusted away long ago.'

'Well it's here, and it's definitely not rusted,' Einor Val noted.

The Ma'goi stepped forward and placed both hands on the portcullis. '*ya kalya,*' he said softly and pressed his hands against the cool metal.

A faint sound like the rustling of paper could be heard. The bars were suddenly veined with cracks, which opened as the party watched. Soundlessly the bars crumbled.

'Wanna bet, I could find a use for that,' Anyon whispered.

'Remain here,' Queron ordered, pointing at Roland. Roland nodded, gesturing for Jason and three of the Damear warriors to remain as well.

Queron entered the tower. As he did so, he raised his right hand before him and a red light appeared on his palm. As he blew gently at the light, the red ball left his palm and hovered at head height several paces ahead of him.

In the light cast by the floating ball, the party entered the lowest level of the tower. They followed a short hall until it ended at four openings. Three were open doors leading into small rooms while the fourth was the base of a set of spiral stairs leading upward.

'Perhaps we should withdraw and cut some torches?' Einor Val suggested.

'Do so,' Queron ordered.

Einor Val and the remaining Damear warrior retraced their steps and soon returned with an armful of torches. Queron placed his left hand above the end of one of the torches, and whispered. The tip glowed, then burst into flame. Using this one, the rest were soon lit.

'You come with me,' Queron said, pointing to the remaining warrior. 'The rest of you divide yourselves into three groups and search this level.'

15

KOBALOS

Guyon and Jerram began to search the room they had been assigned by going over every inch of the walls. The room was roughly triangular in shape with the longer wall being slightly curved. The internal walls were constructed of the same type of close-fitted stone as the outer wall.

As they searched the litter-covered floor, Jerram discovered a large stone in the corner which looked out of place amongst the others.

'Guyon!' he called. 'Come and see what you make of this.'

Guyon knelt by the block and placed one hand upon it. '*nokuna.*' Her eyes narrowed as if she was trying to see through the rock. 'There's something down there,' she said finally.

Moving back slightly, she placed both hands, palms flat on the closest edge of the stone. '*ngiralin,*' she said in a firm voice.

With a loud grinding noise, the stone began to lift at the edge where her hands rested. Slowly the rock rose until it was vertical. Jerram glanced up at Guyon and found his companion leaning against the wall, her face beaded with perspiration.

'Perhaps it would have been simpler if we had just lifted it,' he laughed.

'Perhaps.'

'The others will have heard the noise and be here soon,' he said as he watched her push herself from the wall.

'Then we had better hurry,' she replied.

Taking the torch from Jerram, Guyon peered down into the hole. A set of stone stairs could be seen in the flickering light. She stepped into the hole; Jerram looked about the room and towards the entrance, as if willing someone to arrive, but no one did. With a shrug, he drew his dirk and followed.

The stairs were steep as if made for small feet, and the air was stale. Reaching the bottom of the stairs, the pair found themselves in a small room with an opening on the far side.

Guyon took off across the room. She looked neither left nor right as she passed through the opening. In the torchlight they saw another room, even smaller than the one they had just left. Voices could be heard on the stairs behind them and this seemed to urge Guyon on.

'I can feel it,' she said softly. 'It's so close.'

Jerram could see nothing in the half light of the torch so he stayed by the open door. A light flicked behind him signalling the approach of others. He did not know what Guyon could feel that had excited her so. All he could sense about the place was great age.

'Here!'

Jerram looked back towards Guyon when he heard her sharp exclamation. Quickly he moved to her side. She was pulling a long stone from the wall. When it was finally free, she dropped it and reached inside. Nearly the entire length of her arm disappeared into the hole before she stopped. Her face lit up with a broad grin as she began to withdraw her arm.

'What have you found?' Anyon asked.

He was behind Jerram and could not see the beautifully engraved stiletto Guyon held in her hand. The handle was carved bone with strange designs worked into it. The blade was long and thin and gleamed brightly in the torchlight. The pommel was a large clear gem which seemed to draw in the light rather than reflect it.

'What have you found?' Queron asked.

Guyon turned around and held up the stiletto. Queron did not reach for the weapon but merely stood there examining it.

'A nice enough novelty,' he said, 'but I have little use for it. You may keep it.' With that, he turned and began to climb the stairs. Guyon was the last to leave. As she was about to place her foot on the bottom stair, she stopped and raised the stiletto once more.

'*ngungyen,*' she whispered.

A faint light appeared deep within the gem and grew steadily larger, filling the room with a cool white light.

'*kringgun,*' she said. The light increased even further until the entire room was bathed in a soft light.

She whispered another command and the light disappeared. Slipping the stiletto into her belt she started up the stairs, a faint smile on her lips. The weapon held a magic of its own that could be called forth on command. Guyon would be able to use the artefact to light their way in the deepest darkness and not have to draw upon her own strength.

The group returned to their camp at the river's edge and settled down for the night. Everyone was interested in Guyon's find in the tower, and questioned her until they realised that she was going to say little on the subject.

Guyon lay on the cold ground for some time willing herself to sleep, the stiletto grasped tightly in her right hand. Somehow the feel of it was comforting. She had been born the daughter of a slave, and had therefore inherited her mother's dilemma. Her plain looks and quick mind had kept her out of trouble as she had grown older. One night she had stumbled upon an unguarded way into her master's library. From that time onward, she had spent every free moment poring over the leather-bound tomes that filled the library from floor to ceiling. One entire wall was given over to nothing but volumes containing information about the Arts and it was from

146

these books that she first learnt of the Fortalice. Her master spent a great deal of his time travelling, gathering many other books and scrolls to add to his already impressive collection. It was forbidden for anyone to enter his library so all kept their distance, unknowingly allowing Guyon her free rein.

A few years passed and Guyon felt it was time for her to leave. She approached her mother about escaping from their slavery, but her mother refused to listen. She knew all too well the fate of recaptured slaves. Guyon, although she deeply wished to be free and journey to the Fortalice, would not leave her mother.

Several years later, Guyon went to visit her mother only to find that she had been sold and that none knew of her whereabouts. That night Guyon left her lodgings for the last time. If not for the simple spells she had learnt in her master's library she would have been captured and returned to slavery many times. This only reinforced Guyon's desire to learn more about the Arts of magic and the power they controlled and when she finally reached the Fortalice, she found everything she needed to quench her deep thirst for knowledge.

As she had approached the Moribund, she had sensed a presence which had eased her longings. With the stiletto in her possession, she felt as if she was somebody for the first time in her life, but as she gripped the weapon firmly to her breast, she could sense that there was still more to come. It was as if a part of her was still missing, a part which would soon be with her again.

For five more days the odd group propelled the longboat upriver. On the fifth day they found the river's banks were gradually rising higher above the now fast-flowing river.

'Rapids ahead by the looks of it,' Chrestella warned.

'Even if we could row against the current,' Einor Val said, 'the banks are beginning to steepen and soon we won't be able to beach the longboat.'

'Make for the eastern bank,' Queron commanded.

147

The bow of the longboat cut through the foliage and touched the eastern bank. One of the Damear warriors leapt from the longboat and secured the bowline to a rather crippled-looking tree. He was turning and indicating to the others that all was secure, when something flashed from the thick undergrowth and struck him on the temple.

Gideon, Roland and a Damear warrior leapt to the stricken warrior's aid. They were met by a cloud of rocks and clubs which rained down upon them. Gideon and the other grey warrior fell before their attackers showed themselves. Goblins seemed to burst from the undergrowth in all directions, and before anyone could join those on the bank, they were awash with attackers.

'Cut the rope!' Queron ordered.

One of the Damear warriors slashed the bowline, freeing the longboat from the bank. Chrestella had strung her bow and stood to fire it but the current which had captured the longboat made an unstable base. Forced to sit once more, she turned to Queron.

'It would cost us all our lives if we were to stay and give aid,' he answered.

'But we could have at least tried,' Alaric shouted.

'Look!' Anyon called.

Roland was standing with his back to the river. Gideon was on hands and knees beside him as he shook his head trying to clear it from the effects of the blow he had just received. Roland's sword was cutting a silver pattern about himself and his injured charge. The goblins were cavorting just beyond the reach of his sword, darting in and out when Roland's attention was taken elsewhere. Many goblins lay still at his feet, while many more writhed on the ground in pain.

'Man the oars!' Einor Val shouted.

Quickly they leapt for the oars and began to pull towards their struggling companions. Gideon was now on his feet, though rather unsteadily. He had drawn his sword and was trying to help Roland with their defence.

Queron made no effort to stop them as they rowed

towards the bank. He spoke only as they approached within rock throwing range.

'That's close enough,' he ordered.

Mycroft and Einor Val both turned and faced the Ma'goi. It was quite clear to Queron that they were about to argue with him. Before they could speak, Queron raised his right hand to his chest and clenched his fist. As they watched the Ma'goi's right hand began to glow red. At this sight, they decided it was not wise to push their luck and argue the point.

'If we hold this position they will be able to swim to us,' Queron explained.

Gideon proved the Ma'goi correct by throwing his sword at a goblin and diving into the river. Roland leapt at the closest goblins swinging his sword above his head. The goblins fells back in disarray allowing Roland time to turn and run for the river's edge. He had just sheathed his sword when he reached the bank and dived off into the swirling water.

'A rope,' Mycroft shouted.

Anyon snatched a coil of rope from the bow locker and hurled one end out towards the struggling Roland, who caught it and hung on with both hands. Quickly he was drawn towards the longboat where he was dragged over the side to collapse beside Gideon.

'Thank you,' was all Roland could say between gasps.

Anyon simply placed a hand on Roland's shoulder and nodded.

'Now what?' Einor Val asked. 'We can't row against this current for much longer, and we definitely can't go ashore.'

'It was as if they were waiting for us,' Mycroft said.

'They were,' answered Queron.

'But how did they find out we were coming?' Alaric asked. 'We must have outdistanced those we encountered on the beach. How could word of us have reached this far up river so quickly?'

'Perhaps it didn't,' Queron replied.

'How so?' Einor Val asked.

'Just because we are travelling this river for the first time,' Queron explained, 'doesn't mean these goblins have not been through this before. Many others have made attempts to reach Musero, perhaps even by the same method we ourselves are now using. I don't believe these creatures knew we were coming. I think that there is a village, or whatever they live in, near here, for the purpose of catching travellers once they're stopped by the current. There are probably scouts watching us right now, waiting to return with others.'

'Then what are we to do?' Guyon asked.

Queron glanced at the young female before answering. 'We chose the eastern side of the river because it was the easiest, the western bank being too overgrown, too difficult.'

'So what has changed?' Anyon asked.

'That has changed.' Queron pointed to the eastern bank at the waiting goblins. They had helped themselves to the armour and weapons of the two fallen warriors. Some were building a fire, while several were preparing the dead warriors' bodies for cooking.

'Then let's get off this godforsaken river,' Ivo cursed.

'And by the Lady let the other bank be free of death,' Alaric softly prayed.

'I pray to the High Lord you're right,' Gideon added.

Cautiously they entered the overhanging branches of the western bank. Drawing the oars inboard, they grasped the branches and drew themselves deeper into the tangle of foliage. Cries of anger and screams of rage reached them from the far bank.

It was impossible for them to reach the bank because of several low branches. Queron studied the situation for several seconds before giving his orders.

'Einor Val, take a party and clear the shore. Set up a perimeter of at least fifty paces. Report when this is done.'

Einor Val took all in the longboat save Queron, Anyon and one of the Damear warriors. Noting the lie of the land, Einor Val quickly positioned his sentries and reported the all-clear to Queron. Once this was done, Queron had Anyon cut away the offending branches to allow the longboat to be drawn up onto the bank.

After unloading the longboat they cut armfuls of foliage and quickly covered it. Then, throwing saddle-bags and bed rolls over shoulders, they struck out south-ward, following the course of the river. With the river as a guide, they intended to search out more of the sentry towers; it would also give them protection on one flank should they be attacked.

'If all travel by river ends here because of the current, why would there be more sentry towers?' Anyon asked.

'Perhaps they portaged their boats around the rapids and entered the river higher up,' answered Einor Val.

'Then why aren't we doing the same?' Anyon asked. 'That seems to make a great deal of sense to me.'

'Because we are likely to find more of the creatures waiting for us there,' Einor Val explained. 'If it has been done before, then the goblins will be expecting it to be done again.'

'If that's right,' Anyon asked, 'why are we following the river? Aren't we walking into another ambush?'

Einor Val stopped suddenly, causing Anyon to walk into him. Einor Val turned and the expression on his face told Anyon all he needed to know. Einor Val set out once more, moving quickly forward to whisper in Roland's ear. The young wanderer listened to what Einor Val had to say, then nodded, and moved after Alaric.

Einor Val reached back over his shoulder and drew the coif up and over his head. He then slid his hand down his leather baldric until it reached the haft of his war hammer. Removing it from his belt, he lifted it and held it loosely in front of him. Anyon did the same with his axe and watched as others in their party armed them-selves. The Damear warrior, Gideon, drew his knife, having lost his sword in the fight on the river bank.

They had been forced from the river's edge as they skirted a thicket of thorn trees, and now the sound of running water was beginning to get louder once more.

Soon the white water of the river could be seen as it battered its way between the steep banks.

With screams of delight a large number of goblins launched themselves at the party from the undergrowth, trapping them between their attack and the steep river bank. The goblins' delight was short lived as the first of them to reach the party were cut to pieces. Alaric, Mycroft and Roland fought side by side, their swords dealing death before them. The Damear warriors formed a defensive line before their Ma'goi. Sacha, Guyon and Jason kept back, well clear of the fighting, protected by Anyon, Jerram, Ivo, Einor Val and Chrestella. Queron called up globe after globe of light which he sent flashing into the massed goblins.

More of the creatures poured from the undergrowth, but they were no match for the well-armed and well-prepared defenders. However, there seemed no end to the tide of goblins who threw themselves at the defending party with little regard for their own safety. Poorly armed, they were cut down in their dozens and looked like being driven off when a particularly large band appeared led by a tall goblin.

The newcomers rushed the defenders, splitting into several groups as they did so. One group attacked each of the defending parties while a third hung back, awaiting their opportunity. When an opening appeared, they rushed through the weakened defences and fell upon Sacha, Guyon and Jason.

One blow knocked Jason over the bank and out of sight. Guyon stepped forward and was clubbed, unconscious, to the ground, as was Sacha. Two goblins bent and took up the pair while the rest of their brethren closed in about them. With a shouted order from the tall goblin, the group began to pick their way towards the undergrowth.

Einor Val burst through his attackers and took off after his unconscious companions. Queron snapped an order and one of the Damear warriors followed Einor Val out of sight. The rest of the party finished off the remaining goblins. Alaric and Roland found Jason clinging to a tree root, the lower half of his body in the swift current of the river. Pulling him from the water, they took off after the retreating goblins, a wet and angry Jason trailing behind them.

They were easy to follow: dead goblins littered the trail. Some had been killed by the warrior's sword, but for the most part they had been battered to death by Einor Val's war hammer. Without warning, the party stumbled from the trees into a small clearing. The open area was filled with huts and smoking fires and goblins were milling about in confusion.

The sounds of fighting could be heard from the far side of the village. As they passed between the huts, goblins leapt at them from the thatched roofs while others sprung from the huts themselves. Some of the attackers were female, but this did not dampen the ferocity of their attack. Fighting their way through the village, they finally reached the far side and saw Einor Val slashing his way through a crowd of goblins. The Damear warrior was nowhere to be seen, but just on the edge of the trees was the tall goblin and his two brethren, still carrying the unmoving forms of Guyon and Sacha.

Ivo drew back the string of her bow. Her lips brushed the nock of the arrow before she released it. The arrow struck the goblin carrying Guyon in his right thigh. He stumbled and fell. Before he could rise, Chrestella's shaft entered his heart. Ivo drew another shaft and let fly at the tall goblin. The arrow flashed across the open ground and struck him on the chest then careened off into the trees.

The tall goblin turned and fled into the forest followed closely by the goblin carrying Sacha. Ivo had readied another arrow but no opportunity appeared for a clear shot at either of the fleeing attackers.

The village was empty of goblins, the inhabitants having fled into the forest. Jason rushed across and tended to the slowly awakening Guyon.

'That grey-skinned bastard was wearing a mail shirt,'

Anyon cursed as he ran to where the two goblins had disappeared.

'Jerram, Gideon, Chrestella!' Queron called. 'Follow those two.'

Jerram nodded once and entered the trees.

'Einor Val,' Queron continued. 'Take two and search the village. Roland, take another two and search the trees at the edge of the clearing. The rest of you keep close, there may be other dangers.'

A search of the village revealed the remains of the missing warrior. He had made it to the centre of the village before he had been overwhelmed and savagely torn apart.

It was some time later before Jerram and the others returned. They had followed the two goblins for some distance downriver before the trail had simply stopped, vanished.

'How could you lose the trail?' Ivo demanded. 'You are supposed to be a scout.'

'There was little I could do,' Chrestella interrupted. 'The trail simple vanished. One moment it was clear, the next it was gone. I have tracked many beasts and men, but I have never seen the likes before.'

16

NEW PLAYERS

'**S**how me the place where you lost the goblins,' Queron ordered. He turned from Jerram and faced the rest of the party. 'Take anything you need from the village. But be quick, we have no time to lose.'

Coils of rope, blankets, skins of water, and rough packs were gathered from the huts. There was plenty of food, mostly meat, but knowing the goblins' preference for certain meats, they steered well clear of this.

Once everything of use was packed, the party started out. They followed the trail till they reached the spot where the two goblins had vanished. Queron made everyone keep well back from the spot. Taking a chain from around his neck he drew out a large oval medallion which had been hidden beneath his clothes. Holding the medallion before him, he opened it, revealing a small silver mirror.

'*reyin*,' he said in a clear voice filled with authority.

From their position the others were unable to see what was revealed to the Ma'goi; but they could see the effect. His body stiffened and he stifled a curse. It was the first real show of emotion the Ma'goi had made since their meeting on the beach.

'It seems we are not the only ones interested in the city of Musero,' he said.

'The goblins?' Einor Val asked.

'No,' Queron answered. 'Somehow the goblins are part of it but there is a powerful force behind them.'

'How so?' Einor Val asked.

'The two goblins and the captive were transported from this spot by one with great skill in the Arts,' he explained. 'The transportation of oneself requires great stamina and skill. To transport another requires even more.'

'And the transportation of three?' Guyon asked.

'I have never heard of it being done.'

'How far could they be transported?' asked Roland.

'Yesterday I would have answered the distance from here to the village, perhaps slightly further. But now...'

'Let us work on that distance for now,' Einor Val explained. 'The west is out as the river is too far and they would not want to be trapped with their backs to the fast-flowing river.'

'And north would take them back towards the village and us,' Roland added.

'So we are left with south or east,' Queron concluded.

'I think south,' Chrestella said suddenly.

When everyone paused, waiting for her explanation, she continued. 'They ran in this direction. I doubt they would waste time with deception when they were being pursued so closely.'

Einor Val looked at Queron. 'Is there nothing you can do?'

'There is,' Queron answered. 'But it would expose me to those who transported them.'

'We are hardly undetected,' said Anyon.

'True,' Queron replied. 'But by reaching out and searching for them I would open myself to an attack from which it would be almost impossible to protect myself.'

'No loss,' Anyon muttered, just loud enough to be heard by Ivo. The young archer nudged her companion into silence.

'No. We will search to the south,' Queron decided. 'If we move close enough to where the goblins arrived, I will be able to sense it.'

156

The foliage thickened considerably as the party moved further south. They were forced to break from their route many times to bypass large areas of impenetrable vegetation.

Eventually Queron called a halt. 'I can sense it nearby,' he said.

'That way,' Guyon pointed in the direction of the river.

Queron inclined his head slightly at Guyon's statement and nodded. From the expression on his face it was obvious he had learnt more than where the goblins had been transported.

In short time, they found signs of the two goblins. Following the trail, they found where Sacha had regained consciousness and was made to walk. The trail led to a small hut with a smudge of smoke hanging above it.

As they watched, the low door opened and a stooped figure emerged. Once free of the hut, the figure straightened. It was the tall goblin from the village. This time he was not dressed in rags, and the long mail shirt he had obviously worn in the village was in view for all to see.

Also visible was the sword hanging from the right hip, the light helmet with a raised half-visor, and the knee-high boots. A large cloak hung about his shoulders and reached to his ankles. He wore tight black leather gloves and stroked his chin as he surveyed the small clearing in front of the hut. Turning to re-enter the cramped quarters he stopped abruptly.

He straightened and stared at the exact point where the party was hidden. His right hand rose to his helmet and lowered the visor into place as he called a warning. Two forest goblins raced from the hut armed with maces. The tall goblin drew his sword and pointed towards the concealed party.

Queron rose. 'Take him!' he called. 'But alive, I have need of information.'

The party leapt forward to meet the attack of the two goblins. Even though they were better armed than those they had previously met, and had obviously received some training, they were soon dispatched. Roland was the first to reach the tall goblin and soon found himself engaged in a fight for his life against an extremely skilled opponent. Even when Alaric reached his side and joined the combat, the two were hard pushed to force the goblin back.

As more of the party neared the armoured goblin, he began to back towards the trees. His lips were curled in a strange half-smile as he continued his withdrawal. His sword flashed through the air, parrying blows and snaking out in attack effortlessly. He gave the impression that he could stand his ground against the entire party if he desired, and that he was merely playing with them.

As he reached the edge of the trees, he launched a blistering attack before turning and diving into a small bush. As his head passed between the branches, there was a blue glow which encompassed his entire body.

The party stood in silence staring at the bush. Anyon even walked around the small sparse shrub to squat and examine the other side.

'*tugulawarrin curbanmah*,' Queron called. A faint red glow surrounded the bush. Within the red glow a faint blue aura appeared.

'A passage had been opened for him,' the Ma'goi explained. 'He needed only to step into the circle and he would have been transported to whatever destination had been arranged.'

'Can we use the same passage?' Anyon asked.

'Yes,' Queron answered.

Anyon drew his axe and stepped towards the bush.

'But by now the goblin's saviour would know we have located the passage, and as he has not closed it behind his follower, I would say he has shifted the exit to an undesirable place.'

'Undesirable?' Anyon asked, barely slowing.

'Halfway down a cliff, out over the ocean,' Queron explained with a slight smile as he watched Anyon slide to a halt a pace short of the bush.

Anyon looked about the clearing. 'Perhaps we should search here before following.'

The party separated. Some entered the small dwelling, while others searched the immediate area.

'Then we're back to where we started,' Einor Val concluded. 'Following an unknown enemy who could have been transported in any direction.'

'An unknown enemy no longer,' Gideon said, moving away from the remainder of the party.

Einor Val, Alaric, and Roland followed the Damear warrior who stopped by the remains of a small fire just on the edge of the open ground.

'That tall goblin was a Kobalos, a mythical being from deep in the ancient lore of my people,' Gideon explained. 'They are supposed to be the ancestors of the goblin dating back to a time when they were the supreme race in this land. A great catastrophe struck their race destroying all, save a handful, who reverted to the forest goblins we have met to date.'

'He was a damned good swordsman for a myth,' Roland said, stretching his right arm which was still stiff from the confrontation.

'It seems a great number of myths are turning out to be reality in this forest,' Gideon commented.

'Do you think these Kobalos are from Musero?' Alaric asked.

'You think they could be the race of people we were sent to learn about?' Roland asked.

'Why not?' said Alaric. 'We have a dead city located deep in an impenetrable forest. Only perhaps the city isn't totally dead. And the forest isn't so much impenetrable as well-protected. Then we find a being much like ourselves in stature and clothing, with a knowledge of weapons. This being is supported by unknown allies skilled in the Arts. I find it all a little too coincidental for my liking.'

'At least we now know something about our enemy,' Einor Val said.

'Unfortunately they know more about us,' Anyon added as he approached. The four turned and waited for the short axe-man to continue. 'In the hut,' Anyon said.

'What's in the hut?' Einor Val asked.

'Sacha,' Anyon said quietly. His right hand was fisted round the haft of his bloodied axe, his knuckles white from the strain. 'Or rather what's left of her. That tall almond-eyed bastard questioned her to learn more about us.'

'Questioned?' Roland asked, afraid of what the answer might be.

'Tortured,' Anyon spat. 'What he did to her . . .' Visibly distressed, Anyon left the three and walked off into the trees.

'Don't wander too far,' Einor Val called after him. 'There may be more goblins about.'

'I should be so lucky,' Anyon hissed as he cut a small tree from his path with one blow of his axe.

A shallow grave was dug and what remained of Sacha was wrapped in a cloak found in the hut. The party silently gathered round the small grave as Anyon and Kendrick placed the carefully wrapped body in it.

Gideon drew his dagger, holding the blade before his eyes. 'The edge of the knife gives life and the edge takes it away.' As he spoke the words, the Damear warriors also drew their weapons.

'It is an ancient ritual of our people,' Queron explained. 'The blade of the midwife frees the child from its mother and gives it its own life, just as the blade of the warrior frees us from this life in preparation for the next.'

Large stones were placed on the loose earth before the party once more shouldered their packs and left the open ground for the shadows of the trees.

'How could somebody do that to another person?' Ivo asked incredulously.

'He needed information,' Gideon answered calmly.

Ivo had been speaking to no one in particular, but when the Damear warrior answered her she took up the challenge.

'Is that how you would gather information?' she demanded. 'Do you condone what was done back there?'

'It is not my place to gather information,' he answered. 'I am a warrior, but what happened back there was not the work of a warrior.'

'I am relieved,' she answered.

'If they are allied with one of such power in the Arts the information could have been extracted much quicker,' Gideon continued.

Ivo turned a cold stare on her companion. 'You're not really much different from the Kobalos, are you?'

Gideon stopped and grabbed Ivo by the shoulder, spinning her round. 'In my land we have fought for centuries to maintain our freedom. You have no idea what dangers there are in the southern lands.'

'I can see only too well,' Ivo rejoined.

'No, not the Damear,' Gideon went on. 'Below our land, further south, there are places the people of the Fortalice know nothing about. Warlike lands where the creatures live only to fight. For centuries they have hounded our southern border, raiding deep into our territory, killing, looting, even stealing our children.'

'Why?'

'To the east of Damear is a vast wasteland, a land totally without water, impossible to cross. To the west lies the Moribund. Damear is the only way these warlike lands can reach the north and the soft countries that lie there.'

'But why were we followed when we sought knowledge from the western lands?' Ivo asked, realising that, although at first she had doubted him, he was speaking the truth.

'There are a small number of Damear who believe that we should allow the southern nations passage through our lands. They believe that the northern lands are no concern of ours.'

'Then it was they who tried to stop us from reaching the western kingdoms?' she asked. 'All those innocent people in that small fishing village were slain simply so those rebels of yours could reach our small party and stop us on our mission.'

161

'Yes,' he answered. 'An alliance is feared between the forces of the Fortalice and the western kingdoms. Should the vast western army be ferried across Lake Zeridal, the two forces combined would be more than a match for any army the south could muster. And once the creatures of the south were stopped, many believe that the Fortalice and its allies would continue the war until all nations including the Damear fell beneath their might.'

'Then this search is important to both our races?'

'Indeed it is.'

'What are we to do now?' Alaric asked. He, Ivo, Jerram, and Roland were seated by a small fire. The party had travelled for many days since leaving the hut where Sacha had been killed. They had seen no sign of goblins since that day, but they had not stopped their vigilance.

'We were sent to this forest to lure the Damear away from the true mission which was to send a party to the western kingdoms,' Alaric continued. 'Only, once we reached this coast, we found ourselves allied to those we thought were our enemies. Now from Ivo we have learnt that the Damear are probably an unknown ally.'

'Then what does it matter?' asked Jerram.

'It matters that we were sent to search for a myth, a city that was not supposed to exist. Yet here we are, deep in a forest heading towards that mythical city following the trail of a being long since believed dead. Continually attacked by creatures we had not dreamed existed who are aided by a person so skilled in the Arts that his like has not been heard of before,' Alaric replied.

'It seems to me that we have little choice in the matter,' Roland said. 'We are hardly in a position to demand Queron lead us to the coast, and I think that any information we can learn about these southern lands, and the Kobalos, would be of great value to the Fortalice.'

'But what of this city we search for?' Alaric asked. 'Is it possible it still exists, after all this time?'

'It will be there,' Jerram answered. His family archives had showed him that much before leaving.

'A ruin no doubt,' Ivo said.

'What else would be left after all these years,' Jerram added softly.

The forest changed little in the days which followed. There was no warning of anything out of the ordinary until Jerram appeared telling them he had found the remains of a stone wall. It was intact in several places and evidence showed that it had once reached the height of two men. Creepers and vines now clung to what remained of the wall, all but hiding its moss-covered stones.

Stepping cautiously through a large collapsed section of the wall, the party found themselves looking down on a city nestled in a large depression. The city was massive, larger than any city they had ever seen. Its design reminded Queron of his fortified home of Damear. It was built to be defended from its outer wall to the last building in its very heart. Constructed of grey stone the city spread out before them like a giant maze. The streets were overgrown with vegetation and not one building still boasted a roof, yet there seemed something strangely new about the place.

'Have you noticed that there are no trees in the heart of the city?' Jerram pointed out.

'Yes,' answered Anyon. 'And those in the outer sections are only stunted growths, nothing majestic like the surrounding forest.'

'You would have thought that after all this time the forest would have claimed the city totally,' Einor Val mused.

'Let's enter the city and find out first hand why this is so,' Queron suggested and started off down the gentle slope towards the city.

In a few places the paving stones of the street could be seen, but generally the streets were covered with dirt, long since blown in by the wind. Squat shrubs and bushes grew in abundance making the party's passage difficult and slow.

'We have an hour till dark,' Jerram reported. 'Are we to spend the night in the city or do we retire to the higher ground and resume our search tomorrow?'

'We will stay here,' Queron decided. 'Split into groups and look for a suitable place to wait out the night. A place large enough for all of us would be preferable, but with only one or two entrances, in case there are any inhabitants still about.'

A building was found close by which was large enough for their purpose. Single-storeyed, its roof had long since vanished but the walls were still sturdy and would offer good protection should the need arise. The building was split into three rooms: one small room at the rear and two large rooms which opened up onto the dirt-clogged street.

Queron chose the small room as it had only one opening. At this door he posted one of his warriors. The remainder of the group separated into two parties and began to set up camp. Deadfall was gathered and used to block the gaping windows, leaving only one door which opened from the western room out into the street.

'Looks like we get to watch the street tonight,' Roland said.

'Good,' retorted Anyon. 'I doubt I could sleep if I had to depend on that Ma'goi and his men for protection.'

'They have not threatened us,' Alaric said.

'Yet,' Anyon added. 'Don't forget we are still needed. That Ma'goi has done very little for us to date.'

'He helped us find Sacha,' Ivo reminded him.

'It didn't do Sacha any good, did it?' Anyon snapped. 'And as yet, each time we have been attacked, his support has been noticeably lacking.'

'He is saving his strength,' Guyon explained. 'Each time he uses his Arts, he weakens himself slightly. A little rest is all that's needed to replace what he has lost, but sometimes because of the feats he performs, his strength cannot be replaced by a simple short rest.'

'If we were attacked tonight, could we count on him for help?' asked Jerram.

'If the trouble was more than we could handle,' Guyon replied. 'He has used his skills sparingly over the past weeks.'

'Perhaps he feels he may have need of them with us,' Ivo suggested.

'For defence or attack?' asked Anyon.

17

MUSERO

With the morning came a terrifying wind. The vegetation in the streets was bent almost to the ground under the incessant punishment. A deafening howl tore through the building the party sheltered in as the wind found its way through every small opening. It brought an uncomfortable heat with it which had each member of the party on edge. Queron seemed unnerved by the unnatural wind and rise in temperature, and continually consulted his small oval mirror.

The Damear warriors noticed the edginess of their Ma'goi and remained close to him, their weapons loose in their scabbards. The slightest sign of danger would find them ready. As the day wore on, the wind strengthened until it seemed the structure which sheltered them would fall. Then, as suddenly as it had appeared, the wind dropped.

In the stillness there was an even greater threat than when the wind was at its strongest. In the silence of the afternoon, the muttering of goblins could be heard.

'They must have taken shelter in one of the buildings nearby,' Einor Val whispered.

The sound of the goblins increased as they neared the party's building. They passed the silent hidden group and continued on into the centre of the city.

'How many?' Gideon asked.

Queron reached for his mirror but Jerram answered before he could use his skill.

'Nine,' Jerram whispered. 'Well armed and loaded down with stores.'

No one questioned the scout's answer. Instead they quietly began to put together their packs. Once ready, they crept from the building and circled it until they picked up the goblins' trail. There seemed to be a narrow path running down the centre of the street. Moving silently, the party moved off, pausing as often as was needed to listen out for the goblins they followed.

At one point Jerram signalled for a halt and disappeared into the foliage ahead. He soon returned but passed through the party and vanished down the back trail. This time it was longer before he returned.

'There is another party of goblins behind us,' he explained.

'We must let them pass,' Queron explained. 'There must be no warning of our presence.'

'Too late for that,' Jerram explained. 'It will be only a matter of time before one of them looks down and notices our tracks. They are somewhat different to those a goblin might expect to find on a trail frequented only by its own kind.'

'Then they must die,' Queron said firmly. 'Silently and swiftly,' he added, drawing a slim-bladed knife from his clothing.

It was the first time anyone had realised the Ma'goi was armed. Quickly they melted into the foliage to either side of the path. They did not have long to wait before the guttural voices of the goblins could be heard. A band of six came into sight and began to pass between the concealed members of the party.

Jerram stepped from the foliage directly behind the last goblin. Throwing his arm around the goblin's face he slipped his dirk into the surprised creature's back. The goblin stiffened slightly before dying. Other members of the party leapt from cover, taking the remaining goblins by surprise. Not one sound was heard before the last creature slid dead to the ground at Anyon's feet.

'Now we must dispose of the bodies and continue. I'd say it was likely that other bands will use this trail,' Queron said quickly.

The bodies were lifted and carried so as not to damage the foliage. A small house well off the worn trail was chosen and the bodies were unceremoniously dumped there. Returning to the trail once more, the party continued.

The trail ended at a tall building which was in much better condition than those about it. Jerram and Mycroft entered the building but saw no sign of the goblins. The stairs to the next level had long since rotted away leaving the two with a confusing problem.

'There has to be another door,' Roland reasoned as he began to search one of the walls. 'Something hidden but able to be opened from this side.'

Queron and Guyon both closed their eyes for several seconds before turning to face the southern wall. No one was surprised that both had moved simultaneously; it seemed that Guyon was becoming more experienced as they progressed.

Anyon ran a searching hand over the section of wall indicated, and smiled as his fingers brushed a slightly raised stone. Placing his palm on the stone he pressed his weight against the wall. Silently, a small panel of stone swung downward, revealing a dark square hole in the floor beside Anyon. Queron looked towards the hole and nodded. Gideon moved to the edge and peered in. Turning, he shook his head, indicating that it was too dark for him to see.

Queron muttered a word and a small ball of red light sprang from his fingers and dropped through the hole in the floor; Gideon followed close after. Once Gideon had called up the all-clear, the rest of the party entered the red glowing hole.

'It's as if we are stepping into a pathway to hell,' Ivo said to Anyon just before she dropped through the hole.

'Perhaps we are,' he mumbled to himself as he followed. 'But even hell has its treasures.'

The secret door opened onto a spiral staircase. Gideon moved downwards, the red floating ball of light hovering just above his right shoulder. At the base of the stairs a long corridor opened up to the south. Deep in its darkness, Gideon could make out a faint spot of light, a torch in the hand of a goblin.

'No,' Queron called softly as Gideon started out down the corridor. 'It is time I sought help.'

Queron moved to one side of the corridor and removed the oval medallion from beneath his clothing. Opening the medallion he stared long into the small mirror. His lips moved as he spoke several words, so softly that none could hear what was spoken. A faint red glow from the mirror reflected on his face giving him a strange non-human look.

'It is as you believed, High Lord,' Queron said. 'The city exists.'

'You are sure?' came the reply.

'We entered the city yesterday, but I felt a strange presence and refrained from alerting them to your presence.'

'Good.'

'We are now in an underground passageway beneath the city, which lies in ruins above us.'

'The city on the surface was never more than a lure to trap those who searched for what they could not master. What we seek lies deep beneath the city in a crypt long since forgotten even by those who inhabit Musero.'

'Will those who dwell here prove a problem?' Queron asked.

'You will travel by ways long unused. Once you have entered these passageways, the populace of the city will be the least of your problems, for those who built the city you will travel through guarded their secrets well.'

'Then I will travel with care.'

'Do that Queron, my trusted one, for I will have need of the information you will gather.'

'Yes, High Lord.'

'Do you have aid?'

'Yes, High Lord,' Queron answered. 'Few of my own warriors remain, but the fates replaced those I have lost with warriors from the Fortalice.'

'Warriors of the Fortalice, and another,' the voice laughed. 'How fitting that you should be forced to work together in this.'

'Another?' Queron queried.

'One of the assassins of the Mountain of Death.'

'Alamut?'

'The very place,' the voice answered.

'Who...?'

'It matters not. I will give you the information I have gathered. Be ready.'

Queron took a folded sheet of parchment from his pocket and handed it to Gideon. The warrior opened the sheet and laid it on the floor beside the Ma'goi. Placing the mirror's reflective surface down upon the parchment, Queron whispered one word. *'reyin.'*

A brief flare of red escaped from beneath the mirror. Reaching forward, Queron took up the mirror and closed the decorative face, hanging it back around his neck. Gideon reached down and took up the parchment. The side where the mirror had rested held a tiny map, almost unreadable in the near darkness.

Queron took the parchment and placed a finger on the map. *'kringgun,'* he said calmly.

The parchment remained unchanged but the diagram began to grow in size as they watched. Within seconds the map had grown to a size where it filled the entire sheet of parchment.

'With this we will find what the High One seeks and both our lands will benefit.'

Gideon led the way with the light still showing him the passages ahead. Each time they came to an intersection, the red ball of light would branch off, indicating the direction in which Queron wanted the party to travel. Queron moved in the centre of the party, and a second ball of light hovered above him.

'We must be close,' Guyon whispered to Einor Val. 'He uses more of his knowledge and strength to guide us and light our way.'

Einor Val nodded. For the past hour he had been deep in thought about what Queron would try once he had the information the strange voice had spoken of. Who was the assassin in their party? Why was he or she here?

'If the map is to scale then we are five days' travel from the crypt the voice spoke of,' Einor Val concluded.

'And we have food for one day and water for two more,' Anyon said, weighing a waterskin in one hand.

'We will make it,' Gideon said. 'A day or two without food and water is nothing to the warriors of Damear.'

'And what of the return journey?' Alaric asked. 'How would you go with a further seven days without food and water?'

'We'll manage,' Gideon answered.

'Perhaps the general could whip us up something to eat,' Anyon laughed, 'And a nice tankard of ale,' he added quickly.

'I'd even join you in that drink,' Ivo grinned.

The room the party was in had a low ceiling and was bare. A thick covering of dust and rotted furnishings covered the floor. Queron and Guyon were standing in the centre of the room deep in conversation. Since the journey through the darkness began, Queron had spent much time with the young Kungour. She was eager to learn what she could from the Ma'goi and dogged his steps whenever possible.

'What's with them?' Anyon asked.

'Guyon says she feels there is another way from this room, other than the two obvious doors,' Mycroft explained.

'And the general doesn't agree?'

'No, he agrees there's another hidden door close by, but he says it is of no concern to us,' Mycroft said.

'In that case, perhaps we should search it out,' Anyon said and climbed to his feet. He began a slow circle of

171

the room tapping the haft of his axe against the stone wall, listening for any difference in the sound. Others rose and joined Anyon in his search. Soon all save Guyon and Queron were busy tapping and prying.

'Here,' one of the Damear warriors called. He thumped a small raised stone with the pommel of his sword.

A slight grinding noise filled the room as a section of floor beneath the warrior dropped away. With a strangled cry the warrior disappeared from sight. Roland was the first to reach the opening. Peering down, he saw the warrior clinging to the pit's lip. The bottom of the pit was filled with steel-tipped stakes. The light armour the warrior wore would do little to protect him from them. Roland reached down and grasped the warrior's wrists and drew him from the pit.

'The High Lord said that the secrets of this city would be well guarded,' the warrior said softly, staring down at what could quite easily have been his tomb.

'Enough!' Queron ordered. 'We know where we must go.' He held up the parchment map. 'Any detour may prove costly in time... and lives.'

All members of the party glanced into the pit as they filed past. Gideon drew his knife and whispered several words as he passed. Einor Val kissed his index finger and raised it to his forehead. They moved cautiously from that moment on. Guyon pointed out many places where she sensed hidden passages or compartments and on the off-chance they too were rigged with traps, the party steered well clear of these hidden obstacles.

Finally, tired and hungry, they reached the spot the High Lord had marked on the map. They stood in a circular room with carved columns positioned every few paces around the wall. Between two of these columns was the door they had used to enter the room. Between each of the other columns a large decorated stone head was fixed.

Some resembled humans, others goblins — or rather Kobalos — while the rest depicted creatures of myths or nightmares. Queron drew his medallion from beneath his clothing and opened it to communicate with his High Lord.

He crossed to the far side of the room and called for help. While the others watched, Queron entered a conversation with his High Lord. When he had finished, he returned the medallion to his jacket and began to busy himself with the business his master had set him. Queron walked in a small circle whispering words as he did so.

Guyon could see a faint red light appear behind the Ma'goi. Soon a glowing red circle appeared on the floor in the centre of the room.

'A passageway,' Guyon explained. 'He's preparing a passageway for someone.'

'The High Lord,' Gideon whispered, staring at Kendrick in disbelief. 'The High Lord himself is coming to aid us.'

Queron stopped his pacing and began to whisper a different string of words. His glowing light snapped out throwing the room into darkness. The air in the circle first glowed red, then for a brief moment it changed to a bright green, finally it changed to a deep blue as the shape of a man began to appear. The shape grew and solidified until a man stood in the centre of the circle.

Guyon drew her stiletto and held it before her. A whispered word brought the gem in the hilt to life. Bright light flooded the room blinding them all for a moment. As the spots before their eyes cleared, they saw a tall figure standing in the centre of the room. His hair was grey as was his neatly trimmed beard.

'High Lord,' Queron said reverently.

'Wiseone!' Guyon exclaimed in surprise.

In the light thrown out by the stiletto's gem Cymbeline stood before them. The air about him within the circle changed from red through green to blue.

'So at last it is within my grasp,' he said with a laugh. 'After so many decades of failure, I will at last lay my hands upon it.'

'What?' Mycroft asked.

Cymbeline laughed and left the circle. He walked slowly towards one of the stone heads. The one he stopped before was that of a Kobalos with the look of incredible strength and intelligence. Placing both hands upon the head he began to chant a string of words. As the second word left his lips Jerram launched himself across the room at Cymbeline's unprotected back.

Jerram was brought to a sudden halt as if he had struck a wall. He shook his head and tried to reach Cymbeline once more. This time he was thrown across the room to strike the wall with sickening force.

'Too late, assassin,' Cymbeline said clearly when he had finished his chant. 'You should have struck the moment I appeared within the circle, but you paused, and it was your undoing. Unfortunately for you, you will not receive another chance.'

The section of wall between the two pillars Cymbeline stood before began to glow in a deep light the colour of which was indefinite. In the centre of the growing light the stone head seemed unaffected. Cymbeline stepped through the light and disappeared from the room. The light slowly faded until only the glow from Guyon's stiletto lit the room.

'By the Lady, what in hell was that all about?' Alaric asked.

'I have a feeling we've been used,' Anyon said with a curse.

Roland knelt over Jerram. 'He's still alive. Jason, see if you can do something for him. He at least seems to know something about this.'

Queron and his warriors were quiet; the Ma'goi's face was quite pale. The voice of the old man was the voice of the unseen High Lord who had commanded and steered him from the start of this mission. Yet even he could recognise the features of Cymbeline, perhaps the most powerful of the Wiseones of the Fortalice. How was it possible that a High Lord of the Damear and a Wiseone of the Fortalice could be one and the same person?

Jason's ministrations soon had Jerram awake. He was shaken by the blow he had received but there were no broken bones and, after a short rest, he was ready to tell his tale.

18

ALAMUT

All eyes were on Jerram as he began.

'As you have gathered, I am from Alamut. It is a mountain very much smaller than Fortalice but with the same aims. Thousands of years ago the Founder of our order realised what could happen should the direction of the Fortalice be changed either through design or accident. He decided that another Mountain of Power would be needed to monitor the goings on of the Fortalice, aiding it when necessary.

'We did not have the numbers or power of the Fortalice so our existence has been kept a closely guarded secret. Over the last few centuries, our leaders learnt that there was someone in the Fortalice who was directing a powerful nation to the south — Damear.

'Through continuous attacks by southern tribes, the Damear were moulded into a fighting race of great power. The one who controlled them had hoped to wait until the lost city of Musero was finally reached by warriors of Damear; but Edelmar Rhys of the Western Nations was told of what would happen, so he combined the might of the west into a mighty army. Aided by the Seven Knights, the guardians of Alamut, they prepared themselves for the war which would eventually come.

'The news of this army forced Cymbeline to step up

his plans for the discovery of Musero. By sending a force from the Fortalice, under the story of a lure for the enemy, he managed to gather a small skilled force on the edge of the Moribund — us. Then, with the aid of the Kobalos, who had maintained a limited command over the goblins, we were driven inland towards the city.

'The city has an ancient power which blocks many forms of the Arts, and Cymbeline needed to have someone inside the city to call him through a passage that he would open. He was right. I hesitated when he first appeared, not believing my eyes. I really thought that Gurth was the one, aided by either Guyon, Mycroft, or both.'

'What type of power does the city hold, and how will Cymbeline use it?' Queron asked quietly.

'The city holds no power that Cymbeline or any other human could use. It contains the remains of many great rulers from the city's past. Those are their likenesses on the walls of this room, dating from those who constructed the original city, through the many races who followed.' Jerram first pointed to the stone head of one of the strange creatures, then drew his finger about the room in a circle. Halfway through the circle his finger passed the blank wall through which Cymbeline had disappeared.

'Then what has happened?' Einor Val asked.

'Cymbeline has entered a passage which leads back to the time of the death of Xularkon, one of the ancient rulers of this city.'

'What good will that do?' Mycroft asked.

'He will save Xularkon from the death he so rightly deserved and bring him back to this room, in this time. With the incredible skill in the Arts that Xularkon possessed, they will bring the goblins of the Moribund under the total control of the Kobalos, and with the southern tribes already in Cymbeline's control, they will sweep up from the south, destroying all nations in their path. Once this is done, Xularkon, with his loyal disciple Cymbeline, will bring back the rule of the Kobalos with Musero as the centre of power.'

'What of Damear?' Gideon asked.

'If the High Lords continue to follow the will of Cymbeline, then they will join the southern tribes. If they learn the truth behind Cymbeline's plan, then I believe they will stand against their old enemies and aid the western and northern nations.'

'Then we have helped in the destruction of our lands?' Queron stammered.

'In a way, yes,' answered Jerram. 'There is nothing we can do to stop Cymbeline and Xularkon now. But if we can get a warning to the Damear and the Fortalice, then perhaps we can find a way to stop them.'

'It will take us months to return to the Fortalice,' Anyon said. 'By then everyone we see will have grey skin and almond eyes.'

'No,' Jerram said, getting shakily to his feet. 'Cymbeline will take some time to return with Xularkon. We have that time, and the time Xularkon must use to gather his strengths and allies.'

'Then let us be gone,' Queron directed. His confidence had returned and once again he was in command of the situation. 'How long before Cymbeline returns?'

'I'm unsure,' Jerram answered.

'Then let's get the hell out of here,' said Anyon.

'It won't be that easy,' Queron warned. 'Cymbeline is a Ma'goi of great power. The instant he returns, he will search us out and destroy us.'

'He has to find us first,' Anyon countered, heading for the door.

'It will not take him long to locate us,' Queron explained. 'Unless he is weakened.'

'Will his journey have weakened him sufficiently?' Mycroft asked.

'Yes. But not enough for our purpose. However, I have an idea which might just work.'

Queron quickly explained his plan. Einor Val was to lead the party from the subterranean passageways. Gideon and Kendrick would accompany them, while the remaining Damear warrior stayed with Queron. He would stay and delay Cymbeline when he returned, giving the party time to lose themselves in the passages. Before they left, Queron took Guyon off to one side and spoke with her. None of the others could hear what was said.

'I don't think we should rely on the map too much,' Mycroft said. 'Remember it was Cymbeline who supplied it.'

'Then I suggest we find the closest goblin and ask him the way out,' said Anyon.

'You think they'd help us?' Ivo asked.

'I think so,' Anyon answered, holding his axe before him. 'If we were to ask them just right, I'm sure they'd help us.'

'Perhaps the map shows another way out of these passages,' Einor Val suggested.

'It also shows a large system of passageways to the east. We may find goblins there,' Roland said.

'We don't want too many goblins,' Ivo added. 'Just one will do.'

'One it is,' Anyon said with a laugh and headed off in the direction the map indicated. They had not gone far before a trembling could be felt through the stone floor of the passage. The rumbling continued for a short time before subsiding, helping to quicken their pace still further.

'There's a large number of goblins ahead of us,' Jerram explained.

'How large?' Ivo asked.

'I couldn't tell, but too large a number for us to handle,' he answered.

Turning off the main passage, the group entered a smaller corridor which ran northward. Guyon kept the corridor illuminated. The white light from her stiletto seemed so pure compared to the mixture of colours they had encountered in the room of the stone heads.

'Stop!' Guyon called. Slipping the blade of her stiletto into a crack in the stone wall she closed her eyes and concentrated. Turning slowly, she focused on what had alerted her.

'There is a hidden door here somewhere,' she said.

Anyon hung his axe from his belt and began a systematic search of the wall. The thief's nimble fingers travelled over the rough surface until he stopped abruptly.

Guyon moved over and stood behind Anyon as he explored the section of wall.

'There's a loose stone here,' he said.

'Wait,' Guyon said.

The sound of approaching goblins suddenly grew loud in the confined space of the passageway. 'We haven't time,' Anyon said quickly. He placed his right palm on the loose stone and pushed. His eyes closed involuntarily as the stone disappeared into the wall.

A section of the wall slid back revealing a dark square. The door had moved smoothly and silently and must have been maintained regularly.

'Now!' Einor Val cried, ushering the party into the opening.

'Now how in five hells do we close it?' Roland demanded.

Guyon lifted her stiletto and illuminated the small tunnel. Alaric reached forward and pushed a metal lever up against the wall. The stone door slid back into place as silently as it had opened.

The party waited in silence, hoping that Guyon's light had not been seen. After a suitable time, Alaric reached for the lever again. Taking the metal in his hand, he tried to pull it towards him, but the lever refused to move. Roland lent a hand, but still the lever would not budge.

'Stop playing around and open the damned door,' Anyon cursed.

'It's locked,' Alaric whispered. He stepped back from the door and wiped his face with his hand.

In the light Roland could see he was sweating profusely. 'Don't worry. There has to be another way out,' he said, trying to console the obviously distressed Alaric.

There was nothing else for them to do but follow the passageway. Their path was not shown on the map, and each pace took them further from any chance of finding their way from the dark maze.

Cymbeline moved through a corridor of many colours. They swirled and changed as he was drawn deeper into them. In the distance he could see a pinpoint of light which grew steadily larger as he watched. As the circle of light grew, he staggered into it and found himself in a large well-furnished room. Warriors were fighting in the centre of the room as Cymbeline's weakened state forced him to collapse to the floor. His legs were trembling and his eyes refused to focus properly. Several tall grey-skinned Kobalos were locked in combat with armoured priests. They struggled back and forth about the room as more fighting raged about them.

Suddenly, from nowhere, familiar looking warriors appeared. They were wearing an assortment of armour and fought with goblins in an attempt to reach a tall unprotected figure standing on a dais at one end of the room. The figure turned and saw Cymbeline for the first time. Raising both hands before him, Xularkon stepped back, a look of horror on his face. Suddenly the look of horror fell from his face and Xularkon whirled around and ran from the dais only to slip from its edge and crash to the ground.

Cymbeline gathered his strength and rose to his feet. Concentrating on his knowledge of the Arts he whispered a single word. Balls of blue light sprang from his fingers and flashed across the room towards the struggling figures. The target, a robed woman, swung her staff round in time to block the fireballs.

In the ancient tomes Cymbeline had read in his own time, this was the fight in which Xularkon had vanished. Cymbeline's intervention would prevent that from happening. Then a startling thought thrust itself at Cymbeline. If his plan succeeded then Xularkon would indeed vanish, whisked forward through the centuries to Cymbeline's own time. Cymbeline felt a tug at his back and realised that the passage which had brought him here was about to draw him back to his own time.

One of the attacking warriors dropped his sword and drew a weapon from his belt. Whirling the weapon about his head, he let fly at the surprised Xularkon, taking him around the neck. Xularkon's hands flashed to his throat to try to loosen the constricting thongs. Cymbeline reached his side at the same time. He bent over the gasping Xularkon and, knife flashing, cut the thongs from Xularkon's throat. Blood splashed his face as his knife tore at Xularkon's neck. But Cymbeline cared nothing for Xularkon. The future told of Xularkon's disappearance, therefore Cymbeline's plan was destined to succeed.

Grasping the stunned Xularkon, Cymbeline drew him towards his chest just as the passage opened again and drew him back into the swirling colours of the corridor. As they entered the passageway, Cymbeline felt a tearing pain in his right shoulder. As he was drawn back towards his time, he saw the struggling Xularkon drifting off along a different corridor.

Queron readied himself as the wall between the pillars changed to a deep blue. As he watched, a figure tumbled into the circular room. It was Cymbeline. The old Wiseone looked exhausted, totally drained by his experience, and blood stained his right shoulder. A quick smile crossed Queron's lips. Perhaps the effort of the trip was more tiring than he had thought. He may yet be able to stop Cymbeline's plan and win back the honour he had lost by being part of it.

Queron raised a hand. Cymbeline saw the action and raised his hands in defence, but the old man was too slow and the shock on his face showed it. The red light leapt from Queron's fingertips, striking the exhausted Wiseone in the chest. Cymbeline still maintained sufficient power to protect himself from the greater part of the blast.

Hastily he erected a blue barrier about his body, just as a second attack was launched. Queron realised that he could not penetrate the web wall and that a new method would be needed.

As he completed the word, he raised both hands to release the large ball of fire which twisted and spun on the palms of his hands. At such close range the fireball would destroy the blue shield and probably all those who were in the room.

Before the red ball could leave his hands he felt a sharp pain from behind as a sword entered his back. Queron crumpled to the floor. The fireball vanished as the Damear warrior stepped over his body and moved towards Cymbeline.

The Damear warrior knelt besides Cymbeline. 'For centuries the High Priests in secret have whispered of your doings. My heart is your heart, my sword is your sword, my strength is your strength. Take them and bless me.'

Cymbeline smiled at the waiting warrior and reached out a hand to touch his adoring face. At the touch, the warrior crumpled to the ground and, as Queron watched in horror, the warrior turned to dust.

'Thank you for the gift, my loyal follower,' Cymbeline whispered. The strange look was gone and his body seemed filled with a new vigour. 'You are the first of a new order to worship me, but you will not be the last.'

Queron tried one last time to use the Arts against the strengthened Wiseone, but he realised it was too late. The lords of his land had repressed the whispered words the warrior had chanted. In the distant past, warriors of a hidden cult had surrendered up their lives to their Ma'goi in times of great peril. That hidden cult had served Damear well in those ancient times, but their ways were too extreme now, even for the Damear.

As Queron's head dropped to the floor he thought of the number of times he had escaped death on this mission. If only he had died before they had reached the city, perhaps none of this would have happened. As his life-force slipped from him, he felt Cymbeline's gentle touch on his shoulder. Looking up he saw the darkened wall. Soon Xularkon would step through that wall and begin his evil rule over the Kobalos and their allies.

*

Guyon led the party deeper into the passages. The air was damp and musty, and Ivo became more uncomfortable the further they went. There was something about this place which brought back memories she did not want dug up, shadows from her past which she wished left alone.

Suddenly, as if to bring her fears to life, the sound of running water could be heard just ahead. One more bend of the passageway and they were confronted by a wide underground stream. The passageway opened up onto a large paved area; several strangely designed rafts were tied at the water's edge. Two goblins stood guard by the rafts. On seeing the strangers, one ran towards a large bell while the other drew his sword and attacked. Roland drew his sword and met the attack of the second warrior while Alaric rushed for the first, Kilic, his sword, at the ready.

Roland soon dispatched his opponent and turned in time to see Alaric do likewise, but not before the great bell had been sounded.

'Quickly, onto the raft!' Einor Val shouted. He led the way to the first of the rafts.

'The other rafts?' Anyon asked, his axe raised.

'No time!' Einor Val called.

More of the goblins were pouring into the chamber, many carrying small crossbows. Ivo stood on the dock, a horrified look on her face as she stared down at the vessel. 'Not again. Not again.' Her thoughts ran back to a time when she had boarded another raft. That voyage had cost her her brothers. What would this one cost?

'Ivo, quickly!' Alaric shouted.

A crossbow bolt flashed past his right ear, another struck the steering arm of the raft. But Ivo seemed unaware of this as her mind relived the loss of her brothers.

Anyon leapt from the raft and struck the woman in the stomach with his shoulder, doubling her up over his shoulder as he straightened and turned. More crossbow bolts flashed past him as he leapt for the raft as it moved further from the stone dock. One bolt glanced from Jerram's mailshirt while another transfixed Anyon's sleeve without breaking the skin.

Chrestella answered the bolts of her attackers with arrows of her own, but she could not be sure whether she struck anyone or not. Guyon dimmed the light from her stiletto so as not to make them an easy target, but still left them with enough light with which to steer. Bolts could be heard whizzing past and striking the water about them, but none touched the raft. The goblins were in such a state of panic that they were jostling each other as they strove to stop the intruders.

Quickly the current took them and soon the stone pier was far behind them. It was a pity that they did not have time to see to the other rafts because this left the goblins with the means to follow them. Einor Val's only consolation was that none of the rafts had oars and so they could travel only at the speed dictated by the river, which meant they should maintain their lead from any pursuers.

19
INTRUDERS

As the raft left the dock, Guyon increased her light, but it failed to reach the roof of the enormous cavern. The current drew the raft towards the eastern wall. At irregular intervals tall fingers of rock protruded from the fast-moving water. The raft was supplied with long poles which the party used to push themselves away from the towering rocks. Mycroft swung the steering arm with ease as he threw the vessel to the left and the right, avoiding the larger rocks.

They had placed Ivo in the centre of the raft and Jason was examining her. 'She's not injured,' he said. 'Not physically anyway. But she has locked herself away from what's happening around her and I don't know how to bring her out of it.'

'Is she in any immediate danger?' Anyon asked, moving to Ivo's side.

'No.'

'Then leave her,' Einor Val ordered. 'We have greater problems.'

Jason rose and moved to the stern of the raft. Anyon stayed beside Ivo, and brushed a strand of hair from her face. The light from Guyon's stiletto threw intricate patterns on the wall of the cavern. Jason leaned against the high stern rail and looked back over the path they had just travelled. Mycroft had just swung them round a large rock finger when a brief flash of light appeared behind them. Jason straightened and stared astern. The light flashed briefly once more.

'There's another raft behind us,' Jason called.

Einor Val and Roland leapt to the stern of the raft. Jason raised an arm and pointed astern. The three watched for a few moments before the light appeared again.

'Are they any closer?' Einor Val asked Jason.

'I can't tell.'

'Is the light any brighter?' added Roland.

'No,' Jason answered.

'Then they are being carried by the same current as we are,' Einor Val concluded, leaning against the rail. 'Which means, for the moment, we are safe enough. Guyon,' he called, 'is there any way you could increase our speed?'

'Yes. There is a word I could use that would move us faster than the current we now ride. Do you wish me to use it?'

'Not for now,' he answered. 'How long could you keep up the speed you spoke of?'

'Not long,' she replied. 'A few hours, no more.'

'Then let us hope it is the same for those who follow,' he said.

'Even a few hours will bring us within range of their crossbows,' Roland explained.

'I doubt they'll get a clear shot at us amongst these fingers of rock.'

The trailing raft grew no closer as the day wore on. At Einor Val's suggestion, half the party slept while the rest used the poles to keep them clear of the rocks.

'Lights ahead!' called Anyon suddenly.

Einor Val straightened and saw several faint lights dancing ahead of them. He glanced around and saw that the light behind them was now much brighter.

'Somehow they got word ahead of us and have cut us off,' he said. 'Guyon can you help us?'

'I'll try.' She slipped a hand inside her jerkin and drew out a small packet wrapped in a piece of cloth. Unwrapping the package, she lifted Queron's gift. Opening the medallion, she whispered one word.

'There are five rafts ahead,' she told them. 'But only the one behind.'

'So back would seem our safest bet,' Anyon deduced.

'Hardly that,' Guyon explained. 'I can increase the speed of the raft, but I cannot drive us against the current.'

'Then we fight,' Mycroft said.

'Not necessarily,' Guyon exclaimed suddenly. 'There is a side passage leaving the cavern on the western side. I should be able to move us across the current.'

'Do it.'

Guyon returned the medallion to her clothing. *'ngarrin booltaroo loru,'* she said in a clear voice.

Instantly the raft surged forward. Mycroft threw his weight against the tiller, aiming the raft across the cavern in the direction Guyon indicated. The rafts ahead began to angle across to intercept them and the pursuing raft drew closer.

Ahead of them on the cavern's wall a dark shadow could be seen. It was the opening to the side passage they were trying for. Those on the rafts ahead saw what they were trying to do and warning shouts erupted. The pursuing vessel began to draw even closer, so close that several crossbow bolts splashed in the water close by.

'Chrestella, see if you can keep their heads down,' Einor Val shouted over the cries of their attackers. Chrestella strung her bow and began to pick off the exposed goblins on the pursuing raft.

'I don't see any Kobalos,' Roland called.

'Perhaps that is something in our favour,' Alaric added.

'We could do with Ivo's help,' Einor Val said. 'Is there nothing you can do?'

Guyon leaned over the unconscious figure. 'I'm afraid...' she began.

Mycroft reached forward and took the stiletto from her hand. As the glowing stiletto changed hands, the light faded. Mycroft stared long and hard at the gem-pommelled hilt, a soft word was spoken and the light reappeared, softer than the original, but bright enough to see by.

Guyon nodded her thanks and placed a hand on Ivo's forehead. The young archer's eyes fluttered, then snapped open. 'We have need of your help, my friend,' Guyon whispered. 'Rise and help us.'

Ivo climbed unsteadily to her feet and took in the situation at a glance. She took up her bow and strung it, and drew an arrow from her quiver. Systematically she began to drop the goblins on the approaching raft, until only a few remained. These offered no threat, but instead sheltered on the far side of the raft, which had drifted off course. Suddenly their raft staggered, throwing Ivo and Chrestella from their feet. The vessel spun round the unseen obstacle and ended up heading for the dark opening, stern first.

The obstacle had also thrown Guyon to the floor, breaking her concentration and slowing them down. This allowed one of the closing rafts to reach the opening first. In the light from the torches on the goblin raft Einor Val could see a web of ropes stretched across the opening. The goblin raft struck the web and stopped, pinned there by the current which had increased in pace as they neared the dark passage.

Their raft struck the goblins', snapping many of the restraining ropes. A second goblin raft struck them from the rear, severing the last of the ropes and sending all three rafts spinning into the passage. Shouts of alarm echoed from the other vessels as they braced poles and grasped the drifting ropes in an effort to stop themselves from being drawn into the darkness.

As the three tangled rafts entered the darkness, the goblins made no attempt to attack. Instead they seemed frozen in place by fear.

'What now? asked Alaric. 'Shall we finish them while they seem preoccupied?'

'No, leave them,' Einor Val ordered. 'Perhaps we can learn the reason for their fear.'

Guyon left the stiletto in Mycroft's care and moved cautiously towards one of the goblins' rafts. Using the small mirror in the medallion, she slowly obtained the information they needed from the stunned goblins. Their answers were often only one word, and in their terrified state, the questions had to be asked several times before they drew a reply.

She returned and drew Einor Val and Roland to one side. 'It seems we have blundered into a section of the waterways beneath the city which has long since been abandoned. There are creatures living in the river hereabouts which do not like intruders, in fact they are very definite about this.'

'I suppose no one has ever left this tunnel alive?' Anyon asked with a grin.

'It's not the deaths they are afraid of, it's the state of the survivors that has them terrified,' Guyon explained.

'What state?' Anyon asked apprehensively.

Guyon looked down to where Ivo was sitting. Her knees were drawn up tight to her chest and she was rocking back and forth, whispering strange names over and over again.

One of the goblins noticed they were looking and followed their gaze. As his eyes fell upon the rocking Ivo, he let out a scream of dread. Leaping to his feet the goblin pointed at Ivo and screamed again. Racing across the raft he threw himself into the dark waters and instantly disappeared from sight.

The rafts were searched and a store of food and water was found. Alaric shared out the rations and they all sat down to eat. The goblins, too terrified to pose any further threat, saw the relaxed way the party was handling the situation, and this calmed them somewhat. They too took out what meagre rations they had and began to eat.

Guyon continued to question the goblins and learnt that the waterway emptied out into a major river which would eventually take them to the shores of Lake Zeridal. A small village was situated at the waterway's end, but they would have little problem with the villagers — the first sight of the emerging rafts would have the village goblins running for their lives in case the rafts contained any who had survived the journey. At the first sight of daylight, those emerging from the caverns would go mad and attack any and all about them. No one knew why this was so. The only cure for this madness was death.

One by one the torches on the goblins' rafts burnt out, until only the clean white light which radiated from the stiletto remained. The goblins on the two outer rafts had slowly moved towards the centre raft in an attempt to remain in the light. The fear they showed was contagious. Einor Val was forced to set a watch over Guyon and Mycroft to ensure that none of the goblins tried to steal the stiletto or medallion. He also had to ensure that their raft was not overwhelmed by goblins... and then there was the threat of the unknown.

A loud splash had everyone on their feet. Guyon took the stiletto from Mycroft and increased the light, but nothing could be seen. It was only a short time later that one of the goblins was found to be missing. The goblins went crazy when they realised what had happened, and rushed the centre raft.

The party was forced to withdraw to the rearmost raft. Some goblins were killed and several were thrown overboard before the party was secure. Using the long poles they separated their vessel from the others.

Through the darkness which surrounded the goblins' raft, shouts of anger changed to cries of fear. Fighting could be heard from the raft as the panic of the goblins turned to combat. The sounds of fighting increased, echoing around the passageway's curved walls.

Then all fell silent, a deep silence which was as unnerving as the panic of the goblins. The party waited, but no sound came from the darkness.

'ngarrin baringa gidju,' Guyon said clearly. A small ball of green light appeared at her fingertips. It lifted slowly from her fingers and crossed the short distance to the goblins' rafts.

In the green light they could see that the other two vessels were empty. There were no signs of the goblins who had only moments ago been struggling in the darkness.

Einor Val ordered the poles removed and the rafts joined once more. This time a coil of rope was found. Cut into smaller lengths, it was used to secure the rafts in several places. Pieces of the outer rafts were cut into lengths and combined with a small barrel of tar which had been used to waterproof the vessels. Torches were made and set about the raft's outer edges.

'What happened to the goblins?' Mycroft asked, afraid of the answer.

'No idea,' Einor Val shrugged. 'Whatever happened it must have been quick. Guyon, can you tell how long till we reach the light?'

Guyon opened the medallion and consulted the small mirror within. 'A matter of hours.'

'Then as long as we keep the torches burning we are safe,' Einor Val explained.

'Hopefully,' added Anyon.

Ivo had resumed her position in the centre of the raft. She had wrapped her arms around her legs and was sitting still staring off into the darkness which surrounded the rafts. Without raising her head she whispered. 'It won't matter, the torches will go next.'

Anyon looked down at his companion, and Mycroft moved to her side. 'What do you mean?'

'They'll try for the torches again,' she cried.

'Again?' Anyon questioned.

'Quiet!' Mycroft snapped. He leaned closer to Ivo. 'What about the torches?'

'You remember, Ren. They put out the torches before they attacked,' Ivo said softly. 'First they rocked the raft, then they shot water onto the torches, throwing us into darkness. Then they attacked.'

The companions searched the edges of the rafts for any sign of movement. Einor Val gestured for several of the torches to be brought to the centre of the vessel where they could be protected more easily.

The raft lurched to one side.

'They're under the raft,' Chrestella called.

'If what Ivo said is correct, they'll try for the torches next,' Roland said.

'There's little we can do to protect all of them,' Guyon said. 'But I might be able to keep a few safe if Mycroft helps me.'

Mycroft moved to the Kungour's side, the stiletto throwing a dim light about them.

With several whispered words, Guyon produced a green shield about the inner three torches. No sooner was this done than a jet of water erupted from the right side of the raft, striking one of the outer torches. A second and third jet followed close behind the first, taking out the rest of the torches.

Guyon reached out and touched the stiletto, extending the light out to encompass the centre raft. In the steady clear glow a smooth white hand appeared over the edge of the raft. It was soon followed by a second, then a hairless pallid head. An eyeless face stared at the companions from the edge of the raft, turning slightly to take in all of them. Sickly white skin was drawn tight over empty eye sockets; two small slits situated just above the drooling mouth opened and closed as it sought out the occupants of the raft. The toothless mouth gaped wider, sending the putrid smell of rotting fish across the raft, causing some to gag. As the spittle dripped from between the loose white lips, it struck the raft with a sizzling sound, like water striking a hot pan.

'It's watching us,' Chrestella shuddered.

'Impossible,' Anyon laughed uneasily. 'The bastard's got no eyes.'

'But look at the way its head is moving as it switches from one of us to another,' Mycroft answered.

'There's another,' Chrestella called.

Another of the faceless creatures was peering over the opposite edge of the raft.

Guyon increased the light from the stiletto even further but neither of the creatures seemed to notice the brightening light and, if they did, it made little difference to them.

'You know the light won't affect them, Clay,' Ivo mumbled. 'Remember the last time you tried it. You...' Ivo stopped speaking as a strangled gasp escaped her lips.

'Then if not the light, what?' Alaric asked.

Anyon drew his axe and stepped towards one of the creatures. The pale creature opened its mouth and a small ball of liquid flashed through the air and struck Anyon in the face. He dropped his axe and threw both hands to his face, clawing at his eyes. Anyon began to stagger about blindly, trying to wipe the burning liquid from his eyes, and if not for Roland would have stumbled from the raft.

Mycroft dropped the stiletto and leapt to Anyon's side. Between him and Jason they soon had Anyon resting quietly, the burning pain eased. The only light on the raft now was from the three torches in its centre. Alaric took one of the torches and approached the creature which had attacked Anyon. Holding his shield up before his eyes, Alaric extended the torch towards it.

Suddenly the creature released its hold on the edge of the raft and disappeared beneath the dark water.

'Look out! Behind you!' Chrestella called.

Jerram snatched up a second torch and turned to find himself facing four creatures that had climbed unnoticed over the blind side of the raft. One of the creatures spat its liquid attack at Jerram, who threw one arm up to protect his eyes. A second creature spat at the torch in Jerram's hand, extinguishing it.

Gideon swept up the third torch and threw it at the advancing creatures. The torch fell short and landed at the creatures' feet. They leapt back and threw themselves from the raft.

'It's not the light,' Einor Val shouted, 'it's the heat!'

'That's why the stiletto does not keep them at bay,' Guyon realised. 'It's the heat of the torches they can't stand. Bring the extinguished torches and I'll see what I can do to relight them.'

Quickly the torches were gathered and Guyon bent over them. *'ngarrin kudla gidju.'*

Each torch burst into flames. Guyon handed the torches to her companions. 'Shield them with your bodies,' she commanded. 'But don't let the liquid strike you in the face.'

Jerram sat beside Anyon. Even though he had protected his eyes from the liquid, most of it had struck his face, burning the skin around his eyes. Jason was beside the two continuing his work on their injuries.

'How much longer till we're free of this darkness?' Einor Val asked.

Guyon consulted her mirror, whispering several words. 'We should see the light from the opening at any moment.'

'Keep to the centre of the raft,' Einor Val ordered. 'It won't be much longer now.'

20

WALWYN

No more attempts were made to board the raft by the strange eyeless creatures of the dark water. Jason had seen to Jerram's and Anyon's facial burns, smearing a cool white salve over their red blistered skin. But he was unable to do anything for Anyon's eyes except cover them with a light bandage to keep the approaching light from damaging them further.

Guyon kept the small oval medallion in her hands, concentrating on the reflective interior. The skin on her face changed colour and texture as lights of different colours sprang from the mirror.

'There is something close by!' she cried suddenly. She began to move about the raft, the mirror held before her as if trying to find the source of the green light which flowed from the mirror.

By doing little else, Mycroft had been able to extend the light from the stiletto to radiate a short distance from the raft.

'There!' Alaric exclaimed, pointing to the right wall of the narrowing passageway. A large dark opening set above a stone ledge had appeared. But the speed of the raft was carrying them past it.

'Too late,' Einor Val exclaimed.

But Guyon had different ideas. Grasping one end of

a coil of rope, she dove from the raft and, with strong strokes, began to swim for the ledge.

'Ren!' Ivo screamed. As Guyon cut through the water Ivo had to be held down by Jason and Jerram or she would have thrown herself in after her.

Alaric took the remaining end of the coil and fastened it about one of the corner posts of the raft just as Guyon reached the ledge and dragged herself from the water. Rolling from the water's edge, she quickly got to her feet and looked about for something to tie off to. What she found was a metal ring corroded by time embedded in the rock wall beside the opening. She secured the rope just as the slack ran out, bringing the raft to a timber-straining halt.

Roland and Kendrick grasped the rope and began to draw the raft back against the current towards the waiting Guyon. Gideon threw her a second rope which she secured quickly. Then, with Chrestella's help, they too began to draw the raft towards the ledge.

As the raft bumped against the stone ledge, Roland and Gideon made fast the ropes, while the remainder helped their injured companions to shore. Ivo stepped from the raft and looked about her. Shrugging off the arms that aided her, she walked slowly and unsteadily from the water's edge.

'Father?' she said softly, looking about her, totally confused by what had happened, or what she thought had happened.

'That was a fool thing to do,' Einor Val said as he took Guyon's arm and spun her round to face him.

If he had intended to say more the words were frozen on his lips by the look on Guyon's face. Her eyes were wide and her lips were drawn back into a grin that sent a shiver down the ex-Priest's back. He found his right hand moving up to make a warding sign before he realised what he was doing. Forcing his hand down, he continued.

'Well? Now we are here what are we looking for?' he asked gruffly.

Guyon lifted her open medallion. A deep green light

pulsated from the glass, making Guyon's features look more inhuman with each passing second. 'It is near,' she whispered, 'so near.'

Einor Val almost stepped back in horror, but he swallowed hard and held his gaze against the strange stare. Guyon raised her arm with the mirror and pointed across the ledge towards a section locked deep in shadow. Mycroft moved cautiously towards the section, the light forming a circle about him.

'It's another opening,' he shouted, unable to conceal his excitement.

Guyon, followed by Gideon and Alaric, entered the opening and found themselves in a small chamber. The walls were low and cut from stone. In the centre of the chamber was a pillar made of woven timber. A shaft of light fell from a crack in the roof to one side of the pillar. Alaric crossed to the light and began to pull sections of the roof down.

'We should be able to climb out here,' he said. 'It'll save us having to tangle with the goblins which have their village at the end of this passageway.'

Gideon nodded. 'Best to go back and get the others.'

As Alaric left the chamber, Guyon was busy searching one of the low walls. She found nothing and turned from the wall, a look of confusion on her face. She stood in the centre of the chamber and turned slowly, examining all the walls once more. Suddenly she stopped, her eyes opening wide in realisation. Turning slowly she looked for the first time at the woven timber pillar behind her. The timber was grey and woven in an intricate pattern that made one look away, as if the mind couldn't take it all in.

Guyon forced herself to stare deep into the pattern; then, slowly raising one hand, she reached into the pillar at a spot that looked solid. Her arm disappeared into the pillar up to her shoulder. Then slowly she began to withdraw it. Stepping back from the pillar, she examined the object she now held. It was a staff five feet in height. It was made of the same twisted grey wood as the pillar, yet it looked far from dead. A life seemed to flow through the staff and Einor Val realised that the thin length of timber which was woven to form the staff seemed to have no beginning or end.

Mycroft entered the chamber followed by the rest of the party. Anyon's arm was around Jerram's shoulder, and Ivo seemed at last aware of her surroundings. When Mycroft saw Guyon standing in the centre of the room, the staff in her hands, he stepped forward and offered her the stiletto. She shook her head, gesturing for him to keep the weapon. Again Mycroft held the glowing stiletto towards her. As if to explain the reason for her generosity, the staff in her hands broke into light, blazing with a deep green light which filled the room and smothered the dim glow of the stiletto.

Mycroft understood what she had found and slipped the stiletto into his belt, but he doubted the others understood that the woven staff was an object of great power. Somehow the strangely twisted timber amplified the strength of the user. He had no idea how long the staff had lain concealed within the woven pillar, but in all that time it had gradually drawn magic to fill itself with a power greater than he had ever felt before. With that staff Guyon was a match for any Ma'goi they might encounter, perhaps even for a Wiseone.

'Now what?' Anyon asked.

'We get out of this darkness and head for home,' Guyon answered with a broad smile.

Alaric was the last to be drawn through the opening in the ceiling of the chamber.

Jason had rebandaged Anyon's eyes to protect them from the bright midday light, and the two were sitting beneath a tree waiting for the scouts to return.

Ivo seemed her old self as she strode from the trees to report her find. 'Several hundred yards through there,' she explained, pointing back at the trees behind her, 'is a small village. I noticed a few goblins about, but for the most part the village seems to be deserted.'

'It must be the one the goblin on the raft told us about,' Roland explained. 'From what he said, we had better avoid it.'

'Good thinking,' Anyon called from where he sat. 'No need to go looking for trouble...' his hand rose and touched his bandaged eyes, 'looking for anything for that matter.'

'There are three fishing boats which look quite sea-worthy moored just off the beach,' Ivo explained further. There was a slight shiver in her voice that no one seemed to notice.

'Then perhaps...' Anyon began.

'We should pay them a visit after all,' Roland finished.

Einor Val followed Ivo into the trees for a first-hand view of the village. They soon returned and Einor Val quickly set about explaining his plan.

Roland, Alaric, Kendrick and Gideon walked calmly from the trees into the goblin village. They were halfway from the trees to the village's edge before they were sighted. Without a pause, the four marched into the settlement and headed towards the coast and the waiting fishing boats.

The village seemed all wrong. Although there were signs of goblins everywhere, it was obvious the village had been constructed by a people other than the goblins. The buildings were taller than they would need, and they reminded Roland of the coastal villages he had passed on his travels southward towards the Fortalice.

Once Roland and Kendrick reached the narrow beach they began to strip off their clothing and armour. The two then waded out into the warm water. Further from the beach they waded until the water rose to their chest and they were forced to swim. They swam steadily towards the closest fishing boat. Kendrick headed for the stern while Roland cut through the water towards the bow.

The rest of the party reached the beach as Roland grasped the mooring cable. Hand over hand he drew himself from the water. A goblin face appeared over the rail of the fishing boat and stared down at the dripping

Roland. As the goblin opened his mouth to call a warning, a shaft from Ivo's bow entered his mouth. His mouth clamped shut, his teeth clashing together so hard they snapped the arrow.

Roland was soon over the rail and out of sight. Kendrick also dragged himself from the water and disappeared on board. Faint sounds reached the ears of the companions waiting on the beach before Roland reappeared, signalling the all-clear.

Four empty barrels were gathered and roped together to carry their equipment. With Anyon and Ivo grasping the ropes of the makeshift raft, they headed out towards the fishing boat. Quickly the armour and weapons were loaded while Anyon and Ivo were helped on board.

'Somewhat elaborate for a goblin craft,' Alaric commented after a brief examination of the vessel.

'It's not a goblin vessel,' Roland answered.

The companions turned to find Roland climbing from a deck hatch. He held a rope tightly in one hand and, once he was on deck, he began to take up the tension on the rope. First one hand, then another appeared over the edge of the hatch. Finally a dirty rag-clad man was drawn up onto the deck.

'He claims to be the first officer of the vessel,' Roland explained.

'What happened to you?' Einor Val asked.

The man lifted his head and looked around the deck. Mycroft and Jerram were just throwing the last of the goblin bodies overboard. This brought a brief smile to his lips.

'My name is Walwyn,' he said.

'How did the goblins manage to trap you and capture your vessels?' Einor Val asked.

'We were looking for new trade routes when we sighted the village and decided it was worth investigating,' Walwyn answered. 'A small party from each vessel went ashore, and we had just reached the beach when the goblins struck.'

'How did they manage to get those men still on board?'

'They must have swum out and surprised them,' Walwyn answered.

'The goblins are gathering on the beach,' Chrestella called.

Einor Val turned and saw a large party of goblins standing on the beach.

'They don't seem in a great hurry to get their possessions back,' Alaric noted.

'It doesn't matter,' Einor Val explained. 'Let's raise the sail and make for home.'

'I'll do whatever I can to be of help,' Walwyn offered.

'Good,' Einor Val answered. 'See that everything is right with the vessel and lend a hand where need be.'

Walwyn nodded and leapt to where Mycroft and Chrestella were struggling with the mooring cable.

With Walwyn's help, the fishing boat was soon underway. Quickly they moved from the coast leaving the tree-lined beach and goblin village far behind. Though undermanned, the fishing boat itself handled the rough conditions well, and soon a course was set that would take them to a section of coast close enough for the party to make their way back to the Fortalice.

'There was something about that village that still disturbs me,' Guyon began. She was standing in the bow beside Einor Val, the salt fresh wind was tearing at their clothes, while the stinging spray had turned their cheeks a rosy red.

'It did seem all too easy,' he agreed.

'Not just that,' she continued. 'The entire village itself seemed wrong, nothing like what you would expect to see in a village built by fishermen.'

'Then where do you think this vessel came from, and who built the village?'

'Raiders,' Gideon said from behind the pair.

He moved beside the two and stared out over the bow. 'There are raiders who operate along this coast. They attack small vessels and lure others onto the many shoals and reefs that are to be found.'

'Then how did the goblins lure them ashore?' Einor Val asked.

'They weren't lured ashore; they probably built that village themselves in an attempt to expand their rule.'

'And then the goblins attacked?' Guyon asked.

'I'd say so. When they first attacked us they waited until we were fighting amongst ourselves. So I see no reason why they wouldn't wait until the village was finished and all the stores and equipment were brought ashore before attacking.'

'Then Walwyn isn't a trader as he claimed?' Guyon queried.

'By the sound of it,' Einor Val answered, 'I'd say he was a raider, probably the only survivor.'

'Then perhaps we should dispose of him,' Guyon suggested, turning.

'If you do that,' Walwyn said loudly, 'you will never survive your travels in these waters.'

'How so?' Einor Val demanded.

'As you have guessed, I am a raider. I was not the first officer of this vessel but the captain, and not just of this vessel.' Walwyn stepped to the rail and looked out over the expanse of water between the tossing vessel and the thin strip of coast on the horizon. 'I was the commander of all three vessels and it was my task to set up a new base of operations from which to further expand our empire.'

'Empire?' Einor Val laughed. 'Hardly that. You're nothing but a bunch of murderers and thieves.'

Walwyn's head dropped and he was silent. Guyon and Einor Val exchanged a glance, wondering at his silence. Slowly, Walwyn's head rose and he turned and answered them.

'Now we are called murderers and thieves,' he began, 'but once we were a proud nation, a nation which was called upon to end the reign of one of this world's greatest evils. Once large cities dotted this coast line, and from the harbours of these cities great fleets sailed these waters, trading, exploring, and warring when the need arose.'

'What happened?' Guyon asked, not quite convinced of Walwyn's sincerity.

'We were called upon to help in an immense battle to save the civilised peoples from an evil power which was spreading its shadow across the face of the land.'

'Boat! Boat!' Chrestella called from her perch halfway up the main mast.

'Where?' Einor Val called, shielding his eyes as he searched the waters ahead and to the north.

'From ashore!' Chrestella called as she began to scramble down to the swaying deck.

Looking southward, Einor Val, Guyon and Walwyn saw five small black dots moving steadily towards them. As they watched, more dark shapes separated themselves from the coast and followed the others.

'Picaroons!' Walwyn snarled and spat over the side. 'They're the curse of the coast.'

'Who are they?' Einor Val asked.

'Not who, what,' Walwyn answered in disgust. 'They are the offspring of wrecked and deserted mariners, and they prey on anything.'

'What do you mean... what? Offspring between the mariners and whom?' Guyon asked.

'Female slaves, captives, forest goblins, and anything else that stood still long enough. You'll see what I mean when they get alongside.'

'I must admit you have fired my curiosity,' Guyon stated. 'But I see no reason why we should wait for them to get that close.'

'We have no choice,' Walwyn explained. 'Between us and the open waters of the lake is a large series of shoals, it will be days before an opening presents itself.'

'Then why are we here?' Einor Val asked horrified.

'This is the safe side,' Walwyn answered with a shrug.

The rest of the companions had come up from below deck or had put aside their work to watch the approach of the picaroons. As the small vessels neared, the many oars could be seen, giving the vessels the appearance of large beetles skating across the water towards them.

Fifteen of the vessels could be clearly seen, and with their advantage of wind and what seemed the inexhaustible strength of their oarsmen, they grew steadily closer.

Each boat contained fifty oarsmen: twenty-five per side. A further five men waited in the prow with short curved bows. Another group of five stood at the stern of the vessel; Walwyn explained that these would be the steersmen, plus the captain and his bodyguards.

Even Ivo and Anyon were on deck to witness the approach of the picaroons. Anyon's eyes were still bandaged but his hand rested confidently on Ivo's shoulder. Ivo glanced quickly at his bandaged eyes. Having to aid her injured companion had somehow eased her fear of the water and the old memories it dragged up, but she still felt ill at ease as she returned her gaze to the surrounding water.

Chrestella studied the wind, then raised her bow. Waiting for the roll of the vessel, she fired; her arrow arched through the air striking one of the bowmen in the chest. With a shrill scream, the man fell into the water. Not one of his crewmen made an attempt to help him.

'Good shot!' Alaric called excitedly.

'But hardly an answer to our problem,' Mycroft said. 'There are far too many of them for that.'

Ivo stepped forward and took Anyon's hand from her shoulder. Placing his hand on the rail, she stepped back from her companions and strung her bow. Drawing an arrow from her quiver, she sighted on one of the approaching boats. As the fishing boat rolled up she released the shaft.

The steersman of the closest boat slumped to one side dragging the steering oar with him. The boat veered off course, sharply colliding with a second boat. The snapping of oars and the cries of pain could be heard across the open water. The remaining boats seemed unaware of the situation and continued on.

21

PURSUIT

Guyon drew her medallion from her clothing. '*reyin,*' she said calmly. Studying the mirror's surface, Guyon explained what she had in mind. 'The few miles ahead of us seem free of shoals; if I can increase the speed of the vessel, we may be able to outrun them.'

Replacing the medallion beneath her clothing, Guyon whispered several words. At first there seemed no change, then slowly the fishing vessel began to draw ahead of the picaroons. A grappling hook flashed out from the lead boat, snaring the fishing vessel. Roland leapt for the rope, his sword drawn. As he reached the rope, he was forced back by the archers in the bow of the picaroon's boat, now being towed behind the fishing vessel.

Quickly the fishing boat outdistanced all the picaroons, except for the one which had snared them. Each time an attempt was made to reach the grappling hook, a small but accurate cloud of arrows would have that person diving for cover. Large shields were being hastily constructed from whatever was at hand, but these would probably be ready too late.

'We are too near to the shoals!' Walwyn shouted. 'You will have to slow us down or we will be doomed.'

Guyon shielded her eyes and surveyed the waters ahead

206

of the racing vessel, a quick glance over her shoulder at the distant picaroons decided her actions.

'*nemmin*,' she called. Instantly the vessel's headlong rush eased. Raising her staff she pointed it at the picaroons' rope. '*kandari threttin*.' The rope parted and the released vessel quickly settled to a stop.

As Guyon turned from her handiwork, the fishing boat shuddered briefly before coming to a timber-wrenching halt. The companions were thrown from their feet and tumbled across the deck as sails and rigging fell from above, preventing their attempts to rise. A sharp cry rose from the closest of the picaroon vessels as the plight of the fishing boat was seen.

'Arm yourselves!' Guyon called as she rose and saw their attackers approaching. Swearing and cursing, the companions rose to their feet helping to free those among them who were not fortunate enough to avoid the tangle of ropes. Grappling hooks appeared over the starboard rail and their ropes tightened. Several picaroons reached the deck before the companions readied themselves.

More of the picaroons leapt over the rail and joined their brethren in an attempt to keep the companions from the grappling hooks. Most of the picaroons were manlike in appearance and they all wore a variety of armour. However, two of the picaroons were short and stooped, and long tufts of coarse dark hair could be seen through gaps in their ill-fitting armour. Another had a protruding jaw covered in large silver scales.

'If we do not stop them now,' Einor Val called, 'there will soon be too many of them for us to handle.'

Anyon tore the bandage from his eyes and drew his axe. Spinning the weapon over his head he sent his companions diving for cover. Ahead of him he was able to make out the vague outlines of the picaroons. With a battle cry on his lips he leapt forward.

His first blow missed Roland's head by inches, sending him diving for cover, while the second blow was deflected by Alaric's hastily raised shield. Before Anyon was able to lend his companions' more aid, Ivo tripped him with her bow, and Mycroft placed a booted foot on the small of his back.

The picaroons had been as surprised with the attack as had Anyon's companions and, before they were able to press their advantage in numbers, the companions attacked.

Mycroft, Alaric and Roland drove a wedge through the startled picaroons, their swords cutting a bloodied path towards the rail. Jason had calmed Anyon and was dragging him to the far side of the deck while Ivo and Chrestella watched over them. Kendrick and Gideon launched an attack at the picaroons' right flank before they were forced back.

Guyon stood back from the fighting her staff levelled before her. Einor Val stood by her side, protecting her and directing the fight. Calling commands to his companions Einor Val was able to direct them, forcing those picaroons not killed to the rail. Packed tightly against the rail, the remaining attackers were not able to climb to the deck and give aid to their brethren.

'The others are nearing,' Guyon warned.

Einor Val quickly took his eyes from the fight and saw that the other picaroon vessels were indeed closing. 'Can you do anything?' he asked.

'It is possible that I may be able to get the vessel from the shoal, but after that I will be of little use,' she answered.

'If we do not get ourselves free soon there will be no afterwards,' Einor Val said in return.

'Very well,' Guyon said and slowly lowered herself to the deck. Crossing her legs she placed the staff across them and began to gather her strength. A picaroon broke from the group and rushed at the helpless Kungour. Einor Val raised his war hammer and stepped before him.

The picaroon was a hideous mixture of goblin and man. His skin was grey in patches giving him a sick look, and pointed ears protruded from his rough-cut hair. A smile crossed the picaroon's lips as he saw the warrior standing before him. Armed with the strange hammer it would take no time to dispatch him and then he could turn his attention to the woman seated on the deck.

The thought of what he would do with the woman was the last thought he had as Einor Val brought his war hammer down, crushing the picaroon's skull.

The fishing boat lurched abruptly as Guyon used her skill in the Arts to force it from the imprisoning shoal. With all her sails and rigging down, the fishing boat was captured by the tide and drawn towards the coast.

The last of the picaroons on board were slain and the ropes cut, freeing them from their immediate danger; but even as they were drawn towards the coast by the tide, the picaroons quickly closed the distance between them.

'We don't seem to be all that better off,' Mycroft called.

'If we can reach the shore we should be safe,' Walwyn judged.

The picaroons were almost in bow shot when the leaking and damaged fishing boat touched bottom and grated to a halt. The small craft swung broadside to the beach and was instantly awash from the rising tide. Climbing and falling from the stricken vessel, the companions waded ashore and readied themselves to meet the imminent attack of the picaroons.

Beyond the wreck of their vessel, they watched as the picaroons slowed their approach, oars moving rapidly as they backwatered to keep them from the beach. As the companions watched in surprise, first one, then another of the vessels turned and made for calmer waters.

'Definitely not landsmen,' Alaric commented.

'They will only leave their vessels and fight on land if the prize is big enough,' Walwyn explained.

'And we're not big enough?' Roland asked.

'With your weapons and armour you are more than juicy enough prey,' he answered. 'It's just that this section of coast is not very hospitable.'

'Forest goblins?' Einor Val asked.

'No,' Walwyn replied. 'No goblin in his right mind would be caught along this stretch of coast — too dangerous.'

A loud roar echoed from the trees behind the party.

'How dangerous?' Mycroft asked, spinning around.

'The forest hereabouts teems with strange beasts,' Walwyn answered.

'I'm not sure I want to hear this,' Anyon sighed. His bandage had been replaced and his left hand flashed to drag it from his eyes. Jason's hand locked on the axeman's wrist lowering it to his side.

'Ko'achs,' Walwyn explained. 'Large, scaled creatures which hunt the forest's edge and the southern Kadina Plain. Their bodies are about the size of a war horse and are extremely strong with powerful legs armed with long curved claws. Their heads are large and perched on a short neck. Their jaws are filled with short spike-like teeth, capable of puncturing most armours. Their eyes are red and it is said that should they focus their stare upon you, you are lost.'

Anyon tilted his head to one side as if listening for something: then, shaking off Jason's restraining arm, he began to make his way unsteadily down the beach towards the crashing breakers.

'Wrong way,' Jason shouted as he followed him.

'Wanna bet?' Anyon answered. 'You go your way and I'll go mine. And my way is back to the fishing boat.'

'What about the picaroons?' Jason asked.

'Perhaps they'll come back,' Anyon answered as he entered the surf.

Alaric and Roland moved to Anyon's side and, taking an arm apiece, they steered him from the water. Anyon said nothing as they took him further up the beach, but he turned his bandaged head as if searching for the water and the safety it offered.

Another roar reverberated from the trees, closely followed by a second and a third. The calls were answered by others and soon the beach echoed with the terrifying cries.

'A hunting pack by the sounds of it,' Walwyn cried. 'Any of our villages which border the Murtoa or Kadina Plains have strong outer walls to keep the creatures at bay. Though the Ko'ach is rarely seen these days.'

'And if we happen to see one? What would you suggest we use to defend ourselves?' Anyon demanded.

'Speed!' Walwyn shouted, as he began a mad dash across the sand towards the trees.

'What's he doing?' Anyon called.

'He's headed for the trees,' Roland answered.

'Bugger that,' Anyon said with a strained laugh.

Walwyn disappeared into the trees. The companions seemed unsure of whether they should follow him or not.

'He knows this land better than us,' Einor Val said. 'I suggest we follow him.'

The others nodded and, helping a hesitant Anyon, they hurried towards the trees. The roaring grew louder as the hunting pack neared the companions. Anyon wrinkled his nose at a sharp acrid smell that seemed to envelop them. A soft whistle from above revealed Walwyn perched in the branches of a tree.

'Up here,' he whispered.

Quickly the companions climbed into the surrounding trees where they drew their weapons and waited.

Walwyn whispered again. 'The Ko'ach has very poor vision and if we remain motionless they should pass us by. And the smell of the rotting fruit of the juimbin tree should cover our scent.'

With a crashing of timber a large creature appeared beneath the companions. Its body was long and sleek and was held from the ground by large bowed legs. The skin of the creature was yellow and black and its tail flicked continually from side to side. The large head turned as the creature's red eyes searched the foliage for its prey, a blue forked tongue flicked out seeking any sign of the scent of the prey the creature knew was close by.

With a flick of its tail, which sent a small sapling crashing to the ground, the Ko'ach moved quickly from sight. The roar of the disappearing creature was answered by others.

'How long can we stay here?' Einor Val asked.

Walwyn shaded his eyes and glanced up at the sun.

'The beasts prefer the sunlight,' Walwyn answered. 'As soon as the sun sets they will find a lair and holed up for the night. During that time we will be able to make good our escape.'

Roland threw one quick glance upwards. 'A little over two hours to sunset.'

Gideon settled himself into a more comfortable position and sheathed his weapon.

Mycroft held the stiletto before him, throwing enough light for the companions to find their way through the dark forest. Guyon had sought out the Ko'achs with the aid of her mirror and had found them grouped many miles away. At first their progress had been slow due to cramped and aching muscles. But as the miles fell away behind them they gradually increased their pace.

Walwyn had assured them that before first light they would find the end of the forest and reach one of the many settlements which dotted the coastal edge of the Kadina Plain.

A roar tore the stillness of the night. Walwyn stepped quickly to Mycroft's side and threw his cloak over the glowing stiletto, plunging the party into darkness. A second roar echoed through the night.

'It's the hunting call of a Ko'ach,' Walwyn explained.

'But you said . . .' Roland started.

'I know what I said,' Walwyn snapped.

'Then what is that thrice-cursed creature doing hunting after sunset?' Anyon demanded.

Before Walwyn could answer, another roar echoed from the darkened forest, this time from behind the companions. Guyon had drawn out her medallion and was concentrating deeply on the black surface of the mirror within. Roland glanced over her shoulder in time to see a faint light appear. It was impossible for him to tell what the light was or what it meant to Guyon, but he could see by the shifting of her shoulders that she had found what she had been looking for.

Turning her body slightly, Guyon moved the mirror about until the light shone its brightest. Without a word she left the faint trail they had been following and made her way towards the pinpoint of light her mirror revealed as the only safe place.

The hunting calls of the Ko'achs continued for some time until they changed to cries of anger. The hunting beast continued to vent its anger on the night as the companions followed the slight hope that Guyon's mirror offered them.

No light was possible as the party moved quickly after Guyon. But from where Roland followed the Kungour, he was able to see a steadily growing light radiating from the small mirror. Suddenly the trees were replaced by large dark rocks as the party reached the base of a cliff.

Ivo tried to judge the height of the towering wall of rock, but in the darkness it was impossible to tell where the rock ended and the night began. Guyon did not pause to study her surroundings but moved quickly into the jumble of rocks.

Without warning, a shadow from the surrounding rocks moved, leaping into the path ahead of the party. The shadow turned out to be a man. He had landed in a squat position and was slowly rising to his full height. Head, shoulders and chest, he towered over Guyon. He was dressed in strange skins and he held a large broad-headed spear.

The stranger turned and moved quickly into the darkness. None of the companions had had time to react when the man had appeared but Guyon was the first to recover. She moved off quickly after the stranger, trying to keep up with the long-legged man.

Roland was taken completely by surprise when Guyon suddenly disappeared from sight. One moment she was moving swiftly between the rocks, Roland close behind her, the next she was gone. Roland drew his sword and began a panicked search of his surroundings before a strip of light appeared. Guyon stood in the mouth of a cave, a leather curtain grasped in her right hand.

Roland slipped between Guyon and the cave's wall; he was quickly followed by the others. Beyond the curtain Roland found himself in a small, but well-lit cave. Small torches were mounted on the walls, torches that burnt without giving off any smoke or smell. Between the torches hung the skins of exotic animals.

In a narrow alcove the tall stranger stood motionless. His spear was clasped across his dark chest and only the rhythmical rise and fall of his chest betrayed he was no statue. A tall oval shield rested against his left leg.

Ivo crossed to one of the walls and examined a black and white pelt. The fur was smooth to the touch and sent a shiver through the palm of her right hand. In all the years she had spent hunting, she had never felt anything like it before. Her left hand seemed drawn to the skin. As both hands caressed it, a strange sensation passed through her body, as if the skin was enjoying the feel of her touch as much as she was enjoying it.

'The Zenevre are dangerous creatures, Ivo,' a soft voice called. 'Even after death their magic continues to lure their prey.'

A heavily cloaked woman stepped from the shadows at the rear of the cave. Not one of the companions on entering had noticed the patch of darkness against the rear wall, and even as the tall woman stepped forward to great them, the shadow seemed to fade behind her.

'The Zenevre contain a living magic that attracts others skilled in the Arts,' the woman explained. 'Once the prey touches the pelt of the Zenevre it is overpowered by a feeling of wellbeing. While the two remain in contact, the Zenevre draws all the Arts from its prey, enhancing its powers, while draining its prey of magic.' Einor Val stepped beside Ivo and, grasping her arms, drew her from the skin.

Einor Val looked behind him. 'Roland, watch the opening. It won't take those creatures long to find where we are.'

'You are safe from the Ko'achs,' the woman said. 'They will be unable to find you here.'

214

'How is that possible?' Mycroft asked amazed.

Roland lifted the leather curtain a fraction and peered out into the night. He could see nothing. Then he realised that the darkness was total. There were no shapes, no stars, and the silence was deep — not a sound could be heard.

'There is nothing out there to fear,' the woman reassured him.

'Who are you?' Einor Val asked, 'And what has happened?'

'Einor Val, have I changed so much?' she asked. Before Einor Val could answer, she raised a gloved hand. 'Your hunters will not find you now.'

Einor Val seemed unable to answer.

'But for how long?' Anyon questioned, believing she spoke about the Ko'achs.

'You will find that time has little meaning here,' she went on to explain.

'To you, perhaps,' Ivo said. 'But we have information of great importance that we must get to the Fortalice as soon as possible.'

'The information that you bear will be of little use to those at the Fortalice,' the woman continued. 'They have not the means to put it to use. They have no power to stop Cymbeline and his scheme to bring Xularkon back from the past to help him in his plans for power. For it is too late to halt the Ma'goi.' The woman stopped her explanation and turned towards the rear of the cave. On reaching the stone wall she turned to face the confused companions. 'However, there is one way that his plans may be thwarted.'

'How?' Einor Val asked.

'Cymbeline must be stopped from reaching Xularkon and returning with him to this time.'

'But you said it was too late for that?' Roland queried.

'Here, in this time, yes,' she answered. 'But in Xularkon's time in history it is possible.'

The woman raised a hand to her lips and breathed into the palm of her hand. Then, holding her hand before

215

her, she blew once, sharply. A faint blue light left her hand and flashed across the cave to strike Anyon on his bandaged eyes.

A terrifying scream tore through the curtained opening of the cave echoing from the walls. All eyes flashed to the curtain waiting for it to open, revealing a Ko'ach. But the curtain did not move.

Mycroft turned back to the woman in time to see a large shadowed area at the rear of the cave engulf her, then shrink from sight. Roland lifted the curtain as another roar was heard.

When they had entered the cave it was night, but with the raising of the curtain a bright light streamed into the cave. The sun sat on the western horizon signalling the end of a day, a day that must have passed while the companions had been in the cave. But the light of day brought another shock. Where only that night a forest had surrounded them, now a great plain stretched to the horizon.

Xularkon sat on his tall throne and listened to the messengers as they told of the wholesale destruction of the Azyrite Priests. This time they would not thwart his plans. From the moment he had left the southern wastes, he had begun to preach against the power of the Azyr. There had been many listeners, especially amongst the goblins and other lower forms.

Xularkon had watched his followers closely, and over many years he had chosen five score of them to rise above the others. First he had straightened their twisted bodies and then he had strengthened their minds. To each he taught swordsmanship and a small portion of the Arts which would help him regain his throne.

His closest followers he called Kobalos, and he gave them command over his armies. To these hundred he issued the order for the total destruction of the Azyrites, and now as he sat high above them, he heard how his plans were finally coming to a climax.

One of the kneeling messengers raised his head. 'High

One, we have swept the land clear of all those who opposed you.'

Another spoke. 'Your forces are even now awaiting your order to cross the border and take word of your lore to our neighbours with fire and sword.'

'If it is your wish,' the third spoke.

'It is my wish,' Xularkon answered and stood. His great robes flowed about him as he strode the length of the dais. 'But first the accursed Priests are to be destroyed.'

'That has been done, High One,' the first messenger said.

22

CARAVAN

Anyon shouldered the others from his path as he forced his way from the cave's mouth. He raised his axe to shield his eyes from the piercing light and stared out at the open terrain. 'Where the hell's the damned forest?'

Ivo spun the axeman round and examined his eyes. 'You can see!' she exclaimed.

'Good guess,' Anyon answered with a wink, and stepped further from the cave.

Slowly Anyon's eyes became accustomed to the light. Lowering his axe to his side, but without relaxing his grip, Anyon began to examine their surroundings.

'How is that possible?' Mycroft whispered.

Einor Val shook his head and turned from his companions.

Somehow they had been transported back in time. Einor Val had no idea how this was done, but in his earlier studies as a Priest he had read of many things, strange things which his teachers had told him were impossible. But since then he had learnt the truth. All things were possible to those who had faith, and though his faith had suffered as he had grown older, he was sure now that he would be able to follow the path his parents had set for him. He would seek out Xularkon and put an end to his evil reign.

'Einor Val?' Mycroft called.

Einor Val turned back to answer his friend. As he did so, he noticed Guyon leave the cave. While in the cave she had stayed close to the entrance, taking no part in the dealings within. She still took no notice of their new surroundings but seemed to be deep in thought.

'Guyon!' Einor Val called. 'Have you an answer for all this?' He gestured to the plain below them. 'Where are we?'

Guyon shook her head. 'Not where, when.' She glanced over her shoulder at the cave's entrance and a shudder gripped her body.

'Are you all right?' Einor Val asked, placing a hand on his friend's shoulder.

'Yes,' she answered, a faint smile touched her lips.

'What did you mean, when?' Einor Val asked. 'And, where's the forest?'

'The forest will not take root for more than a thousand years,' Guyon explained. 'Somehow we have been sent into the past, a past where we have a chance of stopping Cymbeline from realising his plans.'

'I don't understand. But, whatever happened in there, we have at least lost the Ko'achs, and Anyon has his sight once more,' Einor Val said. 'I think we should move on as soon as possible before something else happens.'

'Yes,' Guyon agreed. 'Tell the others to be ready to move as soon as I return.'

'From where?'

'I must examine something in the cave before we leave.'

Lifting the flap she re-entered the cave and crossed to the rear wall. The smokeless torches still burnt, illuminating the furs. The tall man who had led them there was gone, yet his spear and shield remained in the alcove. On the rear wall where the woman had disappeared there was a series of carvings. Guyon had noticed them from the entrance but had been unable to tell exactly what they represented. Yet somehow she knew that they were of great importance.

A string of small characters danced across the wall

beneath one of the fading torches. The figures seemed to have been burnt into the stone wall rather than cut, the edge of each figure was rounded like no other stone work she had ever seen. Each figure was different from the one which preceded it, in weapons as well as stance. Yet as Guyon studied the figures she could not help but find them familiar. Drawing her medallion she positioned it so that the last feeble light could reach its reflective surface. Moving the mirror across the cut stone wall she quickly captured the reflections of the small figures. Replacing the medallion, Guyon turned her back to the wall and rejoined the others. As she passed the tall alcove, she reached in and picked up the large-headed spear, testing the weight of it in her left hand before replacing it.

'Did you find anything of use?' Jerram asked when he saw her appear.

'I'm not sure,' she answered. 'Perhaps later I will be able to put a meaning to what I found.'

At a call from Einor Val, the party set off down the slope towards the open plain. Nothing seemed familiar as they travelled, yet this had been the exact route they had taken the previous night. As they reached the base of the slope, a sharp cry echoed from the towering cliff behind them.

Einor Val led the way through the cliff's shadow until a small canyon appeared. The sides of the canyon were sheer, unclimbable. The far end of the canyon was blocked, a huge section of one of the surrounding walls had given away. At the base of this gigantic blockage a large caravan had made camp. The defenders of the caravan were busily trying to repel the attack of a strange mixture of creatures.

'Beasts from the southern lands!' Gideon exclaimed sharply. 'By the Great Lord, how did they reach this far north?'

'Let's find out,' Einor Val said, raising his hammer.

Quickly the party left the shelter of the cliff and moved to the caravan's aid. Once the shadow of the cliff had been lifted from them, they felt the full heat of the morning sun. As they neared the beleaguered caravan, a cry rose from the defenders. The attacking beasts stopped and turned to face the new threat.

Two forest goblins leapt for Einor Val, trying to separate him from the rest of the party. But without thought the ex-Priest smashed both aside without breaking stride. Einor Val's eyes were fixed on a familiar tapered pennant flying above one of the stalled wagons.

Roland, Alaric, Gideon and Kendrick forced their way into the heart of the attack raining blows to either side of them. Mail, clothing and flesh were hacked as the four drove deeper into the odd creatures. One beast leapt before Alaric. Catching his blow on its raised shield, the beast stared at its attacker while trying to bury a long-bladed dagger in Alaric's ribs.

Alaric lowered his shield and fended the blow off. The large eyes and gash-like mouth reminded Alaric of a toad and sent shivers of revulsion through his body. Aiming another blow at the creature's head, Alaric hooked a foot behind its leg, tripping it. Before it could rise, Alaric drove his sword past the creature's shield and deep into its chest, then as an afterthought removed the head. He was still unsure exactly what had happened to them or where or when these creatures had come from, but the feel of steel on bone was a feeling he could well understand.

Jerram, Walwyn and Mycroft followed the four, ushering Guyon and Jason between them. Chrestella, Ivo and Anyon brought up the rear. After the onslaught of the four, the beasts were reluctant to close with the remainder of the party, and the occasional well-placed shaft ensured the attackers kept their distance.

Only Einor Val was still under attack as Alaric, Roland, Gideon and Kendrick reached the wagons. Surrounded by leaping shrieking creatures the ex-Priest continued to move slowly towards safety. Ivo and Chrestella halted their flight and began to pick off some of the creatures on the outer edge of the melee. Seeing that this was of little help, the companions made ready to go to Einor Val's aid.

Before they could, a shout arose from one of the wagons and five robed men rushed towards the battling Einor Val. Each man was dressed in long robes with diagonal stripes of black and white. Their hoods had been thrown over their heads, hiding their features.

The first to reach Einor Val wielded a long thin club, the head reinforced with metal rivets. The second used a quarter-staff with great efficiency. Each tip was wrapped with a thin metal sheeting to give the long staff deadly weight. The next two swung heavy maces, their short handles ending with a weighted spiked ball. The last used a flail, a short-handled weapon with a chain and steel-spiked ball affixed to one end.

The five fought in a wedge and soon had smashed their way through the creatures to stand around the exhausted Einor Val. At the sight of the robed figures the creatures had redoubled their efforts to reach Einor Val. A loud groan rose from the creatures as Roland led the companions in a charge at their unprotected flank.

Dropped weapons and severed arms fell to the ground at the companions' feet, but still the beasts refused to give up their attack. Those creatures cut down but not killed outright grasped at legs, burying their teeth deep into armoured limbs. When the companions reached the robed figures and Einor Val, they opened out to form a tight circle.

'We must fight our way to the wagons!' Roland shouted over the fighting.

'It will be of little use to hope for safety in the circle of wagons,' one of the robed men called. 'Now the hounds have found us they will not be stopped until we, or they, are dead.'

Roland gave no answer, instead he skewered a tall furred beast which had sprung up before him. The beast snarled as it tried to pull the blade from its belly, adding the blood from its now lacerated hands to that of its wound. Roland wrenched the sword from the beast and brought it down on the head of another attacker. This beast resembled a man, save for the forked tongue which flicked out from between yellow fangs.

As the creature fell, it reached out for Roland, only to have its head crushed by the armoured boot of one of the robed figures. Soon the creatures began to thin. From the corner of his eye, Alaric saw that many of the men from the wagons had armed themselves with cross-bows and were firing shaft after shaft into the backs of the now howling beasts.

Finally the last of the attackers fell and the party set about dispatching the wounded creatures that continued to drag themselves towards Einor Val and the robed figures.

Mycroft straightened from cutting the throat of the last of the beasts as the men from the wagons reached the site of the combat. A slow look around showed him that all his companions stood, though all were wounded. It was difficult to see the severity of the wounds as each of them was covered in the foul-smelling blood of their attackers.

The party was led to the wagons where large tubs of water were placed on fires. Each of the companions stripped off his or her armour and clothing and began to wash the sweat and blood from their aching bodies in the slowly warming water. Soaps and liniments, as well as ointments and bandages, were provided by a short richly clothed woman.

She busied herself with the companions until she was sure there was nothing else that they would need. With the last wound treated and bandaged, fresh clothing was provided: soft padded underclothing and light scale-mail shirts, supple leather breeches, high boots of black leather with wide matching belts, and basin-like helmets which supported a chain-mail veil. The helmets, basnets, were well-padded and the aventail hung down behind them to protect the neck. A smaller section could be hooked across the face leaving only the eyes unprotected.

Each of the companions retained their own weapons,

223

though Ivo and Chrestella helped themselves to a small-sword apiece. Only Einor Val was missing. When they had entered the circle of wagons, he had been led away by the robed figures.

As Roland relaxed in the shade of a wagon, the short woman approached him. 'Is all in order, swordsman?' she asked.

Roland made to rise but the woman waved for him to remain seated.

'It is the least we could do for your timely intervention.'

'To me it seemed that our arrival only aggravated the beasts,' Roland observed.

'It was not you the beasts wanted,' she said quietly. 'It was the Priests.' She glanced over her shoulder as she spoke, whispering something that Roland failed to hear.

Her right hand dropped to her belt where her purse hung. 'If I had not been short of coin,' she explained, 'I would never have allowed them to join the caravan.'

'They seem capable enough,' Roland commented.

'They are.' The woman moved closer. 'They are amongst the greatest fighters in the known lands.'

'Is that bad, especially with such a large caravan?'

'The reason they are victorious in combat is because their order has no friends — they have to be good fighters or they would not survive. They travel and live in a land of enemies. The Priests of Azyr are ignored or attacked on sight by every civilised country.'

'Why?' Roland glanced across towards the wagon flying the black and white pennant.

'They speak their mind,' the woman answered. 'This is not a thing that the ruling classes condone. To be told in no uncertain terms, and by lowly Priests, that they, the rulers of large countries, are wrong, goes against the very nature of things.'

Roland merely nodded.

'But enough on this depressing subject,' she said. 'I am Kayte, and you are welcome to the hospitality of my caravan as long as is needed.'

'My thanks. Are you journeying far?'

'East to the Phlegethon River, then south to Xularkon's capital.'

'Xularkon!' Roland exclaimed.

'A hard one to deal with,' Kayte nodded. 'But the profits are worth the extra trouble.' She leaned close. 'I'd appreciate it if you did not repeat our destination. The Priests are hated and sought by many, but most they ignore; however, Xularkon is their sworn enemy. They have pledged his destruction.'

'Have you met with Xularkon?' Roland asked.

'No. None see him save his closest advisers,' Kayte explained. 'Since he walked out of the southern lands with nothing but the clothes on his back he has kept himself apart from outsiders. I remember the time well.

'It was only twenty year ago that he appeared. The further north he travelled, the more goblins flocked to listen to his tales. Old hatreds and long-standing wars were forgotten as more and more followers were drawn to the tales of riches and plunder.

'Within years he had a following of thousands; one walled town after another fell under his control. Soon others flocked to his banner, and Xularkon began to expand his influence further afield. It was when he reached the edge of Lake Zeridal he ordered the hunting down and slaying of the Priesthood.'

'But why have the Priests rated such special treatment?'

'It was whispered around Xularkon's palace that he woke one morning after having a terrifying dream. Servants swear that he woke screaming the word "Azyrite". Xularkon sought out many wisemen in an attempt to find an answer to his fears, but whatever he learnt is known to only himself as those who aided him soon disappeared.'

'How far do the Priests travel?'

'When we reach the Phlegethon River the Priests and I part company — they have their own path to travel.'

A Priest climbed from the back of the wagon and walked slowly towards Roland. As he crossed the camp, he threw back the hood of his robe revealing the calm features of Einor Val.

23
PRIESTS

'Why the robe?' Roland asked.

Einor Val seated himself on the edge of a crate. 'I might ask you the same about the armour.'

'Hardly the same thing,' Roland answered, pointing to where several of Kayte's men were reloading a wagon. They all wore the same style of armour which had been supplied to the companions.

'True,' Einor Val grinned. 'But after they saved my life, I found it hard to refuse their offer of clothing and armour.' Einor Val opened the robe and revealed a black and white striped tabard over a suit of ring-mail.

'Besides, I learnt that they are enemies of Xularkon and are journeying towards his capital in search of armour... or something.'

'Armour?'

'That's what they told me,' Einor Val said. 'I can't say I understand everything they told me, but from what I did learn, we are going to have a hard time reaching Xularkon.'

'Not if we stay with the caravan,' Roland answered. 'It seems it is travelling to Musero. But I doubt the owner will allow the Priests to travel that far. There seems to be little love for the Priests in this land.'

'So I have been told,' Einor Val answered. 'But they

travel only to a small village on the Phlegethon River where they must wait for another of their order.'

'That's of no concern to us. If we stay with the caravan, we may be able to enter Xularkon's capital easily enough.'

'And then?'

'We'll worry about that when we get there,' Roland said, slapping Einor Val on the shoulder.

'Perhaps.'

'To sit here all day is costing me money!' Kayte shouted. 'Hurry with the wagons or we may find ourselves with more guests.'

Many of her men threw nervous glances at the sprawled bodies of their attackers. Already the flies and many smaller carrion-eaters were attracted to the rich spoils. With the noonday heat fast approaching, the bodies would soon begin to pollute the air, calling creatures of greater danger to the small canyon.

The companions spread themselves out amongst the wagons in order to learn what they could about the new land they had entered. Travelling eastward they were running parallel to the coarse they had taken in the stolen fishing vessel.

As the caravan approached a long sloping ridge, one of the scouts appeared. Sprinting down the slope, he arrived at the lead wagon barely able to speak.

'Kobalos!' he croaked between long shuddering gasps of air. He pointed wildly at the ridge, his eyes brimming with fear.

'Curse the motherless spawns of hell!' Kayte swore. 'What in all the hells are they doing so far north? I had expected to meet a few goblin outposts,' she smiled at Roland and winked. 'Easily bribed; but Kobalos are totally different.'

The teamster of the Priests' wagon drew the team to a halt and made to leap down from his seat. He suddenly straightened, his face frozen with fear. A slight wince of pain and he lifted the reins to urge the team forward. The teamster dropped one hand to reach for the small of his back but another flinch of pain forced his hand to return to the reins.

A small patch of red began to stain the lower back of the teamster's shirt. The stain was around a small hole in the coarse material and was the same size as the matching hole in the wagon's canvas behind him.

Roland leaned from the seat of his wagon and saw that the black and white pennant had been removed from the rear wagon.

'Will any of your men talk?' he asked.

'To harbour Priests for any reason is instant death. There are no exceptions. If the Priests are discovered it will mean the death of every person in this caravan.'

'They could fight alongside the Priests?'

'Against the Kobalos?' Kayte asked. 'They are afraid of dying, but they are not crazy. Most will run, some will beg for mercy, but all will die.'

Roland said nothing more but turned his attention to the ridge. A small cloud of dust could be seen before the first of the Kobalos appeared. Roland was shocked to see that the Kobalos cresting the ridge rode a type of Ko'ach, smaller than the ones which had hunted them, but definitely Ko'achs.

There were five in the party that approached the now stalled wagons. Each Kobalos rode tall in a large leather saddle strapped well back on the mount. A chain halter and reins were the Kobalos's means of control. Each rider steered his mount with his left hand, while his right supported a long lance.

The Kobalos wore banded-mail with red leather boots and belt. A small round helmet with chain-mail aventails rested upon their heads. Long swords hung from their hips and large round shields were slung across their left shoulders.

The Ko'achs halted a short distance from the lead wagon. The riders made no move to dismount. Quickly Kayte climbed down from her seat and made towards the mounted Kobalos. One of the Ko'achs raised its head and roared, pawing the air before it. Kayte stopped her advance and took an involuntary step back. This drew laughter from the rider of the beast.

Drawing herself to her full height, Kayte continued her walk until she stood before the mounted Kobalos. After a brief conversation, she returned to her wagon and climbed to her seat. Taking up the reins, she flicked the team forward. Roland threw a quick glance at the waiting riders and then at Kayte. Her face was white and her forehead soaked with perspiration.

'Are we free to go?' he asked.

She nodded and swallowed hard. 'They search for an escaped slave.'

'Didn't they want to search the wagons?'

'There was no need. Anyone who lies to a Kobalos does it only once, and when they are finally caught, as all are, they are taken to their place of birth, or the harbour through which they arrived and executed in a most hideous way.'

Roland stood in his seat and swung out from the side of the wagon. The Kobalos were riding westward in an extended line. The heads of the mounts were close to the ground, searching for the scent of their prey. Roland resumed his seat and hoped that the escaped slave, when caught, fell to the Ko'achs, for in this strange land they seemed to offer the quickest of deaths.

Einor Val sat quietly in the rear of the wagon listening to the soft talk of the Priests. Even though they were moving deeper into a land controlled by their greatest enemy, the Priests spoke only of home and loved ones left behind.

One of the Priests, Annot, sat off to one side. He spoke little, mainly only to answer questions put to him by his companions. It had been Annot who had commanded the group in the fight with the strange creatures. His sharp orders had rung out over the screams and noise, keeping the Priests moving as if they were one.

Of all the Priests, Einor Val felt himself drawn to Thais. He had learnt that it was at Thais's suggestion that the Priests had helped Einor Val and his friends. As he watched, Thais broke into laughter. Warner, Hoshea, and Osmond soon joined him. Annot merely smiled and nodded his head.

A sharp call from the wagon's driver signalled the caravan's arrival at the Phlegethon River. Einor Val lifted a section of the canvas and peered out at the broad river. Vessels of all sizes moved about on its reflective surface, many were making for a small cluster of huts not far from where the wagons had stopped.

The rear flap was raised slightly and Kayte thrust her head into the hot interior of the wagon. 'It will be dark in a short time, so you will be able to enter the village unseen.' She left without waiting for an answer.

'Rather she means that we will not be seen leaving her precious wagons,' Annot explained as he began to gather what few possessions he had.

'If not for her, we would still be many days' travel from this place,' Thais added. 'And time grows short.'

'Why do we risk all to help these people when they refuse to help themselves?' Annot demanded.

Warner, Osmond and Hoshea glanced at one another, searching for any sign that they too thought this way.

'We do this not for these people, or even for ourselves,' Thais answered. 'We do this for the land and for the greater power it conceals.'

'And him?' Annot asked. He turned his head slightly and looked hard at Einor Val. 'Are we doing it for him?'

'Perhaps,' Thais answered.

'Someone approaches!' Osmond whispered.

The canvas flap was thrown open and a black and white robed figure appeared. In the dying light of day, the black sections of the robe merged with the darkness about it leaving only the bright white patches, thus giving the figure a strange twisted shape.

'It is time,' the newcomer announced, drawing the attention of the Priests. 'We are at last whole and our mission will soon be completed.'

'Then, he is the one?' Thais asked.

'Need you ask?' the new Priest answered. 'Did you not feel it the moment you saw him?'

Thais nodded and placed a gloved hand on Einor Val's shoulder.

'Welcome, brother,' he said.

'Our new companion is confused. I'd best explain,' the new Priest said as he waved for them to climb down from the wagon.

'I am Bede, the *soul* of our small Priesthood. It is my responsibility to guide you in the right direction,' he explained. 'Thais is the *heart*. Through him we see our true surroundings and find what must be done. Annot is the *mind*. He joins us and wields us as one against our enemies. Warner is our *shield*, while Osmond's our *armour*. And you, our newest companion, will be the *helmet*. It will be you three who protect us as we near the end of our search.' Bede turned to the last, and youngest member of the group. 'And Hoshea is our salvation, for he is the *sword* that will strike deep into the enemy's heart.'

As Bede finished his explanation, all Einor Val's thoughts of leaving the Priests and returning to his companions were gone. It was as if his life had been set in motion for this one purpose.

'What do you mean he's gone?' Ivo demanded.

'Just that,' Roland replied. 'He left last night with the Priests.'

'Left for where, and why?' asked Ivo. 'After all this time, why would he suddenly up and leave when we are so close?'

'I don't know,' Roland shrugged. 'Perhaps he thought he owed them something after they helped him.'

'And we haven't helped him?' Alaric retorted.

'Forget about him,' Anyon laughed. 'Once those Priests get their claws in you, they never let go.'

'Well, now what?' asked Alaric.

'We stay with the caravan and journey inland to Musero,' Roland decided.

'Not me.' Walwyn had approached unseen and was standing beside one of the empty wagons. 'I'm heading downriver.'

'To find the seafaring nation you once spoke of?' Roland asked.

'Yes,' Walwyn answered. 'This is my chance to learn if the stories are true, to see for myself if my people were really something more than pirates.'

'Good luck,' Alaric said warmly. 'You did not start the journey with us and have no obligation to see it through.'

'If you had any sense, you'd find a far country, some place where Xularkon can never reach, and settle down,' Walwyn advised.

Alaric, Ivo and Roland watched as Walwyn lifted his small pack down from the tail of the wagon and made his way towards the small village.

'The barges are loaded and Kayte is waiting,' Mycroft called. 'Are we to journey further?'

'Yes,' Roland answered.

'Though some not as far as others,' Guyon said softly.

Looking into her small mirror, she examined the first of the two small figures she had copied in the cave. One wore armour and somehow seemed separate from the others, while the second was superimposed over what Guyon now could discern as a sail. Einor Val's aid would be more direct, while Walwyn's would come at another time.

The barges moved slowly upriver, drawn against the current by large oxen. At the end of each day's travel, a village would be reached and there the oxen and their handler would be changed and the caravan would spend the night. After the third day's journey, the river banks seemed full of goblin soldiers. These were far removed from the poorly dressed savages the companions had met previously. These goblins wore armour and carried a great assortment of well-kept weapons.

Large groups of them were moving downriver on both banks. At the head of each company rode one or two Kobalos.

'They don't seem very curious,' Anyon commented.

'They have more important things on their minds,' Kayte explained. 'They ride to a place of gathering from where they will move northward, beginning a new time of conquest.'

'Of murder you mean,' Anyon grumbled.

'Quiet!' Kayte snapped, throwing a nervous glance about her. 'There are many who wait for the chance to denounce a traitor and bring themselves to the attention of Xularkon.'

'Hardly likely out here,' Anyon answered with a shrug, but his voice had lowered noticeably.

'You'd be surprised where the followers of Xularkon are to be found,' she warned.

Anyon turned back to his study of the river bank as a particularly large company of goblins appeared. Their armoured bodies were covered by a sand-coloured surcoat, and they wore tall grey boots which reached their knees.

'By all that's profitable!' Kayte cursed. 'Those are goblins from the southern border. Xularkon must be risking all if he dares strip his border with the Land of Sand.'

'Sand?' Roland questioned.

'It is the southernmost land, beyond even Xularkon's reach. Vast expanses of sand and nothing more save the abominable creatures who dwell there. It was from those very dunes that Xularkon himself appeared so long ago, and since then he has guarded that border to the point of fanaticism.'

'But now he withdraws his troops for a different campaign,' Roland mused. 'This sounds like the making of a truce.'

'Or worse yet, an alliance,' Ivo added.

'No alliance is possible with the creatures of the sand,' Kayte explained hurriedly. 'They congregate in few tribes and their main pastime is survival. To this end, they frequently raid Xularkon's land after food and whatever else they can steal.'

'Whatever has happened, the situation in the south has changed dramatically,' Roland began. 'No longer, it seems, is Xularkon forced to fight on two fronts.

For whatever reason, it bodes ill for the surrounding lands.'

'Indeed it does,' Kayte continued. 'If Xularkon is able to gather a large enough per cent of his forces, none of the lands to the west will be able to stand against them, and I will lose a lot of business. This is most distressing.' Kayte reached for the purse hanging from her belt as she spoke.

Ivo shook her head in disgust and turned to watch the river bank. Kayte's only fear seemed to be loss of business. She cared little for the loss of life that would precede a force such as the one Xularkon was raising. They must reach Xularkon in time to stop him.

She turned to Roland. 'Did Xularkon succeed in his drive to the west?'

'From what I have been able to learn about him, it seems he started his forces moving westward in good order, but after their first major victory, his plan of attack changed drastically and his army split into several smaller units which terrorised the western lands for some years before being finally driven out.'

'That hardly seems the type of attack Xularkon would plan,' Ivo observed. 'From what we have heard, he attacks a land or city, then secures it before moving on.'

'After this campaign, his forces were always on the run, withdrawing after each battle until they massed about the walls of Musero itself,' Roland continued.

'And Xularkon?'

'When the city finally fell there was no sign of him, many believed he had fled southward, swallowed up by the sands from which he had first appeared.'

Alaric placed a hand on Roland's and Ivo's shoulders. 'There's a river guard-post just ahead. Be ready in case of trouble,' he whispered.

Alaric left the pair and went to warn the remainder of his companions, while Ivo and Roland crossed to the bow of the barge. In the distance, the river narrowed slightly, and it was at the narrowest point that a large group of goblins could be seen waiting on the eastern bank. Many barges and other craft were moored side by side while goblins moved about their decks.

Ivo nudged Roland and inclined her head towards the closest bank. Amongst the sparse vegetation, more goblins could be seen. These carried large heavy crossbows and were keeping a close watch on the barge as it passed.

'Insurance,' Roland whispered. 'The only chance of escaping the guard-post is to cut the tow cable and use the river's speed.'

'And that's where the crossbowmen come into play,' Ivo added.

Roland nodded. 'At this range, they'd cut the crew and passengers to pieces.'

Kayte had ordered that the barge be halted and made fast to the other waiting vessels.

'I may be able to speed up our passing slightly if I offer a few well-chosen gifts to the post's commander,' she explained. 'Though occasionally, to one's annoyance, you do meet an honest officer.'

A rope was thrown from the bank and the barge was drawn in close enough for Kayte to leap ashore. Followed by a small number of her crew, two of whom carried a small but heavy chest, she began to push her way through those already waiting.

While Kayte moved slowly forward to carry out her business, the companions gathered on deck. They stood or sat where they could, watching the frenzied activities going on before them. While they watched, they talked and laughed, pointing and shouting at the crowds. Only a close look revealed that each carried a small bundle: rations and water wrapped in a light sleeping cloak.

As well as their own weapons, many had taken up pikes and staves, examining and toying with them as if bored. As Jerram watched he could feel the tension building. One shout of warning and the deck would have erupted in violence.

24

RIVER VOYAGE

Kayte and her small party of crewmen soon returned, minus the chest. She was smiling broadly as she boarded the barge, but her smile quickly disappeared when she saw her passengers. Positioned about the deck, each was armed, with small parcels at hand. A strange look was in their eyes as they waited for her to speak. She realised that her earlier assessment of these people was true. They were no ordinary travellers, and the wrong word spoken now could spell death for her, her crew and many of those ashore.

Forcing a smile, she stepped forward. 'Luck was with us,' she said calmly. 'The commander was an old acquaintance of mine and the gift was received in good faith.'

As Kayte watched, her passengers relaxed slightly. Hastily acquired weapons were replaced and several of the group moved from the barge's rails to talk quietly with their companions. The bank was now in total confusion as the oxen for Kayte's barge were whipped forward. Shouts and curses erupted from the teamsters as the teams of other barges blocked their path. Merchants shouted their anger when they realised what was happening. Kayte leapt to the rail and shouted orders while trading insults with her fellow merchants.

With all that was happening, it was not for several hours that the disappearance was noticed.

236

'Gone?'

Gideon nodded. 'I went looking for him some time ago, but he was not on deck. Thinking he had gone below to escape the noise, I thought no more of it. But eventually I went below to find him.'

'But where could he have gone?' Roland asked.

'Fallen overboard?' Mycroft put forward.

'Idiot!' Anyon laughed. 'How could he have fallen overboard in this weather? I've seen rougher water in a bath tub.'

'But not all that often,' Ivo added quickly.

Anyon ignored her. 'He's bolted, just like the others. He's decided he's had enough and has done something about it.'

'He would never leave,' Gideon argued. 'Not while there is still a threat to Damear.'

'Wake up, Gideon,' Anyon said sharply, leaning forward as he spoke. 'Don't you realise that we are the only threat to Damear. You said yourself that there were many in Damear who still follow the teachings of Xularkon and await the predicted second coming. What if Kendrick was one of these?'

'Impossible!' Gideon cried. 'I have known Kendrick since we were small boys. I would have known if he was a Xularkonite.'

'Would you?' Ivo asked.

Gideon said nothing. He leaned back against the timber rail and closed his eyes. Everything they had said had a ring of truth but how could he believe his companion was a traitor to their homeland.

'Whatever the reason he's gone and there's little we can do about it,' Ivo said pragmatically.

Anyon slammed his axe down on the rail, drawing everyone's attention. 'The problem is not what we can do about his disappearance, it's why he disappeared. Why would he choose now of all times?'

'Because we're deep enough into Xularkon's territory to make escape impossible,' Alaric answered.

'Then the quicker we leave the waterway and lose

ourselves in the traffic along the river, the better,' declared Jerram.

Guyon said nothing. She drew on the chain supporting her small medallion, bringing the ornate oval shape into the light.

'*tugulawarrin kendrick*,' she whispered.

The expression on her face remained the same but her eyes dropped from the mirror to the deck beneath her.

'*reyin.*'

One of the barge crew screamed. Roland, Alaric and Gideon spun round, swords drawn. Quickly they searched the deck for trouble, but found none. Then they realised that the crewman was staring at Guyon, or rather the mirror she held. The crewman's arm rose slowly until it was pointing towards Guyon.

'Demon!' he cried.

The crew had rushed to their companion's side at the sound of his scream. Now they turned their attention towards Guyon.

'Demon!' another of the crew shouted.

'Guyon, I think you should put the mirror away,' Roland advised, stepping between her and the gathering crew.

'What's their problem?' asked Anyon.

'Obviously there are no Ma'goi in this time,' Jerram explained. 'And the few who are beginning to learn the Arts are considered demons.'

'There is another reason,' Guyon explained as she closed the medallion and slipped the mirror out of sight. 'Kendrick is still on board.'

'Where?' Gideon asked.

'Below deck, with his throat cut.'

Ivo and Chrestella slowly backed away to where their bows rested against the barge's rail. Jason and Anyon moved to protect the two archers as Jerram and Mycroft also drew their weapons.

Kayte appeared from behind her men and surveyed the scene before her. 'A pity,' she said, shaking her head. 'I had hoped to deliver you alive to Xularkon. It would have proved quite profitable. Add the information about the Priests, and the entire trip would have been worthwhile.'

'You planned to betray us all along?' asked Mycroft.

'From the moment I first saw you. We were camped in that forsaken canyon at the request of the Priests, and as they were paying me quite handsomely, I could see no point in refusing.'

'Especially as you intended to sell them into the hands of Xularkon as soon as you could!' Anyon shouted.

'Just business,' Kayte laughed. 'The Priests said that they awaited the arrival of someone special, someone who would aid them in their cause.'

'But why kill Kendrick?' Gideon asked.

'He might have heard something that could have proved costly to me. One of my men caught him lurking below after I had discussed my meeting with the outpost commander. So you see, he had to die.'

'As do you!' Gideon yelled. His left arm whipped up from his side and the concealed knife spun across the deck towards Kayte, but she had expected something like this. As Gideon's hand released the knife, she leaned to one side, allowing the spinning weapon to pass by her shoulder, finally to embed itself in the chest of the man standing behind her.

'Kill them!' she screamed.

As one, the crew drew whatever weapons they carried and leapt for the companions.

Ivo and Chrestella had time for only one shot before they were forced to drop their bows and hastily draw their knives. Alaric, Roland, Mycroft, Gideon and Jerram took the brunt of the attack. Only six of the crew bothered with Anyon, Ivo, Chrestella and Jason. Seeing only four of the strangers, three of them armed only with knives and two of them women, made the attackers confident.

This confidence soon vanished as Anyon leapt forward, his axe raised above his head as the deck echoed with his shout of anger. One of the crew slipped past Anyon's defence only to die suddenly. Jerram crouched and wiped the blade on the dead man's jacket. He had moved with such speed that Ivo had not realised he had attacked until the crewman had fallen.

Guyon levelled her staff. '*doom-gara pulugge*,' she called.

The furthest end of the staff briefly glowed green before a small brightly coloured ball detached itself and flashed across the deck to strike one of the attackers. Stiffening, the man screamed as the ball expanded, covering his body with a web of thin sparkling light.

One of the crew came to his aid, but when he touched his screaming companion, he too became covered with the web. The remainder of the crew did not stop their attack, but they gave their two trapped companions a wide berth. As the fine webs disappeared the screaming stopped and the two men dropped lifeless to the deck.

The overconfident crew soon found themselves fighting for their lives as the armoured companions forced them back across the deck. Two more fell to Guyon's deadly web before they decided they had had enough. Some dropped their weapons and pleaded for mercy while a few who could do so threw themselves from the barge into the river's current.

Kayte shouted an obscenity as she raced across the deck and leapt the starboard rail. Her shout was cut off abruptly as Ivo's thrown knife took her between the shoulder blades. She hit the water and never surfaced; a faint trace of pink quickly drawn away by the current was all that remained.

Anyon placed a gloved hand on Ivo's shoulder and looking down at the waters mumbled, 'Paid in full'.

After watching the fate of Kayte, the remaining crew threw themselves over the side in an attempt to escape.

The teamsters had stopped at the sound of fighting and had awaited the outcome. They owed Kayte no loyalty but with her death their contract was over. With the skill gained by years of repetitious work, they quickly removed the team's harness. Without another look, the teamsters began to steer their beasts from the river's edge.

As soon as the harness was released, the barge was taken by the current. Guyon placed both hands on the staff and closed her eyes. *'ngoppun,'* she whispered.

The movement of the barge stopped. Then it slowly began to move upriver once more. The barge's speed steadily increased until they were moving at the pace of a galloping horse. Sweat beaded Guyon's forehead as she drove them further upriver. Each minute had them that much further from the pursuers who would soon take up their trail.

After two hours the barge turned slightly and struck the bank hard. No one was injured in the incident but Guyon was lying prone upon the deck. Her hair was plastered to her face and her breathing was ragged. Jason knelt beside her and raised her head.

'She's totally exhausted,' he told the others.

Jerram knelt down and, lifting Guyon in his arms, made for dry land.

'Release the barge,' Roland ordered. 'The further it is found downstream, the further from us they will start their search.'

Jerram, Mycroft, and Anyon threw their weight against the grounded bow of the barge, pushing it out into the current. Soon the vessel was spinning its way downstream.

'Let's find a sheltered place and rest,' suggested Roland. 'We could all do with a warm meal before we continue.'

With the fire doused and their bellies full, the companions settled down to wait out the remainder of the day. Guyon was sleeping peacefully now under the steady watch of Jason. Roland realised that if not for Guyon's actions, they would by now have fallen into the hands of the Kobalos and goblins who would already be searching for them.

He knew that Guyon needed all the rest she could get, but time was short and, regardless of how she fared, they would have to leave the hastily built camp as soon as the sun disappeared.

Roland could not be exactly sure but he believed that they were only days from Xularkon's capital, Musero. Even though the terrain had changed considerably, he had compared the time taken on their previous journey to the number of days travelled so far and was sure they were close to their goal.

Anyon rested beside Ivo. Even though the two still traded insults, it was obvious that they were drawing closer together. Jason sat beside Guyon, occasionally raising a hand to her brow. Beside him was Mycroft, a faint light radiating from his stiletto. Gideon sat alone. Since learning of the death of Kendrick he had said little, keeping to himself where possible.

Chrestella and Alaric were a good distance from the camp. They were beside the river and had the watch until last light. Jerram sat on the far side of the camp. Since the battle on the barge, he seemed changed. Finally he was one of the group. Roland could still not bring himself to believe what Ivo and Chrestella had said about Jerram's fighting skills. But he had to admit that when they had thrown the dead bodies of the crew over the side a great number had died from knife wounds to the neck.

Jerram raised his eyes and caught Roland's attention. Roland nodded to the unspoken question and began to climb to his feet. The sun was caressing the western horizon, throwing a haze of gold amongst the trees. Without an order being given, the companions rose and packed away their meagre supplies. Jason roused Guyon. She got quickly to her feet and beamed a large smile at her gathered companions. As she turned towards Roland, he noted that her eyes did not reflect the smile. They seemed sunken and dark, showing just how tired Guyon really was.

The companions travelled for two days before they found any sign of civilisation. The sun had just risen above the eastern horizon, and already there was a heat haze forming in the distance. The companions had stopped beside a wide well-travelled dusty road. There were several other small camp sites bordering the road, so theirs just became one of many.

Jerram soon left the camp site and crossed the road to the closest of the camps. Roland was deep in conversation with Alaric and did not notice Jerram's return.

'We may have stumbled upon some good luck for a change,' he explained. 'Those camped about us are mercenaries and malcontents here to seek their fortunes under Xularkon's banner.'

'Did we draw any attention when we arrived?' Alaric enquired.

'None seemed to have noticed our arrival in the dark,' Jerram replied. 'To most of those I spoke with, we are just another group waiting for our money and guides.'

'You said most, what of the others?' Roland asked.

'They don't give a damn. These are the sorriest looking bastards I have ever seen. The mercenaries are of a low quality and for the most part they are outlaws fleeing justice.'

'How did you find out all this?' asked Alaric.

'They aren't hiding anything,' Jerram continued. 'Quite the opposite, in fact. At the moment, they are happy to just sit here beside the road and drink themselves into a stupor.'

'How long have they been waiting,' Alaric asked, glancing up and down the road at the morning activity of the camps.

'Some for more than a fortnight, the rest just a few days. If we remain right here and become part of this madness, we may just be able to make it to Musero undetected.'

'Musero?'

'That's where they are to be taken for the first part of their training,' Jerram answered with a laugh.

Roland studied those moving about between the camps trying to trade whatever they possessed for drink. As the day wore on and the temperature rose, waterskins and casks changed hands many times and several fights broke out. For the most part the fighters were allowed to continue until there was a winner to claim the prize, sometimes something as small and invaluable as a tiny leather flask. The losers remained where they fell, in the dust of the road with only the flies for company.

'At this rate there won't be many left to train,' Mycroft noted.

'I think that has just come to an end,' Chrestella observed as she dropped down beside them.

Coming down the road was a small mounted column of Kobalos. There were at least twenty of them and they were followed by about fifty goblins wearing mail and at least two hundred humans wearing anything from rags to polished mail armour.

'It seems the training begins,' Ivo whispered as the leader of the Kobalos reined in his mount.

He said nothing as he surveyed the road and camps about him. Slowly he raised his hands and removed his helmet, placing it on his right thigh, his right mailed hand still resting on it. As he searched those gathered, he flicked his head several times, throwing out his long dark hair.

Turning his head again, he snapped four sharp words to those who waited behind him. His left fist shot up and pointed to a small camp beside the road. Quickly the Kobalos leapt from their saddles and crossed the dusty ground to where the surprised camp waited.

After disarming the occupants, they were dragged to the closest stand of trees by two squads of goblins while the dismounted Kobalos followed. Ropes appeared as if by magic and were thrown over low-hanging branches. Those in the other camps watched in silence while the occasional nervous giggle came from the dusty ranks of humans already on the road. As they screamed, the captives' hands were tied and the nooses were placed about their necks. When this was done, the goblins once more turned to the mounted Kobalos commander.

He gave a sharp nod and replaced his helmet in one move. As the screams changed to strangled gasps, the Kobalos commander kicked his mount forward. The remaining Kobalos raced for their mounts and followed their commander down the road, while the goblins remained to chase the still stunned humans onto the road to join the rest of the volunteers.

'So ends our training,' Anyon whispered.

25

CONSCRIPTS

The mounted Kobalos moved at a steady pace and the human volunteers were forced to keep up with them. Even though they greatly outnumbered the goblins, and in some cases were even better armed than their guards, there was never any trouble. The occasional glimpse of the armed Kobalos riding just ahead of the column, or simply the dust cloud marking their progress, was enough to keep even the unruliest volunteer in line.

'What if we don't stop in Musero,' Ivo wondered, 'but skirt the city and keep marching?'

'Then you'll be able to put your training to good use,' Anyon answered.

'But how would we escape?' asked Chrestella. 'We are watched at all times.'

'If we wait long enough there will be a battle,' Anyon said around a mouthful of cold greasy lamb. 'And in the confusion we will slip away.'

'But that would mean facing soldiers who share the same beliefs as us!' Jason exclaimed, shocked.

'So?' Anyon shrugged. He gave the bone in his hand one last longing look, then flicked it over his shoulder and began searching for something else to eat.

'You wouldn't draw the blood of an ally?' Jason asked, his voice rising slightly.

'Quieten down,' Anyon warned. 'The last thing we need is to draw attention to ourselves. You saw what happened to the last bunch who caught the commander's attention. Besides, what does a few more killed mean if it allows us to escape and find this Xularkon?'

Jason seemed unable to answer. He just sat and stared at Anyon as the axe-man began to work on another rather dubious looking bone.

The sun was setting as the long column of volunteers reached the outskirts of Musero. With a few coarse orders, the volunteers were herded into tall timber-walled enclosures. Large bins of bread were placed in the centre along with several barrels of water and a few vats of thin soup. Anyon swung his pack from his shoulders, threw it to Alaric and, with a smile and the faint sound of whistling, crossed to where their evening meal waited.

'Can you believe him?' Jason asked. 'How can he be so callous and uncaring?'

'It's just his nature,' Ivo answered quickly.

'It's a nature we are all going to have to learn,' Mycroft added, 'if we are going to survive here. I heard some talk that we are to be used as reinforcements against the western army. If we don't want to end up in some battle with the western forces I suggest we part company with our new travelling companions some time tonight.'

Silently the others agreed.

As Anyon bent to take up one of the small wooden bowls provided for the volunteers, he kept his right arm tight to his side, trapping the empty waterskin which hung there. He was one of the first to reach the waiting meal and was quick to fill his bowl and stuff several pieces of the dark coarse bread inside his tunic. He stood aside and sipped at his soup while he waited for more of his fellow conscripts to feel the pangs of hunger.

When a suitable crowd surrounded one of the water barrels, Anyon began to slowly work his way in towards the water. Unseen by any goblin observer, Anyon dipped and filled his waterskin; then, holding the bulging skin close to his body, he made his way back to where his companions sat and ate.

Putting his back to the compound's wall, he slid down to a sitting position, then slowly placed the full waterskin down beside his pack. Anyon knew what his companions thought of him, but he didn't care. Not one of them could survive in some of the places where he had been forced to live. He let his eyes wander the inside of the compound, as the volunteers slowly settled themselves down for the night.

Anyon drew his knees up close to keep the chill from his legs. As he did so his right hand dropped to the small knife hidden in the top of his boot. Although they had not been disarmed by their overseers, Anyon slid the knife from his boot and kept it concealed in the palm of his hand.

All the time he had continued his examination of the compound. Finally his eyes fell on his companions. All were readying themselves for sleep, except one. Mycroft was sitting a few paces to Anyon's right, a faint smile on his lips. Anyon tried not to look down at the hidden knife to see if it was visible. Mycroft must have noticed the effort because his smile broadened as he drew his hand from behind his back.

Protruding from the closed fist was the blade of his dagger. Anyon allowed himself to relax and smile as he realised that perhaps he had not been so clever after all.

Anyon rose and slowly sauntered over to where Mycroft sat. Easing himself down beside him, he said nothing. Sitting that close to Mycroft, Anyon could just make out the movement of Mycroft's hidden right hand.

'Will you need a hand?' he whispered.

Mycroft nodded.

Anyon slowly moved his left hand behind his back and slipped the blade of his knife between two of the slender poles which made up the wall of the compound. Anyon slid his knife down until it rested on the leather thongs which secured the timber poles. Then he slowly began to cut through the thongs.

Even though his knife was razor sharp, it was awkward work trying to cut without allowing anyone to see what he was doing. Most of those in the compound were asleep, but there were a few who still sat about and spoke in low whispers.

Mycroft coughed softly to gain Anyon's attention. Inclining his head slightly, Mycroft indicated a section of the compound's wall. Anyon stopped his cutting and watched the wall for some time before he saw what Mycroft meant. Moving slowly along the outside was a stooped goblin sentry. Every few steps he would bend and examine the wall. Anyon realised that he was looking for broken or cut thongs, and when he reached the section of wall where the companions rested, he would find just that.

Anyon turned back to Mycroft, his mouth open to ask a question. Mycroft shook his head. Anyon could now see Mycroft's arm moving rapidly back and forth; he was risking being seen by the other conscripts in an effort to finish his work before the sentry reached them.

With a slight snap, the lowest thong parted. Mycroft moved himself from the wall and lay down. When he was sure that his movements had not drawn any unnecessary attention, he rolled over on his stomach and began to work his way through the opening he had made.

Anyon threw a quick glance towards the fast approaching sentry. Another look at Mycroft showed that the goblin would reach him before he was through the wall and safely hidden in the shadows.

The sentry was only paces from Mycroft when another shadow appeared. This time it was a Kobalos who, with a sharp order, had the goblin springing to attention. The Kobalos moved closer to the sentry and stooped to examine the spot the goblin had been so interested in. He reached down into the dry grass and lifted something from it. Holding it close to his face, he examined it in the faint light. From the sounds he made it was obviously something of value. Slowly his head turned to the left, and he stared straight at Mycroft. A cruel smile twisted his alien features.

Straightening, the Kobalos sent a crashing backhand blow to the sentry's head, sending him spinning into the shadows of the trees beside the compound. The Kobalos took one step towards Mycroft, pocketing the object he had retrieved. Suddenly he stopped. The smile froze on his face.

Slowly the Kobalos began to collapse, but an arm appeared from behind, supporting him under one arm and across his chest. Jerram's head appeared over the Kobalos's shoulder as he quickly and silently lowered him to the ground.

Mycroft pulled himself through the wall and looked up at Jerram in total disbelief. It seemed that only moments before he had started his attempt to cut his way through the wall, Jerram had been lying a short distance from him fast asleep. But here he was.

'How...?'

Jerram silenced Mycroft's question with a raised finger and waved for Anyon to join them. Anyon dropped his right hand to his pack and turned, a large smile on his face, to get the attention of his companions, only to find them watching him. That caught Anyon by complete surprise and his smile disappeared suddenly, turning to bewilderment. It seemed that everyone had known what he was up to.

Roland and Alaric were smiling. Ivo was finding it hard to stifle her laughter; she looked away, but a brief look back revealed the comical look still on Anyon's face. Ivo raised both hands to her mouth as Roland moved to the hole in the wall and began to ease his way through it.

A slight disturbance caught Anyon's attention. One of the other conscripts had rolled over and was watching wide-eyed as Alaric took Roland's place at the hole. Anyon raised his axe in warning but the man began to rise to his feet, kicking off the thin blanket he had been using as a cover. Guyon placed one hand on Anyon's shoulder, while she spoke a word and pointed her staff at the rising man. He stopped and looked about, a surprised look on his face. Then he shook his head and lowered himself back to his waiting bedroll. Drawing the blanket up over his shoulder, he rolled, turning his back to the wall and the companions who sheltered beneath it, and dropped into a deep sleep with no knowledge remaining of what he had seen.

Quickly the party melted into the darkness. Moving as swiftly and silently as possible, they pushed their way through the trees surrounding the timber-walled compound until they found themselves at the beginning of a narrow paved street.

'What now?' Anyon asked, placing a hand on Ivo's shoulder, making her jump. Since leaving the compound, Anyon's attitude had changed considerably.

'Quiet, you idiot,' Ivo hissed.

Anyon merely shrugged and, without waiting for his question to be answered, started off down the street.

'Where does he think he's going?' Alaric asked. He kept his voice as low as possible and stayed hidden in the shadows.

'He's probably forgotten where he is and thinks he's going to help himself to a horse and ride out of this mess,' Ivo answered.

'Perhaps we should follow him,' suggested Chrestella.

Slowly they followed Anyon down the street. By now he was well ahead of them and occasionally disappeared around a corner, remaining from sight until the party quickened their pace to once again see Anyon's familiar gait as he continued his untroubled stroll.

'For now things are going well, but what happens when the sun rises and the city with it?' Mycroft questioned.

'Anyon seems to know what he's doing,' Gideon answered.

That drew a laugh from Ivo. 'I doubt it.'

Rounding one corner, the party found the street deserted. Realising that Anyon could have entered any one of a number of buildings, they quickened their pace once more. As they passed one rather sorry looking building, they heard the mumbled sounds of conversation coming from within. The door to the building was open a fraction, so Roland placed his hand against it and lightly pushed. As the gap widened, the party could see a large dimly-lit room. One voice could be heard above those in the large room.

'Anyon!'

Anyon paid no attention to the newcomers, concentrating instead on the job at hand. Several rather tall, ill-dressed characters were pressuring him from all sides.

'This is it!' one called.

'Your luck's finished now, you short bastard,' another growled.

Anyon ignored them, elbowing them out of his way to give himself more room. With a quick flick, he stooped and released the dice. They bounced across the uneven floor and came to rest in a small circle scuffed in the dust.

'Damn! What luck!' one of the watchers cried.

Anyon simply straightened and reached for his winnings.

'Perhaps it wasn't all luck,' the tallest of the watchers said and bent forward to take up the dice. Anyon's right foot shot out and tripped him. Finding himself falling forward, the taller watcher grabbed one of his companions for support, pulling him down with him. The last of the watchers seemed stunned by what had happened, but before he could do anything, Anyon brought his axe up and hit him in the face with the flat of the blade.

With his hands pressed to his face, and blood streaming from between his fingers, the last watcher stumbled backwards into the watching companions.

'Enjoying yourself?' Ivo asked.

Anyon turned and smiled, but said nothing as he continued to collect his winnings.

'Where in the five hells do you expect to spend that?' Roland demanded, pointing at the handful of coins Anyon held to his chest.

'Who cares?' was Anyon's reply. 'At least I've been working on our problem.'

'How will your cheating at dice help us?' Ivo asked, a faint edge to her voice.

'Perhaps it has helped you more than you know,' came a familiar voice from the shadows at the rear of the room. 'This building is well off the goblins' patrol routes. We were hiding in the cellar when I heard Anyon's voice.'

Weapons were drawn before the owner of the voice revealed himself.

'Einor Val!' Mycroft laughed. He sheathed his weapon and took a step towards his companion.

'There is little time for hellos,' Einor Val warned. 'The men Anyon was dicing with are deserters and already they have been missed and a search mounted. Soon these buildings will be alive with goblins.'

'Which way?' Chrestella asked.

'There is a door which leads into a narrow alley,' Einor Val explained.

'And these?' Gideon asked, eyeing the three deserters.

'Leave them,' Einor Val threw back over his shoulder. 'When they are found the search should be called off.'

'But they have seen us; what if they talk?'

'I doubt they'll be given the chance to talk,' Einor Val said quickly.

Soon they were racing down a narrow alley. They saw no lights nor heard any sounds, other than the ones they themselves were making. Einor Val turned sharply and disappeared into an open doorway. The room was small. What little furniture it contained was covered in dust. A door at the rear of the room took them into a large room with no windows. Einor Val crossed quickly to the far corner and threw a worn rug to one side, revealing a small trap door in the floor. He grasped a metal ring and pulled the door open. Not waiting to see if the others followed, he dropped through the open trap door to the room below.

As Ivo dropped to the floor, she smelt the moist air and a shiver ran up her spine. She had not realised which way they had run in the darkness, but they must have made straight for the river.

The trap door closed with a bang and a bright light sprung from nowhere. Einor Val touched the burning taper to an open lamp. As the wick caught, Einor Val shut the face of the lamp and a faint light filled the room. Standing behind Einor Val were the strange Priests they had first met at the caravan. Each wore a large hooded cloak; several of the cloaks hung open exposing the armour and tabard beneath.

26

CONFRONTATION

Bede drew a shuttered lamp from beneath his cloak. 'We must hurry.' Drawing his cloak closely about his armoured body, he turned and moved quickly down a narrow sloping passageway.

Thais and Hoshea also withdrew lamps from beneath their cloaks. Thais handed his lamp to Chrestella and followed his companions, with Hoshea bringing up their rear. Mycroft shrugged and followed the Priests into the darkened passageway. The others followed.

In silence they moved quickly down the passageway. Before long the damp air became almost overpowering and it seemed to Ivo that she was drowning as she struggled with her fear. She threw a glance at her companions, but none of them seemed to notice her dilemma. She drew a deep breath and continued.

Slowly a bright light appeared and grew before them. Bede stopped and closed the shutter of his lamp before placing it on the muddy floor of the passageway. 'Before us is a way into the city above,' he whispered. 'There will be guards, but they will be few in number.'

Turning from them, he drew a short reinforced club from beneath his robes and headed towards the light. Each of the other Priests drew similar weapons and followed.

'It seems we have little choice,' Alaric whispered, drawing Kilic.

Anyon nodded, as did Roland. Chrestella moved her bow from her shoulder and strung it. Gideon mumbled a short Damear prayer as he readied his weapon. Jerram, Jason and Mycroft also armed themselves, and Guyon raised the woven staff before her. As her companions readied themselves, Ivo stood still as she fought to drive the smell and sounds from her mind. Finally Anyon noticed Ivo's problem and crossed to stand beside her. With his axe held firmly in his right hand, he cupped Ivo's right elbow in his left hand and squeezed firmly.

None of the others noticed Ivo's trauma, and she was drawn along with them by Anyon. As they blinked and shielded their eyes trying to restore their sight in the light after the half light of the passageway, they saw that they were beside the wide subterranean river which had been their means of escape when they had first visited the city in their own time. Several dead sentries were stretched out in the shadows.

The passageway angled upwards and then suddenly dropped back to the level of the river. Soon they found themselves at a narrow section of the river. Before them, several large rafts had been roped together to form a rough bridge over the fast-flowing river. Shouts could be heard from behind them as the dead sentries were discovered.

Anyon was the last across the bridge and he spun about, his axe raised. 'Cut the ropes and set the rafts adrift!'

'No!' Roland snapped. 'We will need at least one of the rafts if we are to escape.'

Anyon shook his head. 'We'll find another way.'

Roland pushed Anyon aside and pointed at the closest two rafts. 'Cut the furthest one adrift. That will stop the goblins and still leave us two rafts.'

Mycroft glanced over his shoulder and saw that the Priests had not stopped and were almost out of sight. 'Chrestella. Ivo. Stay here and do as Roland suggested. If you can keep the goblins from crossing, we will meet you here and take our chances with the river's current.'

He glanced down at the river passing beneath them and a slight shiver passed through him at the thought of throwing themselves into that swift dark current.

Mycroft led his remaining companions in pursuit of the Priests.

Roland looked about and saw that the Priests had already moved off and were running towards another opening not far from where he stood. Several goblins lounged by the opening. When they saw the Priests, they leapt to their feet only to be driven to the ground by the first Priest to reach them.

As Roland passed the dead sentries, he saw a dirty blanket had been spread upon the ground. Small dice and various items of little value lay in the centre of the blanket. Anyon moved towards the blanket but a shove from Mycroft sent the short axe-man stumbling forward, a soft curse on his lips.

Chrestella watched them as they disappeared from sight. She felt a pang of fear and disappointment as she realised that she might not see them again. She turned to Ivo and saw that her companion was also taken aback by their situation.

Ivo, however, had not noticed the departure of her companions. She was back on the underground lake once more, her brothers beside her as they rowed around the edge of the still dark waters. The sound of water lapping against the side of the raft and the smell were still with her from those days. Her surroundings had released the memories and they had come flooding back.

'Ivo!' Chrestella shook her once more. 'Ivo! What's the matter? The goblins are trying to cross to the rafts. We have to do something.'

But Ivo was lost in her past. With a snarl of anger, Chrestella pushed Ivo to one side and drew an arrow from her quiver. Carefully she took aim and released the shaft. With a small cry of triumph, she watched as one of the goblins pitched headfirst into the swelling waters. Shaft after shaft she fired, until she had but two left. Looking about her she saw Ivo's quiver, still full.

Ivo felt the touch and opened her eyes. She could make out a dark shadowy figure bending over her. The shadow spoke. 'Quickly! A few are in the water and will be here shortly.'

Ivo stirred in her dream, remembering the figures in the water and how her brothers had tried to protect her. No. Not again. It was not going to happen again. Pushing the shadow from her, she climbed to her feet and drew a long feathered shaft from her hip. Raising the bow, she aimed and released in one fluid motion, sending the shaft into the throat of a goblin.

The shadow tried to stop her, but she pushed it aside. Nothing was going to stop her from saving her brothers.

She turned to the figure beside her, a figure which had never been in her dreams until now. 'Tell them that I did my best.'

Ivo fired into the massed goblins until her quiver was almost empty. Chrestella stood to one side, waiting. She could hear her friend talking, calling out names which had no meaning to her. As the first of the goblins began to climb from the water, Ivo dropped her bow and drew the short-sword at her waist. She cut three goblins from the side of the raft before Chrestella could join her.

Ivo spun round and hissed. 'They're mine. Go!' There was such feeling in her voice that Chrestella took several paces back. 'Go!' Ivo screamed.

Chrestella turned and began to follow the path taken by the others. She glanced back over her shoulder at one point and saw Ivo down on one knee, slashing at the goblins as they tried to climb from the water. One hand was at her side and Chrestella saw that blood was seeping from between her clenched fingers. In two minds whether to go back and help, Chrestella hesitated. At that point a goblin rose up from the side of the raft. Its club fell swiftly striking Ivo on the back of her head. Without a sound she toppled forward onto her face and was still.

Chrestella spun and ran along the passage. There was nothing she could do to stop the flow of goblins across the rafts, but she had to warn her companions.

*

The party had travelled for only a short distance before they surprised a large number of goblins moving in the opposite direction. The goblins fell back before the onslaught of the Priests, and it looked as if the party might win through, when suddenly a Kobalos appeared. Quickly the Kobalos organised the goblins and stopped their retreat. Soon the greater numbers of the goblins began to take its toll.

Hoshea raised his mace. 'We must silence the Kobalos, or they will hold us here until reinforcements arrive.'

Mycroft turned to Guyon for aid, but she had her eyes tightly closed, her body taut as she fought an unseen enemy. As Mycroft watched, her face began to redden and her forehead beaded with sweat. She flinched and grimaced, and her head began to roll from side to side. Mycroft realised that she was locked in a combat with Xularkon and that she would be of little use to them.

Once more the Priests forged their way into the mass of goblins. Bede almost reached the far side before they were repulsed. Just as it seemed that the goblin numbers had held fast, Jerram, who had moved forward in the centre of the formation with Anyon, called out.

Anyon spun round and cupped his hand to take the booted-foot of Jerram as he leapt into the air. With the added strength of Anyon, Jerram was able to clear the heads of the goblins who had stopped their advance. Rolling to a halt, Jerram quickly came to his feet, his dirk ready. The Kobalos made no move towards him. With a shake of his head, the Kobalos overcame his surprise and drew his sword. There was a strange half smile on his lips as he moved confidently towards the crouched Jerram.

As the sword swung down, Jerram rolled forward and to one side, slashing upward as he did so. The blade of his dirk cut through the fabric of the Kobalos's jacket but failed to penetrate the mail shirt beneath. Again the tall Kobalos seemed surprised. He stopped momentarily and glanced down at the cut sleeve. Then, for the first time, the Kobalos showed anger. With sword raised, he leapt for Jerram.

Thais stepped on the arm of a dead goblin and lost his footing. Quickly the goblins closed in about him. Warner and Osmond moved to their comrade's aid but not before Thais had taken several wounds.

Without warning, a piercing scream rose above the sound of steel. The Kobalos slumped against a stone wall, one hand fisted around the handle of Jerram's dirk. The fighting ceased as the goblins watched in horror as their leader slipped slowly to the floor. One of the goblins turned his back on the dying Kobalos and raised his short curved sword, pointing it at Jerram. Many of the goblins followed the pointing sword, some even took a half step towards the unarmed man.

Alaric realised the importance of the moment and slipped a dart from his belt. With a quick flick he let fly with the dart, taking the pointing goblin in the temple. With a gasp, the goblin dropped to the ground. By now the goblins had lost heart completely, and it took only a slight effort to send them on their way.

The Priests moved off on the heels of their attackers, Thais supported by two of his comrades.

Jerram retrieved his dirk before following. Slowly he gained on the Priests and his companions until he was almost upon them. Passing through a large archway, he skidded to a halt. The room was huge with a raised dais against the furthest wall. A high-backed throne sat on the dais. A tall Kobalos stood beside it, a crazed look on his face.

'You have interfered with my plans for the last time,' he raved. 'I am Xularkon and it is my destiny to rule this world and all upon it.'

Bede reached up and opened the visor of his helmet. 'We shall see,' the Priest called. 'For we are here to help you fulfil your destiny.'

That sent Xularkon into a rage. Screaming at the top of his voice, he ordered all those in the room slain. From narrow doorways on either side of the room, dozens of goblins appeared. Some attacked the Priests, while the majority formed a wall protecting the raving Xularkon.

The Priests formed themselves into a wedge formation and slowly began to battle their way into the goblin defenders. Xularkon strode back and forth across the dais as he screamed more orders at his forces. His hands were gripped tightly into fists and held before his chest. As he called for more troops his voice cracked several times revealing his panic to the attackers.

Thais, though wounded, took his place in the wedge. Xularkon raised one hand. Red flame shot from his fingertips and raced across the room towards the battling Priests. In a flash of light, the flame struck a wall of green light, curling the flame back upon itself and sending it down on the defending goblins.

Guyon lowered her staff as she waited for Xularkon's next attack. Jerram, Anyon and Roland stood before their companion, shielding her from the attacks of those goblins who broke free of the fighting. Alaric and Gideon had joined the Priests in their effort to reach the screaming Xularkon. Mycroft stood beside Jason at the door and watched in amazement as Guyon turned back Xularkon's attack.

'The power of that staff is incredible,' he said just loud enough for Jason to catch the words.

'How so?'

'Xularkon's strength is awesome,' he answered. 'I can feel it from here, reaching out as he tries to bring his goblins under control and combat Guyon at the same time. But, I can also sense a madness in his magic, an insanity which weakens him.'

Booted feet could be heard coming from one of the side passages. Mycroft drew his sword and leapt for the opening just as four goblins reached it. The first fell to a straight blade through the chest. The second was backhanded away as Mycroft drew his blade free. He turned the curved sword of the third goblin and buried a dagger deep in the creature's chest as he felt the cold steel of the fourth goblin take him low in the side.

Reaching down, he grasped the goblin's hand, trapping the blade in his body, and brought his own sword

261

round to cut the goblin's throat. Leaning back against the cool stone wall, he pulled the blade free. His eyes felt heavy, as he began to settle to the floor. A shout brought him back.

Jason was battling three goblins. He had one by the throat and was repeatedly driving his knife into the creature's chest. The other two attackers were slashing at his exposed back and shouting with excitement.

Mycroft pushed himself from the wall and stumbled to where he could dispatch the first goblin from behind. He killed the second as it turned. Jason was on the floor, his hand still locked about the goblin's throat. One look was enough to tell Mycroft that the ex-healer was dead.

The Priests battled further into the press of goblins, gaining ground with each minute, but Thais had been weakened greatly by his wounds, and fell before the dais was reached.

The last of the goblins fell back to the dais and formed a semicircle before Xularkon, who had continued his attack on Guyon. Each blast of red fire was met by the raised staff and smothered in a green light. From a side passage, four Kobalos appeared. Drawing their swords, they quickly joined their lesser brethren on the dais.

The skill of the Kobalos was amazing as they met the attack of the six remaining Priests. Stopping their advance, the Kobalos began to push the Priests from the dais. Roland led Anyon, Alaric, Gideon against the last of the goblins. Jerram stayed beside Guyon as she still struggled to keep Xularkon's power contained.

Suddenly the rear wall of the room darkened and a figure stepped from the darkness.

Anyon raised his bloodied axe and cursed. 'Cymbeline!'

The Wiseone strode forward. He seemed confused by what he saw, but quickly his eyes reached the cowering figure of Xularkon, and a faint smile touched his taut lips.

Xularkon fell back, his hands rose to his lips as if to tear a cry of fear from them. His attack against Guyon forgotten, Xularkon turned to run from the room, but slipped from the edge of the dais and fell at the feet of the closest Kobalos.

Xularkon raised one arm and pointed at the tired Cymbeline who had made no move to enter the room further. 'Stop him!' Xularkon cried. 'Don't let him take me again, not again!'

The Kobalos looked confused but turned to face Cymbeline as ordered. The three remaining Kobalos continued to press their attack. Warner overextended himself and was cut down by one of the Kobalos. Without even a glance, his killer stepped over his still twitching body to launch a blistering attack against Osmond.

Chrestella burst into the room. 'Hurry! They are right behind me!' she shouted and, drawing her sword, turned to face down the passageway. Gideon backed quickly from the fighting and ran to join her just as the first of the goblins appeared.

Xularkon crouched by the edge of the dais, his fisted hands shielding his face. Cymbeline now realised who he faced. How Guyon and the others had journeyed back in time to this crucial moment was lost to him, but he realised that if he did not do something soon, all his planning and sacrifices would have been for nothing.

He raised his hands and sent twin balls of red lightning towards Guyon. With a flick, she struck the balls aside with the staff and then, for the first time, attacked. Lowering the staff to waist level, she gripped it firmly with both hands and sent a shaft of green light spearing towards the surprised Cymbeline. He was momentarily taken aback by the audacity of the attack, but with a brief movement of his lips, a wall of red light appeared before him. The green light struck the wall and fragmented, lighting the entire room in one brilliant flash.

One of the Kobalos, the one nearer to Cymbeline, died on the green flame and another was slightly blinded by the return flash. That cost him his life as Bede leapt forward and drove his mace against his opponent's exposed head. As the Kobalos fell, three more entered the room, each armed the same as the others but also carrying short throwing spears. Taking the situation in instantly, one of the Kobalos hurled his spear, taking Bede in the side. The other two followed suit. Anyon batted one spear from the air, but the second struck Osmond full in the chest. As blood gushed from his mouth, the Priest dropped slowly to the ground.

The Kobalos then drew their swords and rushed forward. Einor Val, Warner and Annot were still fighting the first three Kobalos and could not face this new attack. Jerram moved forward and faced the three alone, but only for a short space of time, as Anyon appeared beside him.

'This is the wrong place to be,' Jerram laughed.

Anyon smiled. 'Wanna bet? They look to have rather heavy purses.'

As Jerram and Anyon, shoulder to shoulder, met the attack, the goblins reached the door and the waiting Gideon and Chrestella. About a score of goblins tried to force their way into the room, but they were held at bay by the two defenders. The sheer weight of numbers proved too much for Gideon and Chrestella, and they were pushed back. As that happened, many of the goblins began to swarm around them.

Chrestella dropped one with a short thrust, tripped a second and blocked the blow from the third. But the fourth goblin drove his sword deep into her side. Before she could strike back, another goblin caught her by her hair and slit her throat. Left alone, Gideon slowly backed into the room cutting to left and right as he fought to keep the goblins at bay.

Blood spattered his face and chest, and his mail shirt hung in tatters. His arms were crisscrossed with bloody cuts as he took wound after wound; but he refused to die. As he backed slowly into the room his lips twitched as he repeated his funeral prayer over and over again. Finally a blow struck him on the side of the head and he folded to the ground, trampled by the goblins as they sought out new victims.

Guyon sensed rather than saw the danger, and swung

the staff about. Small balls of light sprang from the end of the staff, each one striking a goblin in the chest. Screaming, the goblins fell to the ground, rolling in pain as they tried in vain to extinguish the magical fires that consumed them. But even as she swung back to face Cymbeline, a burst of red fire struck her and threw her back against the wall. The staff dropped from her fingers as she fell.

With a laugh, Cymbeline leapt from the dais and dragged Xularkon to his feet.

Mycroft pushed himself up from the floor and drew the stiletto from his belt. Reversing it, he threw it at one of the Kobalos with what little strength he had left. The glowing weapon spun end over end and finally buried itself deep in the neck of its target. Mycroft watched the stiletto strike before folding to the floor.

Alaric and Roland went to Jerram and Anyon's aid. Annot, Warner and Einor Val fought the Kobalos toe to toe, none gaining or giving ground. All of them knew that as soon as more goblins reached the room, it would all be over. However, what they saw enter the room was the last thing any of them had imagined.

Gripping her bow, Ivo staggered into the room, her hand clutching her side, blood oozing between her fingers. Her hair was matted and bloodied, her face locked in agony. Through a haze of pain, she saw Einor Val and the two Priests, their backs to the wall, fighting the three Kobalos. In the centre of the room Jerram, Anyon, Roland and Alaric faced the remaining two Kobalos. And just on the edge of her vision, she saw Cymbeline dragging Xularkon towards the wall of shadows.

Lifting her bow, she forgot her pain as she nocked a retrieved arrow. Slowly she drew the bow taut as she raised it and sighted on the back of her intended target. With the slightest touch of her lips upon the string, she released the shaft. The arrow shot across the room, striking deep just as Cymbeline and Xularkon stepped into the darkness. The last thing Ivo saw as she fell to the floor was Cymbeline release his grip on Xularkon.

27

ESCAPE

As Xularkon disappeared from sight, the five Kobalos stopped their attack and withdrew to the dais. They seemed unsure of what to do next. The sound of booted feet and the clank of weapons heralded the arrival of a large party of goblins and another two Kobalos, one of whom was a full head taller than his brethren. One was dressed the same as the others but the taller one's armour bore intricate patterns worked in silver and small gems. Quickly the five explained what had just happened. The two new arrivals listened, glancing from the shadowed wall to the waiting Priests and companions.

Finally the taller Kobalos spoke. His speech was fast and guttural, similar to that of the forest goblins, but the Kobalos and the waiting goblins understood him well enough. Two of the Kobalos leapt from the dais and, with the goblin company in close pursuit, sprinted for the shadowed wall.

The remaining Kobalos separated, but within minutes one returned with another company of goblins. This company was loaded down with weapons of all descriptions. Following their Kobalos, they marched across the room and disappeared into the shadow.

Anyon knelt beside Ivo. Slowly he raised her head to his lap and pushed the blood-soaked hair from her face.

Her breathing was irregular, and she had lost a lot of blood. Her eyes fluttered open. At first it seemed as if she could not see Anyon, but then her face brightened as her eyes focused on him.

'There's nothing for you here,' she croaked.

Anyon drew her head tighter into his lap. 'Wanna bet?'

Ivo smiled, and closed her eyes.

Mycroft was propped against a wall. Both hands were pressed to his injured side. Roland knelt beside him, reaching for his bloodied hands.

Mycroft smiled and shook his head. 'Too late, my friend.'

Roland smiled back at Mycroft, and then looked to where Guyon was being lifted to her feet by Annot and Warner. Alaric looked down at Chrestella's still form, her body half blocked the doorway she had died defending. Not far from her, Gideon lay sprawled in death. Gideon's words came to him. 'The edge of the knife gives life, and the edge takes it away.'

Jerram checked the last of the Priests: dead, all of them dead. Jason was also gone; the ex-healer had stood little chance. He had never been anything of a swordsman, but he had done what he could.

Another company of goblins rushed into the room. They didn't spare the injured party a second glance as they made for the slowly shrinking shadow.

Einor Val watched the goblins disappear before speaking. 'We're going to have to get out of here. Every goblin in this place must be making for this room, and the portal can't stay open for much longer.'

'But what of our companions?' Annot asked. His voice lacked strength, and he leant against the wall for support.

'They come with us,' Guyon said, pushing herself from Warner's grip. Staggering across the room towards Mycroft, she almost fell, but Warner was soon there to support her. Placing the butt of her staff on Mycroft's chest, she whispered several words too soft for even Warner to hear. Mycroft's breathing became easier and some colour returned to his face.

She turned and even more unsteadily made her way towards Ivo. 'It is all I am able to do.' Reaching the injured archer, she placed the staff upon her chest. Ivo's eyes opened again and a faint smile came to her lips.

'They have sufficient strength to survive the rigours to come,' Guyon said. 'But we will have to leave now for I have used the last of the staff's power in saving them.'

Anyon lifted Ivo gently to her feet, and made for the door through which they had entered earlier. Alaric looked towards the shadowed wall.

Roland placed a hand on Alaric's shoulder. 'Anyon's right, my friend. There will be more danger beyond the portal than we will find here.'

Warner still supported Guyon, and Roland helped Mycroft to his feet. Jerram moved ahead of Anyon.

'I'll scout ahead.'

Alaric followed Jerram, while Annot and Einor Val brought up the rear.

Jerram led them quickly to the waiting rafts. Crossing the first to the outer raft, they cut the ropes and allowed themselves to be taken by the current. The entire party sank to the floor of the vessel, too tired to do anything as they slipped into the darkness.

Alaric moved beside Roland. 'How will we control the raft's direction if have lost the power of the staff?'

Roland shrugged, but it was lost in the darkness. 'The river took us to safety once, it will do so again.'

The party slept.

Guyon was the first to awake. Something had told her that it was time for her to act. '*ngoppun.*' Instantly the raft veered to the right. Guyon could see nothing in the darkness, but she knew that they had entered the small side passage. The raft touched the side wall of the river sending a shiver through those who slept. Roland sat up, his senses told him that something was wrong.

'Alaric!' he called, reaching out and shaking the sleeping form next to him. 'Cut sections from the raft and make torches.'

Alaric cut several long pieces from a low box in the centre of the raft containing the rations and water. Searching in the box, however, he could find nothing to light the hastily prepared torches.

'Here.' Guyon held out her hand and Alaric touched her fingers with the end of the torch. *'kulkun.'* The tip of the torch broke into flames.

Alaric quickly lit the other torches from the first. He handed one to Roland who moved to the edge of the raft. The noise and light had woken the others and Alaric handed out torches to Annot and Einor Val as well as keeping one for himself.

'We're in the side passage,' Roland said, as he straightened from his inspection. 'Somehow we left the main stream and entered the smaller river where those strange creatures live.'

'Will live,' Guyon reminded him. 'Will live. We last encountered them well into the future. They have not as yet been condemned to their vigil.'

Anyon looked at her suspiciously. 'Why are we here?'

'I have to return something,' Guyon said, holding up the staff.

The party was able to dock the raft at the same point they had reached the last time they travelled the river. Only Guyon left the raft. In the darkness, she had no trouble finding her way to the small room with the woven pillar in its centre. Carefully reaching into the pillar, she placed the staff in its heart.

'Here you will rest and regain your power until I need you again.'

Returning to the raft, they were soon underway once more. Free of the passageway, the companions said their farewells. Mycroft and Einor Val were to stay in the past and journey to the north and find the Fortalice in its infancy. It would be many, many centuries before the Fortalice would help in the affairs of those countries bordering it, but Mycroft had decided that he would continue his studies in the Arts while Einor Val wished to continue his training in weaponry.

Jerram, with Annot and Warner, were heading north-west. It was Jerram's hope to reach Alamut as it was beginning to take shape and help ready it for the times to come.

Guyon said nothing of where she intended to go but convinced Roland, Anyon, Alaric and Ivo that they should return to the strange woman's cave where they were sure to find a way back to their own time. They weren't sure how she could promise them this, but they were not going to mistrust her now. As Guyon watched the four of them moving eastward along the lake's edge, she laughed to herself. She had heard Anyon make mention of travelling north to Alaric's home where they could help him regain his title and, of course, be rewarded handsomely.

Guyon heard a slight noise behind her and turned to find a tall dark-skinned native standing there. He carried a broad-headed spear and large oval shield. He smiled as she noticed him.

'Home?' he said softly.

'Yes,' she answered. 'Home.'

EPILOGUE

In the waste's vastness a shadow appeared. A deep black shadow which seemed to have a depth beyond all imagining. The shadow was suddenly interrupted as a figure appeared at its centre. Arms flailing, Xularkon stumbled from the darkness and took several paces before waking to his surroundings. Weakened by his journey, the heat of the air around him drove him to his knees. His clothing was torn and stained and for some reason his weapon was missing.

Then he remembered...

Those priests. Those damn priests. If not for them he could have defeated his nemesis.

Clenching his fists he drove them repeatedly into the burning sand. Again those damned priests had aided his nemesis and had stood between him and the power that was rightfully his; but it mattered little. Slowly he raised his head. His jaw stiffened with determination. His face was as grey as the sand around him but his eyes were filled with colour — red, the colour of the blood he would see spilt. In the distance through the heat haze he could just make out the green edge of the southern wastes. Beyond its northern border he would find willing followers to his banner and soon he would be in a position to impose his will over all.

All who survived...

As Xularkon stepped forward a strange feeling touched his consciousness. The waste was all too familiar, and the thoughts which raced through his fevered brain seemed to echo dreams of a past time. Shaking off those distractions, Xularkon lengthened his stride, his fatigue forgotten. He would take his rightful place in history, but this time he would destroy those accursed priests before they had a chance to interfere with his plans.

ARMOURY

ACHICO	Twin weighted bolas.
ANHINGA	Small dart.
AVENTAIL	Form of mail armour worn to protect shoulders, neck and part of face.
BALDRIC	Shoulder belt of leather used to support a sword.
BARD	Complete protective armour for warhorse.
COIF	Close-fitting mail hood.
GREAVES	Armour for lower leg.
HAUBERK	Shirt of mail protecting head, trunk, arms, and legs above the knees.
LORICA	Leather armour covering breast and back.
SABATON	Armour to protect feet.
SURCOAT	Long loosely-fitting coat without sleeves.
TABARD	Short garment split up both sides with short flared sleeves.

Martin Middleton
Circle of Light

*'The journey will be hard and many times you will meet
Dark forces at work upon this world… We have
awaited your return for centuries, Death Lord…'*

The King of Nuevah is dead, murdered by his own
brother. Evil forces threaten to plunge Nuevah into
Darkness… unless a lost prince — ambushed and sold
into slavery years before — returns to claim his rightful
throne.

Four Vahian soldiers embark on an epic journey in
search of the lost prince. They are joined by a young
bondservant called Teal, whose instinctive skill with
weapons reveals the mystery of his birthright. Teal finds
a ring in the subterranean city of Perdu which gives him
mystic powers and enables him to draw together others
with identical rings and similar abilities. Under Teal's
guidance, the seven Usare must use the combined
might of the rings to form a Circle of Light against the
forces of Darkness who threaten to engulf all the lands
in war.

Teal's perilous odyssey leads the Usare across many
strange lands and sets them against horrifying
creatures, savage foes and age-old magic. As they
venture closer to the Dark forces, Teal learns of a
terrifying ancient prophecy… that he alone must fulfill.

In the vein of the novels of Raymond E. Feist, Stephen
Donaldson and Julian May, *Circle of Light* is a
breathtaking combination of fantasy, heroism and
adventure, a mythical saga that takes the reader to the
very edge of imagination.

Martin Middleton
Triad of Darkness

'And what is the force we must render powerless?'
'The God Erebus — Devourer of Souls.'

The evil that threatens all the lands has not been eliminated by a Peace Treaty, merely temporarily held at bay.

Teal, the hero of *Circle of Light*, is the only one who can stop the Dark forces that hunger for absolute power. He uses the magical abilities he has gained as a Usare — a ring bearer — in his epic struggle with the most dangerous enemies he has yet encountered.

With the help of his Circle of Light, and many new friends, he undertakes a remarkable journey through mythical lands, where he must do battle with the creatures that follow the Darkness... and with the Darkness itself.

In this breathtaking fight between good and evil, Teal's odyssey also becomes a journey of discovery, as the truth of his heritage — and his power — is at last revealed.

Martin Middleton
Sphere of Influence

She is the Darkness... She is the underlying evil which has lain upon the world for an eternity, waiting for the first touch of life so She could corrupt it, twist it to Her ways... She has decided to use her powers to start a war which neither side can win. And after this war, She will claim the pitiful survivors as Her own.

Teal the Death Lord, hero of *Circle of Light* and *Triad of Darkness*, has banished the Dark Gods from his world and secured an uneasy peace in the lands under his dominion. But the cost has been great — the Gods of Light have been forced to follow the Gods of Darkness into oblivion. If Teal is to return the Light to his lands, he must also unleash the forces of Darkness and once again do battle with evil.

Teal and his companions set out on a perilous quest for the source of the Darkness. It is this source that Teal must destroy if a time of mass destruction and unparalleled bloodshed is to be averted...

In an awesome confrontation between good and evil, Teal comes face to face with his destiny... and must make the ultimate sacrifice if he is to curb the Darkness's ever-expanding sphere of influence.